Refinery

A Novel

by

Jim Killen

iUniverse, Inc.
New York   Bloomington

iUniverse books may be ordered through booksellers or by contacting:

iUniverse
1663 Liberty Drive
Bloomington, IN 47403
www.iuniverse.com
1-800-Authors (1-800-288-4677)

Because of the dynamic nature of the Internet, any Web addresses or links contained in this book may have changed since publication and may no longer be valid. The views expressed in this work are solely those of the author and do not necessarily reflect the views of the publisher, and the publisher hereby disclaims any responsibility for them.

ISBN: 978-1-4502-6027-5 (sc)
ISBN: 978-1-4502-6029-9 (hc)
ISBN: 978-1-4502-6028-2 (ebook)

Printed in the United States of America

iUniverse rev. date: 10/07/2010

To my brother, Tom, who first made me a teller of stories

Contents

Acknowledgments ix

Prelude xi

Chapter 1 1

Chapter 2 26

Chapter 3 45

Chapter 4 53

Chapter 5 66

Chapter 6 82

Chapter 7 98

Chapter 8 106

Chapter 9 114

Chapter 10 131

Chapter 11 153

Chapter 12 167

Chapter 13 179

Chapter 14 189

Acknowledgments

Behind the headlines telling of industrial disasters, there are many untold stories of human hurt and heroism. This is a fictional effort to tell such a story.

This story started to develop some time ago. I was talking with a couple of refinery workers about the industrial disaster that took place in Bhopal, India. In that catastrophe, several thousand people died from inhaling methyl-isocyanate gas that had escaped from a chemical plant. One of the men got a pensive look in his eyes and said, "I just believe that if that had happened over here, someone would have done something to keep all of those people from dying." The other man nodded. When I heard that statement, I realized that the man was saying something about himself, and about the others like him, and about what they expected of themselves and of each other. The story began to develop then and continued to come together as I watched the things that have happened in the lives of people I know and in the world in which we live. Now it is ready to be told. I hope that you enjoy it. I hope that something in it speaks to you—or, maybe, for you.

I want to thank those friends who are more familiar than I with the petro-chemical industry, who read my book and corrected my technology: Howard Hayre, Jason Killen (my grandson), Martha Pepper, Matthew Young, and Michael Greene. I want to thank those who have critiqued my writing to make me a better story teller: Jim Sanderson, John Dufresne, and Rogayle Franklin. And thank you to Liz Harris, Cindy Busch, and Juanita Shook, who corrected my errors in punctuation and other grammatical problems. Finally, I want to thank the people at iUniverse for helping me to get my story to you.

Prelude

"I can't believe this is happening." Jared Philips mumbled these words to himself as he clutched the chain link fence by the runway of the old Ellington Air Force Base and watched a column of thick black smoke rise from the Apex Oil Refinery just a few miles away. He knew that he had just escaped death in a major industrial disaster. But he had a gut feeling that he was witnessing the disintegration of something even bigger than a part of an industrial complex. Jared's boss, the plant manager, had asked him to help him explain the scope of the damages to some high company officials who were flying in from New York. Jared thought that might be the toughest task of the whole day.

Jared chuckled as a private joke flitted across his mind: *I knew if that damned dragon ever got loose, he would play heck with everything.* Then he remembered what he had heard about his two friends, Sarge and the Deacon. He felt an emptiness in the pit of his stomach. He felt a great sob rising in his throat but stifled it.

Jared realized that this was the first time that day that he had been able to stand still long enough to think about how he was feeling. He was physically and emotionally exhausted. He was dirty and sweaty, and there was a rip in the leg of his coveralls. His face felt like it had been sunburned, and he felt an intense pain in both of his hands that he had not felt before. He realized that he was clutching the rough wire of the fence so hard that he was hurting himself. He released his grip, crossed his arms against the fence, rested his head on them, and tried to get himself ready for what was coming next. Jared wondered what would be the impact of the things he had witnessed—and what would be required of him.

Chapter 1

Six weeks before the disaster, Jared had driven down Highway 225 in Pasadena, Texas, for the first time. He was on his way to begin his career as an engineer with Apex Oil and Refining Company. Jared found himself being more impatient than usual with the morning traffic. He was not late, but he was eager to get to his destination. He felt that he was on his way to keep a date with destiny. Since he was a young boy, Jared had wanted to be an engineer. It had taken him seven years of hard work and heartbreak to get here. Now he wanted to get on with it.

Finally he drove through the gate of the Apex Oil Refinery. This was the flagship refinery of one of the country's biggest oil companies. He admired the orderly way in which the tanks and towers and buildings and abstract sculptures made of pipe were built. Jared thought it looked deceptively serene. He knew about the alchemy that was going on inside of those towers and pipes to turn sticky black crude oil into thousands of products needed by the people of the world. By comparison, the plant where his father had worked was much smaller and looked rather old and rusty.

Jared felt fortunate to be going to work at Apex. This had not been his first choice for a job. In college, he had thought about working for a big engineering firm. He had applied to several big firms and interviewed with a few. But the only job offer had come from Apex. Now that he was here, he was getting excited. He thought, *All right, this is where I belong!*

Jared had been told to meet Al Scardino, the senior process engineer, in the company cafeteria. As he stepped out of his car, he caught a whiff of the smells that always seemed to hover around an oil refinery—smells that sent most people looking for a residence in some other part of town. Jared remembered how his father had always said, "That just smells like money to me." He heard the muffled sounds, the low rumble, and the hiss that let him know that industrial processes were going on all around him.

1

As Jared approached the glass door of the cafeteria, he thought for a fleeting second that he saw his brother, Arthur, coming to meet him from the other side. He quickly realized that he had caught a glimpse of his own reflection in the glass. Jared thought, *Boy, I wish he could be here going to work with me today. I'm afraid it's gonna be a long time before he can go to work anywhere.* Jared shook his head and brushed away a tear that had come to his eye. He used the reflection to check his appearance, a habit left over from his navy days. He had tall and athletic build. He had a fair complexion and light brown hair. He knew that many people thought he looked younger than his twenty-seven years, but he had decided not to let that bother him. He wore khaki pants, a golf shirt, and a new pair of oxfords with steel toes. His new plant security badge hung on his shirt. He thought he would pass inspection for his first day of duty. He opened the door and went in.

The cafeteria was a large, pleasant, plain-looking room. A large coffee urn stood next to the door so that those who came early could get free coffee. There was a cafeteria line, and an assortment of tables and chairs. Jared noticed a group of tables pushed together in one corner as if in preparation for a meeting.

One man sat eating breakfast and reading a newspaper. A woman, dressed for office work, sat at another table eating pancakes. The man didn't look up. The woman did. Jared nodded to her and smiled. She nodded back. Jared got a cup of coffee and found a place where he could sit and watch the people coming into the cafeteria without being too conspicuous. He had to wait for Al Scardino. He also wanted to get his first look at the other people with whom he would be working.

As Jared was cooling his coffee, a fidgety little man came in wearing blue coveralls with a company logo over the pocket and a white hard hat, the company uniform. All but the management and technical personnel wore it. Jared knew that the coveralls were probably made of Nomex, a fire-retardant material that was a safety requirement in most petrochemical plants. This man also wore motorcycle boots with his pant legs tucked into the boot tops to make them more conspicuous. He glanced around as if he were looking for someone, filled his cup with coffee, and sat down at the group of tables that were pushed together.

People continued to drift in alone or in small groups. Some filled their coffee cups and then left the cafeteria. Some sat to visit. Jared noticed that a group of men had joined the man in the motorcycle boots in the corner. Eventually an older man came in wearing the blue Nomex coveralls. He seemed to be an especially energetic person for his age. His grey hair was cut in a military burr. The little man in the boots called out, "Ten-hut!" and stood and saluted. Everyone else laughed. The older man sat down, and the conversation in the corner got a little livelier. Jared heard the men poking fun at each other, each one determined to give as good as he got.

The cafeteria was gradually filling up with people and the sounds of conversation. Jared heard an explosion of profanity from behind him. The man who had been reading his paper when Jared came in had stood up and was shouting at another man, who was filling his cup at the coffee urn. The man by the coffee urn answered with a blast of profanity of his own. He advanced across the room toward the other man. His right hand was clenched in a tight fist, and his arm was cocked as if to deliver a knock-out punch. His left hand held a cup of coffee. As he advanced across the room toward his adversary, they both turned the air blue with cuss words. Jared noticed that everyone was watching this display and smiling. Nobody seemed worried. When the man reached the table where the other stood, they sat down and drank coffee together. Jared imagined that this might be a traditional ritual for these two friends.

Jared went to get some more coffee. He bent over the coffee urn to refill his cup. When he stood up and turned around, he found himself looking at two young women in blue coveralls who had just come in. One was a pleasant-looking redhead, a little overweight but attractive. The other was a real beauty, a brunette. Her company coveralls really showed off her spectacular figure. She had dark brown hair that had been brushed until it shined and a face that looked like a model in a cosmetic commercial, even though she wore no makeup except a little lipstick. Jared thought she was even prettier than Judy, his ex, had been. The thought of Judy still stung a little bit, but Jared reminded himself that he had decided to put that behind him and move on. That brunette sure looked good to him.

Jared stood facing the two young women and feeling a little taken aback. They both smiled at him and said, "Hello." He said, "Hi," and there was an awkward moment when Jared thought about starting a conversation. But he settled for saying, "Have some coffee. It's good." Then he turned and went back to his table. He heard the ladies giggle softly behind him. They went to sit down with the first woman Jared had seen, who he assumed was a secretary. As they sat down, they looked at Jared again and smiled. Jared smiled back and nodded. Jared told himself that he would have to try to get acquainted soon, but right now, he had to meet Al Scardino.

Jared heard the little man in the motorcycle boots making another announcement. "All right, you guys, clean it up. Here comes the plant hypocrite."

Another older man came into the cafeteria and stood by the coffee urn. He was a little thicker through the middle than the other one. He put down his cup and stood staring at the man in the boots making gestures of mock exasperation. As he walked toward the table, the man in the boots said, so that everyone could hear, "Hey, what would you do if I slapped you in the face?"

The other shot back, "I'd knock a knot on your head, that's what I'd do."

The self-appointed MC said, "See! See! That proves you're a hypocrite. The Bible says you're supposed to let me hit you again."

The older fellow said, "Baloney! I'm religious but I ain't stupid." Everyone laughed.

Jared sat watching the antics of the people who were gathering, and he smiled. They reminded him of his father and his father's friends. He had been thinking a lot about his father lately. His father had really wanted both Jared and his brother to go to college. He had planned the family budget to make that possible. He was proud that Jared had become an engineer. That is what he had wished that he could have been. Jared knew his father was feeling good about the things his son was doing now.

Suddenly, all of the conversation in the cafeteria stopped. Two men walked into the cafeteria, caught up in an animated conversation. They wore slacks and short-sleeved dress shirts. Jared guessed that the taller and older of the two was the plant manager, Joe Summerfield. And he assumed that the other man might be the assistant plant manager, Michael Miller. They filled their coffee cups and continued across the cafeteria, still deep in conversation. Summerfield was doing most of the talking. He had a mellow baritone voice and was impressive in his appearance. His hair was grey and thinning, but Jared thought that, as a younger man, he had probably been quite handsome. He moved with self-confidence. But he seemed to be all worked up over something. Michael Miller was shorter, younger, and solidly built. He was mostly listening and nodding. Just then, they noticed Jared.

The taller man asked, "Are you Jared Philips, our new engineer?"

Jared stood and said, "Yes, I am." Now everyone in the cafeteria knew who he was.

"I'm Joe Summerfield, and this is Michael Miller. We're glad to have you aboard. We've been looking forward to meeting you." Jared noticed that, even though the conversation Summerfield had been having was still obviously on his mind, he had put it on hold to give his full attention to meeting a new person.

Jared shook hands with both men and said, "I've been looking forward to meeting you too. I'm really glad to be here at Apex."

"You met Al Scardino yet?"

Jared said, "I'm supposed to meet him here this morning."

Summerfield said, "Good. He'll get you oriented. He's supposed to bring you by to see me later. But just in case something happens and I miss you, my wife and I want to invite you to dinner at our house on Wednesday. We have three new staff members coming on this week, and we want to get acquainted with you."

"That's very nice of you. I'll look forward to it."

Summerfield smiled and said, "See you later," and then the two men went on their way, taking up their conversation where they had left off.

Jared felt a wave of anxiety wash over him. He reminded himself that, like all new employees, he had been hired for a six-month trial period. If he could not meet the expectations of these two men and Scardino, he might be unemployed again in a very iffy job market. He had confidence in his ability to do the work. But experience had taught him that lots of things can happen that are beyond anyone's control—and he had to have this job. He didn't want to let his dad down. And he felt that it would be important for him to be able to help his brother, Arthur, get through college if he needed help. Arthur who was married and had a little baby with Down syndrome, had joined the National Guard to meet his military obligation while being available to the family. Then the local Guard unit had been activated. Arthur had just come home from his second tour of duty in Iraq with a serious injury. Since Jared's dad had lost his refinery job, he would not be able to help Arthur as much as he had hoped to. Jared felt it was his obligation to step in and help his brother if help was needed. Jared really needed this job.

Jared realized that gloom had settled over him as he remembered all of the things that had gotten in the way as he was coming to this place in his life. He felt a knot forming in his stomach. He started talking to himself. *Hey, you can do this. Just play the hand that's been dealt you, and you can do something that will make your dad proud. Now suck it up and get ready to do whatever you have to do.*

Jared saw from the clock on the cafeteria wall that it was almost time for the plant whistle to blow. People began to get up and leave the cafeteria. The two pretty girls looked at Jared and smiled just before they left. Jared smiled and nodded. Then he heard someone behind him calling his name, and he turned around. A short, balding man with a belly that hung over his belt gave Jared a friendly smile, held out his hand, and said, "Al Scardino, the guy who's looking forward to making you do most of the work." They laughed and shook hands. Then Al said, "Come on, let me show you what you are getting into."

The conversation between Joe Summerfield and Michael Miller continued down the hall and into the office suite. They went into Summerfield's nicely furnished office. There was a desk of dark wood and upholstered chairs. A large framed picture of the company's founder hung on the wall. But the office was dominated by a large window that offered a panoramic view of much of the refinery. Joe closed the door and handed Michael a letter on company letterhead, saying, "This is the letter I've been talking about. I've highlighted the parts that bother me most."

Michael read the whole letter. The highlighted parts read, "It is common knowledge that we work in an increasingly competitive business environment. We would like for you to submit plans for increasing the profitability of your installation. One of the things that you should do is to seek ways to decrease the cost of operation, especially in the areas of employee compensation and maintenance expenses. Look for ways to replace older employees, whom we must pay premium wages, with employees who can be compensated at a lower rate. Also look for ways of outsourcing work to contractors. Finally, you need to minimize the maintenance expenses for non-essential equipment." The letter was signed by William Stone, Assistant to the Chief Executive Officer.

Michael nodded, "I've been telling you this was coming. When I went back to work on my master's of business administration degree, I was surprised at how much they talked about this. I thought I was going to learn more about running a refinery, but all they wanted to talk about was what a company has to do to make its stock attractive to investors."

"Do you know anything about Stone?" Summerfield asked.

"I've met him. He's an arrogant little guy. Graduated at the top of his MBA class at Harvard. The company hired him and fast-tracked him right to the top. I expect that they're counting on him to reorganize everything."

"The MBA seems to be the key to the executive office everywhere. You know, I'm the last plant manager for Apex who has an engineering background. I'm glad to have a guy like you around who has both."

Michael smiled and said, "I'm glad that you're glad."

"But you tell me, what will it mean to have a company run entirely by people who know how to inflate stock values but don't have the foggiest notion about how to run a refinery?"

"That question keeps me awake at night."

Joe began to walk around the room and wave his arms as he spoke. He was trying to get something off his chest. "These people don't seem to realize that some of those older guys they want us to get rid of have a lot of expertise that can be valuable to the company."

"It worries me too. But I'm just telling you that this is the way that the industry is going, and we're going to have to work with it."

"I know that, but I think we should try to stay ahead by reaching for excellence and for creative new solutions and processes. Look at the American steel industry. They didn't modernize their plants. Now a major American industry is just about gone. And the same thing has happened to most of American manufacturing. I could see the same thing happening to the refining industry. Oh, hell, you've heard me make that speech a dozen times."

"You know I feel the same way you do, but finding a way to compete through excellence is going to be hard. We haven't found the secret yet."

Joe snorted, "Short-term profit can't be everything."

"No, but it is something. Think about it. When you buy stocks other than Apex, you may ask questions about how the companies maintain their plants and about their long-term plans. But most investors just ask how much the stock is likely to appreciate and pay in dividends."

"To tell you the truth, I never thought about that. I put all of my investment money into Apex stocks. This is my company."

Michael looked surprised. "I admire your loyalty, but for your own safety and your family's, you really ought to diversify your investments. Remember what happened at Enron."

"Yeah, I know you're right. I'll do some thinking about that."

"I hope you will."

Joe opened a file folder that was on top of his desk and took out a sheet of paper. "Let me show you the letter I've written to Stone."

Michael read silently and then aloud, "As you know, the Apex Pasadena Refinery has been, for many years, the most profitable plant in the company. I understand how important it is not to rest on our laurels. I would like to try to increase our profitability by increasing our productivity. To that end, I think it may be important to keep some of the older employees whose expertise can be valuable." Michael stopped reading, looked up, and said, "I want you to know that I appreciate what you're trying to do. But I feel like I need to warn you that you may be sticking your neck way out to do this. People like Stone don't like to get any reply except 'Yes, sir.'"

"Do you think I shouldn't send it?"

Michael said, "I think you ought to think about it for a day or two before you send it. I believe that sending this will be more dangerous than you think."

Joe paused, looking at his friend, and then said, "Okay, I'll think about it." He took the letter back and shoved it into the file folder. Then he sat down, leaned back in his chair, and smiled a little bit. "I've been asking myself if I'm getting all churned up about this just because I'm about the age of some of the guys they want me to get rid of. I could retire any time and become a serious golfer and enjoy all of the benefits that everyone keeps talking about."

"Are you thinking about retirement?"

"Not really. To tell you the truth, I'm having too much fun. I've never done anything that I liked more than running this refinery. I just hope you don't get impatient. I want you to be around to take over when I'm ready to hang it up."

Michael smiled. "I'll still be here if the company will let me."

Al Scardino took Jared on a tour of the office suite. He introduced him to the secretaries and to as many of the other management and technical staff as he could find. The office suite was pretty plain and utilitarian in its decor. A few family pictures and company appreciation plaques hung on some of the office walls. But most of the offices had large windows offering views of parts of the refinery. Somehow, that made the office suite impressive. Jared met the secretary he had seen drinking coffee with the two younger women in the cafeteria. He made a special mental note of her name, Mrs. O'Brien. She would be his way of getting an introduction to the brunette. In the business office, the chief accountant, Mrs. Sanchez, seemed especially glad to meet him. She said they were expecting another new staff member to arrive on Wednesday. Al saw that the technical manager, who was in charge of all engineering functions of the refinery, was talking on the phone. They passed his door and went into the offices of the electrical engineer, the mechanical engineer, and the systems engineer in charge of keeping the plant control systems up and running. They met Marvin Elrod, the plant maintenance superintendent. Elrod was a tall and lanky man with a deeply tanned and furrowed face. Jared noticed that he was apparently the only man wearing company coveralls in the office suite. In each place they stayed just long enough for an introduction and an exchange of pleasantries. Al explained briefly what each staff member did.

Al and Jared arrived outside of Joe Summerfield's office just as Michael Miller was coming out. His secretary said she was sure that Mr. Summerfield would want to see them.

Summerfield welcomed them cordially. He asked Miller to come back in and told his secretary to call Ken Allison, the technical manager, to come in. Allison came in, and Summerfield introduced Jared to him. Then he invited everyone to sit down in the comfortable chairs he kept arranged in a circle at the far end of his office. He gave Jared a little pep talk about what a great place the Pasadena Refinery is and welcomed him again to the technical staff. He reminded him of the invitation to dinner on Wednesday and gave him directions to his home. Ken Allison didn't say much during the visit, but after the meeting was over, he shook hands with Jared again and said, "Welcome aboard. You'll be working under Al's supervision, but if I can be of any help, I'm right down the hall."

When they were alone again, Jared commented, "Ken Allison didn't have much to say. He seemed to have something else on his mind."

"He probably does. He has a big job and only about a third of the staff he needs to do it. But he's a good guy. You'll like him when you get to know him."

Finally, Al ushered Jared into the process engineering office. It was a spacious room with cabinets designed to hold blueprints and large tables where they could be spread out. One wall was taken up by a large window that offered a view of much of the refinery. There were other file cabinets. There were four cubicles for staff engineers. Al pointed to the cubical nearest to the windows and said, "That's my mouse hole. The one next to it is yours."

Jared looked into his new home base and saw a steel desk with a computer in the middle of it. There was one desk chair and a filing cabinet. It would be up to him to make it feel like home.

There was a suit of company coveralls folded up on the desk with a hard hat on top of them. Al explained, "If you ever need to go down into the plant, you will have to wear those Nomex coveralls. It's a plant safety requirement. They always start you with a large size. If they fit, someone will pick them up and stencil your name on them. You won't need them much."

Jared picked the coveralls up and looked at them. "Large will probably be about right for me. Who goes in those other two cubicles?"

"No one. When I first came on, there were four process engineers on staff. After a few years they reduced the staff to three. Then, within the last couple of months, John Kubrich, the old senior process engineer, retired, and Dietrich Schmidt took a job with a big engineering firm. They promoted me to be the new senior process engineer and hired you to be the rest of the staff."

"Well, what do we do?"

"Just as little as we can," Al said, and then he laughed. "They really don't expect much from us so I have decided to give them just what they expect."

Jared gave him a quizzical look. Al went on, "Our job is mostly to plan the rates and operating conditions of the refinery units. Then we monitor the processes and see that everything is running smoothly and to act as troubleshooters if anything goes wrong." Al went to the table where he had spread out a large engineering drawing. It was a map of the entire refinery. He talked Jared through an explanation of the plant. He said, "The planners laid this plant out in six sections, Sections A, B, C, D, E, and F." Al pointed to the sections on the large drawings as he spoke. "Each section has a combination of units that is designed to accomplish certain functions of the refinery. Each section has a computerized control center where the operators work. Of course, the refinery is always changing and evolving as new processes are developed and as processes are modified to meet market demands." Al explained the basic functions and processes that were carried on in each of the sections and then added, "I'm sure you realize that these processes are considered secret. We don't talk about them to anyone outside of the company."

Jared understood most of what Al said because of his training. He asked a few questions, which Al answered. Al said, "The detailed drawings of each unit are in those cabinets. They're also on your computer." Throughout Al's explanation, Jared kept looking up and glancing out the window as if he were trying to see in the refinery outside the things that were represented on the drawings. But Al kept focused on the drawings. Then Al took Jared to the computer on his desk. He told him to drag in another chair, and they sat down together. He explained the plant control system and showed how their computers were connected to the various sources of information in each of the units. For the next couple of hours, Al explained the procedures they were to go through daily to monitor the functioning of all of the units in the plant. Jared took notes furiously. When Al finished, he said, "Well, that's about it. Any questions?"

Jared turned his chair to face Al and said, "That doesn't exactly sound like doing as little as you can to me. What did you mean when you said not much is expected of us?"

Al looked a little embarrassed. "Well, I just thought I'd better warn you. I expect that you are full of big ideas like I was when I came here right out of college. Dietrich Schmidt and I came at the same time. We were classmates at Texas Tech. He was really smart, one of the most creative engineers I've ever known. When we first came, the company expected creative work from us. They wanted us to find new and better ways to do things. We actually did some pretty interesting things. Dietrich noticed that we had a large network of steam generators, most of which were not optimized. He asked if we could install turbine generators to make electricity and optimize the steam network. The company gave us the go-ahead to work on it. When we had it worked out, they let us put the systems into place. It cost them a bunch of money. But now the plant produces all of its own electric power and some to sell. It's paid for itself several times. It was fun to be part of something like that."

"I'll bet it was. I've heard of that process. Did it actually originate here?"

"Well, some other plants had done something kinda like it, but one application of it sure as heck did originate right here."

"I would like to get involved in some things like that."

"I was afraid you might. That's why I thought I'd better warn you. There isn't much encouragement to do stuff like that any more. Joe Summerfield is a good guy. He has an engineering background. He tries to run a tight ship. He's interested in creative engineering. But the company won't give him any money for updating and expanding facilities. They even make him pinch pennies on maintenance. The last couple of times that someone came up with a creative idea, Summerfield sent it through to the head office. Head office said they'd give it consideration and, if they thought the idea had merit, they'd send it to their engineering contractors for development. We never heard anything more from them. Finally, Dietrich got disgusted and decided to go with one of the big engineering firms so he could be where the action is. He went with Brown and Daniels."

When Jared heard the company name, he winced a little inside. That was the company that had been his first choice as an employer. "What about all of those changes and all of that evolution that you talked about?"

"Most of it is market driven, and it just comes down from above. They don't ask us much."

Jared said, "My dad says that most of the modifications he has seen in his plants and the others around it amount to one kind of downsizing or another."

"Well, when I look around, I can see what he is talking about, but fortunately I don't see that happening here, yet. Still, I don't see any real expansion or creative development either. And, as I said, what there is comes down from above."

That explanation rubbed Jared the wrong way. He shook his head. "I hate to hear you say that. I think the refinery should be where at least part of the real creative action is."

Al nodded. "It ought to be. I don't know what the people in the head office are thinking. It's almost as if they don't think they are gonna be in business long enough to justify the investment of big bucks in maintenance and modernization."

"That idea makes me real nervous. I've read a lot about some of the shortsightedness of American business and industry, but I never actually had to bump up against it."

"Well, now you have," Al said. "But let's not hold the funeral yet. Let's just do the best we can within the limitations that are set for us. We can still have some fun with this job. But if you have any ideas about doing something big, I am afraid you may be disappointed."

Jared got a pensive look on his face and said, "I think my dad is expecting me to do something big."

"Your dad?"

"Yeah, my dad." Jared walked to the window and looked out as he talked. "My dad is a really interesting guy. He is a really smart man, smarter than I will ever be. But he didn't get to go to college. He went through a union apprentice program and became a master electrician.

Then he went to work in a refinery. He wasn't content with just fixing things that were broken. He wanted to figure out how everything worked. Not just the electrical things but everything. He used to go to the college bookstores and buy used engineering books and read them. Eventually he started coming up with ideas about how to do things better. They actually let him improve some of the electrical systems, but they didn't pay any attention to most of his other suggestions. He used to tell me about his ideas, and you know, when I got to college, I found out that some other people had come up with the same ideas and gotten them patented."

"What's your dad doing now?"

"Well, they eventually retired him—before he wanted to retire. Staff reduction. He went to work as a counter salesman in an electrical supply house. Every day, he drives by the old refinery on his way to work and watches it rust out and thinks about the big things he coulda done if he'd been an engineer. Now that I'm an engineer, he thinks I can do anything, and he is counting on me to save the oil industry."

"What do you think?"

"Well, I think I know I am not nearly as able to do anything as my dad thinks I am. But I think the industry is important, and I hope that I will eventually be able to do something significant to make it better. Yeah, I guess I really do want to do something important to make the industry better."

"Oh my! Well, welcome to frustration farm."

Jared smiled, "Well, I'm not frustrated yet. I'd better get busy figuring out all that I'm supposed to be doing."

Jared spent most of the day poring over the engineering drawings of the plant and getting familiar with the computer programs that he was expected to use. He thought it was significant that Al had made no offer to take him out into the plant to see the units themselves. Al obviously thought that his job was to be done in the office. Finally he asked Al if it would be okay for him to spend some time each day going out and becoming familiar with the plant itself. Al said that would probably be a good idea. He said Jared could use the last two hours before quitting time each day to go out and look around.

Jared printed off a copy of the basic plan of the entire plant. He changed into the fire-retardant company coveralls. As he was doing that, he had a silly thought that he was like a knight putting on his armor to go out on some knightly errand. He put on his hard hat and went walking.

After Jared left the office, Al went down the hall to the restroom. He met Miller on the way. Miller asked, "How is our new man working out?"

"I think he is going to work out just fine. Every time I explained something, he started nodding his head before I got through. When I was showing him around, it was almost as if he had been here before. Now he's gone out to explore the plant for himself. I think we may have another Dietrich Schmidt on our hands."

"That's good."

"Is it—really?"

"Yeah, I think it is—really."

Jared had not gone far before he realized why Al preferred to stay in the office. In the midafternoon it was hot in the refinery. Summer in this part of the country is famous for heat and humidity. The refining processes generated additional heat, and the structures blocked most of the air circulation. Jared mopped his brow with his handkerchief and felt his clothes being soaked with sweat. He decided that the heat was something he would have to live with and that it would be okay to be sweaty. He went on walking. First he walked through the whole plant, identifying by sight the different units and buildings on the plan. He identified the boilers, the distillation towers that split crude oil into fractions, the catalytic cracking and delayed coking units that upgraded the heavy fractions into lighter components, and the reformers that boosted the gasoline's octane. He could imagine the processes going on inside them to do the basic work of the refinery, heating crude oil up until it breaks down into its component parts and separating them for their many different uses, from gas to asphalt.

He noticed that some of the units were newer than others. They had been added at different times in the plant's history and incorporated the technology of those times. He noticed the placement of the cooling towers and the generating units that Al had mentioned. He was amazed at the complexes of pipes that he saw. They were more bewildering than he had expected them to be. He saw the places where big underground pipelines entered the refinery, bringing crude oil from domestic oil fields and from offshore lightering stations where crude oil was transferred from oceangoing tankers.

As he walked down the main company street on the east side of the refinery, he passed Sections A, B, and C. Each section had units arranged for different purposes. He found the building where the lubricants were compounded and packaged for shipment. He wandered through it. About halfway through his walk, he found himself at the dock on the ship channel. There were storage barns and shipping facilities. No ships were there at the time. A railroad spur ran by the shipping barn. Near that was a station where tank trucks came to be filled with gasoline for nearby service stations. From there, Jared crossed over and walked up the company street on the west side of the plant. He passed Sections D, E, and F.

When he came to Section F, he decided to take a closer look. He climbed the stairs onto the unit's first floor and found the control room. Four men in company coveralls were working at different tasks. One turned to face him; it was the older man with the burr haircut Jared had seen in the cafeteria. He had a wad of chewing tobacco in his cheek. He spit into a Styrofoam cup that was standing nearby and said, "Can I help you?" He said it without much enthusiasm.

Jared introduced himself. "I'm the new engineer, and I'm just trying to get acquainted with the plant. I wonder if you have time to tell me about this unit."

The man gave him a quizzical look and said, "What is this, some new scam the front office has dreamed up to check up on us?"

Jared laughed and said, "No, this is my own idea. I've spent four years in a university learning about refineries. Now I need to get to know a real one. You look like you've been around here for a while. I'll bet you can tell me a lot about it."

"Yeah, I've been around here for a while, I guess. I came to work as a pipe fitter about thirty years ago. My name is Bill Anderson, but everyone calls me Sarge." He offered his hand, and Jared shook it.

Jared said, "I grew up around refineries. My dad worked in one of 'em. When he found out that I was gonna be an engineer in a refinery, he told me that I oughtta look up some of the old pipe fitters and get acquainted. He said they might be able to keep me from making a fool of myself."

"What did your dad do?"

"He started as an electrician, and then he worked as an operator."

Sarge looked at him as if he were looking over his glasses, even though he didn't have any glasses on. "You ain't givin' me no bull, are you? Do you really want to learn about this unit?"

"Yeah, I really do."

"Well, okay. I can't guarantee that I can keep you from making a fool of yourself, but if you'll let me finish what I was doin', we can go out and climb around a while." He finished making some notes on a form he was filling out and spit his chew into the cup. He looked at Jared and said, "You know, guys around here don't much cotton to bein' told what to do, but there is one rule we all follow: We don't smoke out here. We know that a little whiff of odorless gas could come drifting by just as we were lighting up, and all hell would break loose. So if you have a need for nicotine, you need to develop a taste for Beechnut or Copenhagen."

"Gotcha."

Without saying any more, Sarge turned and led Jared out of the control room onto the unit floor. They spent half an hour climbing around on the unit as Sarge explained how everything worked. Jared was amused at the difference between the ways Sarge explained things and how his professors had explained the same things. Jared asked questions, and Sarge answered. Eventually, Sarge asked a question about something he had always wondered about, and Jared was able to answer it. Jared gave his explanation simply and without any hint of condescension. Sarge said, "Well I'll be damned." and gave Jared an appreciative smile.

They worked their way farther and farther up the unit until they were pretty far up in the air. Finally Sarge said, "I wanna show you a safety valve." Jared knew that a safety valve was designed to relieve pressure on a unit in case of an emergency, but he simply followed Sarge. Sarge led Jared to a vertical ladder that would take them the last sixty feet up to a narrow platform that ran around the very top of the unit. Sarge scrambled up the ladder like a squirrel. Jared followed. When he came to the top and his head came up through the opening in the platform, he saw Sarge looking at him with a sly grin on his face. Jared realized that Sarge was watching to see if he was either winded by the climb or scared by the height. It was a sort of a test of his manliness. He was glad he was still in good physical condition. He climbed onto the platform, laughing, and said, "Hey! Doin' that several times a day could keep a guy in shape." Then he walked around the platform, being careful not to hold on to the safety rail that surrounded them. He felt a little breeze cooling his face, and he commented, "Well, it's nice and cool up here." He looked at the things he could see from there. He identified each of the units that he recognized and asked Sarge questions about some of the other structures. He could see other petrochemical plants from there, and he asked Sarge to identify them. He made a little show of enjoying the height. Then, when he guessed that he had passed the test, he turned to the safety valve on the top of the unit and said, "This is what you brought me up here to see."

Sarge said, "Yeah, that is the safety valve." Then they climbed back down the ladder and worked their way back down to the control room. It was almost quitting time.

By the time they were through, a kind of a relationship was growing between them. Sarge said, "You know, we ain't used to having engineers ask us questions, especially young ones. Most of 'em think they know everything, and we don't know nothin'."

Jared laughed and said, "I know better than that."

"Do you want to meet a couple of other old pipe fitters?"

"Sure."

"Do you drink beer? Aw yeah, you were a college boy. You drink beer."

"Yeah, and before that I spent three years in the navy. I drink a little beer."

"Well, I'm meetin' two other old pipe fitters for a beer right after quitting time. Do you want to join us?"

"Sure. I'll even buy the beer. Where should I go?"

Sarge gave Jared directions to a place called the Five O'Clock Ice House.

The Five O'Clock Ice House was a rambling ranch-style building made of rough-cut wood. It had a large porch across the front. It looked more like a barbeque restaurant. When Jared arrived, he found Sarge and another man sitting on a bench on the porch. It was the other older man he had seen in the cafeteria. His face was tanned and lined, just as Sarge's was, and he had the same mischievous twinkle in his eye.

Sarge waved and said, "There's Apex Oil's new technical genius. Come over and meet somebody."

Jared waved and came up on the porch.

Sarge said, "This is George Christopher, another old ex-pipe fitter. They call him the Deacon around here."

Jared shook his hand and said, "Deacon?"

Deacon smiled and said, "Yeah. I spend a good bit of time at my church, and some folks think that's peculiar."

Jared smiled and said, "Let me guess, you don't cuss."

Deacon said, "Well, maybe not as much as some folks."

Sarge added, "And he don't drink beer neither. He sticks to Dr. Pepper. He says that's 'cause he's religious, but just between you and me, I think he's really an alcoholic and he can't handle it."

"Shucks, my secret's out," Deacon said.

Sarge asked Jared, "Did you have any trouble finding the place?"

"A little. Back home we have a place called the Ice House that actually was an old ice house back when people used block ice to cool their ice boxes. I was expecting something like that."

"This one used to be like that, but several years ago the owners moved to this old barbeque place 'cause it's closer to the plants. It's still a tradition around here."

"Who're we waiting for?" Jared asked.

Sarge offered the explanation. "Mac MacKinzie. He's another old pipe fitter. He's just about to retire from Petrotech, our maintenance contractor. The three of us and our families have been friends for years. Our kids grew up together. We all started together with the construction company that built Sections E and F. When the construction was finished, Apex hired us to run three of the maintenance pipe gangs."

Deacon said, "We were real terrors."

Sarge smiled and went on. "Then Apex decided to outsource their maintenance functions. Needless to say, we didn't like that too much. I bid into a job as a unit operator. The Deacon here went to night school to qualify as a safety technician so he could get some easy money. We stayed with Apex. But Mac took a job as a supervisor with Petrotech. He's still fitting pipe. They kinda put him in charge of the work they do at Apex."

Jared said, "Well, I can see that you three are just the kind of guys that my dad wanted me to meet. By the way, why do they call you Sarge?"

"I guess it was because I had just gotten out of the army when I came here, and they said I ran my pipe gang like a sergeant runs his squad in the army. I never was more than a private in the army. My pipe gang promoted me."

Deacon said, "Here comes the third musketeer."

A new tan SUV pulled up in front of the Ice House, and a tall, balding man got out. He wore green coveralls, the uniform of Petrotech, the maintenance contractor. Sarge shouted, "Hey, there's the man of leisure."

Mac waved and responded, "Six more weeks and I'll be free at last!" He came up onto the porch.

Sarge said, "Mac, let me introduce you to Jared Philips, the new Apex engineer. His daddy was a refinery worker, and he told him that he might learn something by hanging around with old pipe fitters. He promised to buy our beer."

Mac said, "Well, I'll be damned. This is the first time I've ever met an engineer that thought he still had anything to learn."

They went into the Ice House, picked up their drinks at the bar, and settled at a table by a window.

Deacon started the conversation. "Mac, have you got that dream home of yours about finished?"

"Almost. As soon as we get settled, we want to have you all up for a weekend."

Sarge asked, "What are you gonna do with yourself?"

Mac said, "I'm gonna fish, and I'm gonna learn to play golf, and I'm gonna plant me a garden so we can have fresh vegetables, and I'm gonna stop having to smell this damned refinery."

Deacon said, "I hope you don't come out like old Polansky. He bought a farm for his retirement place so he could smell the fresh, clean country air. Then when he moved up there, he found that he was living right between a feed lot and a paper mill."

Mac laughed, shook his head, and said, "No, I checked that out."

Deacon asked, "You gonna have plenty of money to live on?"

Mac said, "Yeah, I think so. We've been watchin' it. We really planned to retire two years ago, but when the stock market took its nosedive, we decided to keep plowing a little longer. When we counted up all we'll have coming in, we think we'll be okay. You guys will probably come out okay too. I'm afraid the companies are not going to let these younger guys come out so well."

Sarge said, "Yeah, we can see the signs of that." Sarge looked at Jared and said, "I'm afraid that may go for technical people too."

Jared nodded, "Yeah, I know. I'm replacing two guys. When these companies decide to get 'lean and mean,' they seem to get meanest to their own people."

Deacon said, "Mac, we're going to miss having you around. To tell you the truth, we're going to miss having you at Petrotech. We've all felt safer knowing that you were makin' them run a tight ship."

Mac looked away, paused, and said, "Oh, the guys will do a good job. They're good people, and they have good skills. Their only problem is that they don't know the plant."

"That's what bothers me," Sarge said.

Mac said, "They don't have any incentive to learn it. They know they'll be working here one week and somewhere else the next. We have a lot of turnover too. Petrotech has been pretty good to me and the other supervisors, but they're pretty chintzy with their raises for the other people. People tend to work with us for a couple of years and then go looking for a better job."

Jared asked, "Are all of the maintenance functions carried out by contractors?"

Sarge said, "At first they were. Then they discovered that wasn't gonna work, so they gave the maintenance supervisor a little pool of craftsmen to respond to emergencies. He has about a dozen mechanics, pipe fitters, welders, electricians, and a whole bunch of computer technicians. We keep 'em busy. But Mac's guys and the other contractors do most of the work."

Deacon grinned and asked, "Have any of them asked you lately what the cat cracker does?" All three laughed. They were remembering a favorite old story. "Tell Jared that story. Jared, this is a good one."

Mac was glad to oblige. "I was workin' with this new young guy, and he was real curious about everything. We were workin' on a particular unit, and he asked me what it was. I told him it was a 'cat cracker.' He asked what it did, and I told him it did just what it sounded like. I carried on until I just about had him believing that it cracked cats. Then I tried to explain to him the function of a catalytic cracking unit. I made my explanation just as long and as boring as I could. I used every big word I knew and even made up a few. He said, 'I'da liked it better if you'd just said it cracks cats.'"

Jared laughed and said, "I'll bet that no one ever asked you that again."

Mac shook his head and said, "No, they still do. Matter of fact, they send all of the new guys around to ask me the same question. It's gotten to be a kind of an initiation for them."

Deacon said, "I understand that they haven't let you slow down at the last. You're doin' a turnaround on two units in Section C before you're through."

Mac said, "Yeah, and I'll be just part of the way through the second one. You know they want us to turn those jobs around in seven days so they can get the units producing again as quick as they can. We use'ta work on a turnaround for several weeks to fix everything that needs to be fixed. Most refineries still do. Now we put lots of people on the job and work around the clock to do just the bare minimum in terms of maintenance. I really don't think we're able to give the units the maintenance they need in that time. But that's what Apex asks us for."

Deacon asked, "Does it bother you that you'll just be part of the way through the last one?"

"Yeah, that bothers me," Mac said, "but I told myself that if I'm gonna retire, I've gotta be able to turn it loose and leave it with 'em. I've been training the new job supervisor for six months. He's a good man. I've written him out a checklist of things to do to shut down a unit and to bring it back up. He ought to be able to do it."

Deacon said, "I sure hope he'll remember everything you told him, especially about the safety stuff."

Mac said, "By the way, speaking of safety, I'm glad Apex sent you over to explain that 'Which Way to Run' plan to our people. That's a good idea. Who came up with that?"

Deacon explained, "It came out of the work of the Apex safety department with the community emergency response teams."

Sarge broke in and said, "Don't let him kid you. You're lookin' at the author of the 'Which Way to Run' procedure. He put it together and sold it to the management."

Mac said, "Well, it's a good plan. I can't imagine why someone hasn't thought of that before. It's good for everyone to know what's the best way to evacuate the plant in case of an emergency. Our guys appreciated it. How did you come up with it?"

"Well, I was sent to represent the company in a Community Emergency Preparedness Committee. All of the community law enforcement agencies and fire departments and civic organizations were working together with all of the area industries to make plans for what to do in case of an industrial disaster. It got me to thinking that we really hadn't done all of our homework. I just sat down and thought through the quickest way to get to safety for people in different parts of the plant under several emergency circumstances. I knew I had to keep it simple so people could keep it in the backs of their minds. It really wasn't hard since I knew the plant. When I showed it to my boss, he liked it and showed it to the big boss. They put me in charge of developing it and training everyone in its use. It's kept me busy."

Mac said, "It's a good plan. I just hope we never have to use it."

Everyone looked somber and nodded. Deacon said, "Jared, folks around here still remember an explosion that happened in one of the chemical plants down the road back in 1989. It killed twenty-three people and hurt more'n a hundred. And in 2005, there was an explosion over at the British Petroleum plant in Texas City that killed fourteen. We don't want anything like that to happen again."

Sarge said, "Mac, Jared said he wanted to pick our minds about things in the plant. Since you're leaving, do you have anything to tell him that might enlighten him?"

Mac said, "You know, I've been thinkin' about that. I remember that one new engineer asked me about something that might puzzle you. He found a lot of old control valves around that don't do anything. He couldn't figure out why. The fact is that the whole plant is hi-tech now. All of the units are run by computerized gadgets. But most of the units were built before they computerized. Those old manual control valves were the controls before the computers came along. When the plant switched over, they didn't see any need to go to the trouble to take out the old valves unless they were in the way. They just opened them and left them in place. If the operators know where they are, they can actually use them as emergency controls in case there's a computer failure. So, if you get to wondering what alla those old knobs and valves are, that's the explanation."

Jared said, "Hey, thanks. That's something I probably would have been wondering about pretty soon. Now I know."

Just then, Sarge interrupted the conversation and said, "Hey, look who's here." Two men were just walking into the bar. Sarge explained to Jared, "The guy on the right is the plant maintenance supervisor, Marvin Elrod."

Mac volunteered, "The guy with him is one of our guys, Buddy O'Neil." O'Neil was not tall, but he had the build of someone who had been lifting weights. His hair looked as if it had been done by a stylist. He walked with just a little bit of a swagger.

Sarge waved his arm and shouted, "Hey, Marvin. Whatcha doin' hangin' around with the riff raff?"

The two men picked up their drinks and wandered over to the table. Sarge asked, "Do you know Jared Philips, our new engineer?"

Marvin answered, "Yeah. I met him this morning when Al was showing him around. I expect you have forgotten half of the names of the people you met by now."

Jared said, "Maybe, but I remember your name. It's good to see you again."

Mac said, "You are runnin' around with some rough company."

Marvin said, "Me and Buddy have been beer-drinkin' pals since high school. He tells me you are pretty rough on the guys at Petrotech."

Buddy said, "Hey, wait a minute. This is my boss. Don't tell him everything you know."

The men made small talk for a few minutes, and then Marvin and Buddy went to a table on the other side of the Ice House to sit and drink.

Jared said, "Marvin has a pretty important job, doesn't he?"

Deacon said, "Yes, he does. There is a maintenance specialist in every section that is supposed to report to him. Elrod is supposed to keep them all on the ball. When they started outsourcing the maintenance work, Joe Summerfield was still the assistant plant manager. He wanted to put an engineer into the position of maintenance supervisor, but the big boys in New York told him to fill the position with an hourly man. Next, he wanted to put Sarge into that position, and that's who shoulda been in it—but Sarge turned it down."

Sarge said, "Yeah, I had some things going on in my personal life just then, and I didn't feel like I was up to doing the job justice, so I passed."

Deacon said, "Marvin was the third choice for the job, but he has been in it ever since."

Sarge said, "I try not to give Marvin any flack. He knows I was offered the job first, and he is a little touchy about it. He really doesn't want any advice from me."

Mac said, "Yeah, and Sarge has a real tough time not givin' advice to anyone."

Sarge turned to Jared and said, "You got any other questions that you want to ask right now?"

Jared said, "No, I guess not, unless you can tell me about those two pretty little ladies who were in the cafeteria this morning."

Sarge said, "You are gonna have to find out about that on your own. We're all happily married men."

Jared said, "Well, there is one other thing. Where are the best apartments for rent around here?"

Deacon said, "Several of our people live in apartments along the beltway. I think there are some pretty nice ones there that don't cost too much. That might be a good place to start."

Mac looked at his watch and said, "I hate to leave good company, but I had better get home. I know Betty has a long list of things for me to do, so we can get on our way when the time comes."

Sarge said, "Do you think the two of you could find time to come to the Apex company barbeque when it comes around in a few weeks?"

Mac looked surprised and said, "Do you think they would let an outsider come?"

Sarge made a face that was supposed to make him look like a big shot and said, "I think I can pull some strings and get a couple of tickets."

Mac said, "That would be great. I always liked those barbeques. It would give us a chance to see all of the old guys who're still around. You're on."

Jared said, "I promised to pay for the beer so I'd better do it." He got up and went to the counter.

Mac turned to Sarge and said, "I know why you are so taken with him. He reminds you of someone else."

Sarge got a pensive look on his face for just a few seconds and said, "Yeah, I guess he does."

Deacon said, "You need to be careful."

Sarge said, "Oh, don't worry. I know who he is and who he ain't. I'll give him hell just like I do everyone else."

Driving away, Jared couldn't help thinking about how comfortable he had been with the three old-timers. It was like being with his dad and his friends again. He remembered the story about the cat cracker and laughed out loud.

It had been a big day for Jared. He made it a little longer by spending a couple of hours driving around looking at apartments. Then he ate a burger at the Dairy Queen and went back to the motel to get some rest.

Jared went to bed early. He was tired. He soon fell into a deep sleep. But in the middle of the night, he woke up in a panic. He had been dreaming. He remembered the dream clearly. He had been running as hard as he could to get away from something. Then he heard something roar behind him, and he was knocked off his feet. When he got up, he found himself looking at a solid wall of fire and felt himself being drawn toward the flames by some invisible force that he could not resist.

His heart was beating hard and fast. He sat up in bed and turned on the light. He looked at the clock. It was two in the morning. He knew he had been dreaming, but he would not say it was just a dream. He had always believed that dreams have meaning. He had never had a dream like that before. He wondered what it was all about.

Eventually his heart stopped pounding. He laughed at himself and thought, *I'd better start goin' to church again. I think I just dreamed about going to hell*. He lay awake for a long time, mulling over the things that were going on in his life. Eventually he went to sleep. But when he woke up in the morning, the memory of the dream was still with him. It stayed with him. He often thought of it and wondered what it was all about.

Chapter 2

On Tuesday, Jared arrived for work early. He walked through the cafeteria hoping to meet that pretty girl who had caught his eye, but she hadn't arrived yet. Mrs. O'Brien, the secretary he had met, was there so he went over and spoke to her. Neither Sarge nor the Deacon had arrived. Only the little guy in the motorcycle boots was there. So Jared got a cup of coffee and went on to his office. Al was not there yet. Jared occupied himself with his computer, familiarizing himself with the specifications of each of the units.

Al came in just as the plant whistle was blowing. "Hey, here's the early bird. Did you learn all about the refinery yesterday?"

"Well, not quite all, but some. I walked around the whole plant, and then a guy by the name of Sarge gave me a guided tour of a unit in Section F."

Al grinned and said, "Sarge is quite a character."

Jared said, "Yeah, he is. I had a beer after work with him and two other older guys, Deacon and Mac. That was quite an experience."

Al said, "Oh, my. You got right into the middle of plant tradition on your first day on the job. Those three used to run three maintenance pipe gangs in the plant. They were real characters. They had a competition going between their gangs. They were like high school football teams. They loved to brag about the tough jobs they'd had to do and how well they had done 'em."

Jared said, "I can picture that."

"Yeah and if they ever disagreed with anything that we told them, and they turned out to be right, they loved to brag about that too. They would tell those stories over and over forever."

"Yeah, I can picture that too."

Al said, "Those three have never gotten over being pipe fitters. They were mad at God and everybody else when the company outsourced their maintenance functions. They all have better jobs now, but they just loved being pipe fitters."

Jared asked, "Did you know that Mac is getting ready to retire?"

"No. I'm kinda sorry to hear that. We counted on him to keep our maintenance subcontractor on the ball."

Jared said, "I got the impression that the old guys don't think the plant is being as well taken care of as when they were doing it."

"Yeah, well, you would expect that from them, but just between you and me, I think they're probably right."

"I suppose they'll all be retiring within a few years."

"That'll be the end of an era."

Jared said, "I would like to pick their brains and see what all I can learn from them before they go."

"Well, okay, but you'd better keep reminding them that you are the engineer and they are not."

Jared spent the day doing the things Al told him were parts of his job. In the midafternoon, Jared asked if he could go walking around the plant again. Al told him to go ahead. Jared got the idea that Al kind of enjoyed having the office to himself for a while. He put on his coveralls and hard hat and went walking. He visited Sections A and B. He found that Sarge had called the chief operators on each of those units and told them to expect Jared. They were all friendly and helpful.

After work, Jared found an apartment and signed a lease on it. He moved his stuff into it.. Then he called a furniture rental company and arranged for some basic furniture to be delivered the next day: a bed, a reclining chair, a TV table, and a breakfast table with two chairs. He wasn't planning to do any entertaining.

On Wednesday, Jared again went to work a little early, hoping to meet that pretty girl he had seen on his first day. The weekend was coming on, and he thought it would be nice to have someone to explore the city with him. When he walked through the door, he saw four women gathered around Mrs. O'Brien's table, including the one he was interested in. He filled his coffee cup and was planning to saunter over, but before he could, he heard Sarge calling him. "Hey, Jared, come on over here and meet some of these mavericks." Sarge and the Deacon were surrounded by good old boys at the tables in the corner. Jared couldn't think of any way to get out of responding. He thought maybe he could get away in time to meet the girl.

He ambled over to the table where the men were gathered. Sarge introduced them all. The first one he met was the little guy in the boots. Sarge said, "This is Billy Bob Jacobs. We call him Hog because he's in love with his Harley-Davidson."

Jared said, "Hi Hog," and shook his hand. Next was a slightly worn-looking man in his late forties. "This is John Slovacek. We call him Pop because he and his wife had their first little one just a few years ago, and he couldn't stop talking about his boy. He still can't." Then there was a tall, lanky man in his midtwenties. "This is Sam Willis. We call him Tex, for obvious reasons." Then there was a middle-aged African-American man. "This is Henry Brown. We call him Brown—because that's his name." Jared shook hands with each man in turn and laughed at the explanations of their nicknames.

Deacon said, "Sit down, Jared, we're just telling fish tales. Do you ever do any fishing?"

"My brother and I used to drown some worms in a little pond near where we lived, but I never did any of this big water fishing like you guys probably do down here. Go on with your tales." Jared sat down facing the group, glad for a chance to listen for a while before he had to talk.

Pop said, "As I was saying, my boy and I were fishin' for croakers off of the jetty, and he hooked something really big. The boy looked at me and said, 'Help me land him, Daddy.' I just said, 'You hooked him, you catch him.' He kept on reeling, and finally he got him up to the jetty, and I got him inta the net. It was a great big old redfish. When I put him in the ice chest, he didn't fit. His head and his tail both stuck out. The boy looked at him, and his eyes got as big as saucers. He said, 'I caught him, didn't I, Daddy?' I said, 'You sure did, boy. You caught him all by yourself.' He was one proud kid."

Everyone nodded and grinned. Brown said, "That's good. I'll bet every kid in his school has heard about it by now. A boy needs some braggin' rights. It'll give him self-confidence."

Pop looked at Deacon and said, "Didn't I see you and another fellow out in your boat that Saturday?"

"Yeah, we were out there trying to catch some specks," Deacon said. "That was my preacher with me, Tim Mathis."

Hog threw up his hands in exasperation and said, "I just don't know about you guys who take kids and preachers along when you go fishing."

Deacon said, "Why shouldn't we?"

Hog threw up his hands again and said, "What if you had wanted a beer?"

Deacon said, "Well, that ain't a problem for me, but if I had wanted a beer I would have had a beer."

Hog persisted. "What if you couldn't get your motor started and you said a cuss word?"

Deacon laughed and said, "Tim has already heard all of the cuss words I know. What do you think, that he'd of called down a thunderbolt on me?"

Sarge broke in and said, "Hog, is it true what I heard about you, that when you go fishing, you take along fifty gallons of gasoline, two cases of beer, and six shrimps?" Everyone laughed.

The men went on taking turns telling tall tales. Jared listened and laughed. When the group began to break up, as everyone was standing, Pop spoke up and said, "As your newly elected union committeeman, I need to remind you to come to the meeting tonight."

Brown asked, "Is anything big coming up?"

Pop said, "No, not really. But we need to keep our attendance up so the big boys will take us seriously." Then Pop caught himself and said, "Jared, you didn't hear that!"

Jared said, "Hear what?"

Jared turned to see if the pretty girl was still there, but she had already gone.

After work, Jared went home, cleaned up, and put on his suit for the dinner at Joe Summerfield's house. He followed the directions he had been given to the professional community in Clear Lake City, a few miles from the plant. Jared was not accustomed to seeing so many big, fine houses concentrated in one place. The Summerfields' house was a red brick two-story with white columns in front. The front yard was nicely landscaped. There were flowers blooming in the flower beds. Jared thought, *This is a really nice place.* Two other cars was parked in front.

Joe Summerfield met Jared at the door and welcomed him cordially. The inside of the house made Jared think of the pictures he had seen on the covers of his mother's *Better Homes and Gardens* magazines. Everything was tastefully chosen, and it went together beautifully. Rich cherry wood furniture stood out against walls and woodwork painted in pastel tones of pink and blue. Jared had the impression that the things he was seeing were very expensive. He could have felt ill at ease in a place like this, but Joe Summerfield welcomed him in a way that immediately made him feel comfortable. "Come into the living room. There are some people I want you to meet. This is my wife, Helen." Helen Summerfield was very attractive. She smiled and grasped Jared's hand in both of hers and said, "Welcome to our home, Jared."

Joe went on. "Of course, you know Michael Miller. This is his wife, Ann."

Ann Miller was kind of a plain woman but with an outgoing personality. She shook Jared's hand and said, "We're really glad to have you in the Apex family. Is there no Mrs. Philips?"

"No," Jared said with a smile, "there was once but not any more."

Everyone could see a little sadness behind the smile so they left the subject alone.

Joe Summerfield went on. "And here is another of our new people, Ed Osborne and his wife, Eileen." The Osbornes, too, were friendly, though a little more reserved. "Have a seat there, Jared. We're waiting for one more person to arrive. Would you like a cocktail?"

Helen served Jared a drink and they sat for a few minutes engaged in the kind of talk people make when they don't want to start any significant conversation because they know it will soon be interrupted.

Just as the clock in the corner was chiming seven, the door chimes also rang, making a strange kind of combination of tones. Joe Summerfield went to the door and welcomed the last guest, a small young woman who wore a rather severe-looking grey suit; her blonde hair was pulled back into a knot behind her head. Jared thought, *In spite of all she is doing to hide it, I think this is a pretty woman.* She had a pretty face, but she wore only a minimum of makeup. Joe Summerfield said, "This is Deborah Olsen. Miss Olsen is new in our accounting department." She was introduced to everyone just as Jared had been. She made eye contact with Jared as she shook his hand, and Jared thought he saw just a flicker of the kind of recognition that usually passes between young people of the opposite sex. Helen Summerfield served Deborah a cocktail and then said, "If you'll excuse me, I'll see about dinner."

Joe Summerfield asked if anyone had trouble finding the house. No one had. They talked a little about what a nice neighborhood they were in. Then Helen came and invited everyone into the dining room.

Salads were already on the table. They were really fancy salads with mandarin orange sections and artichoke hearts mixed with the greens.

Joe Summerfield said, "It's our custom to return thanks before eating." Everyone bowed their heads, and he said, "Eternal God, we give you thanks for these and all of your blessings. Amen."

Jared was a little surprised at this act of reverence. He had grown up in a home where prayers were said, but he hadn't heard one said in a long time. He noticed that no mention of Jesus was made. He wondered if that meant that the Summerfields were Jewish or just that they were showing a courtesy to anyone who might be.

As everyone ate their salad, Jared had a chance to look again at the people around the table. He noticed that Joe Summerfield's face was lined and showing a few of the signs of age, but Jared thought that his mannerisms were those of a younger man. He had about him the air of easy self-confidence that set others at ease. Michael Miller had a full head of dark brown hair and thoughtful brown eyes. He too seemed to be a self-confident person. His respect for Joe Summerfield actually showed in everything he did. Ed and Eileen Osborne were both a little on the plump side, close to Joe Summerfield's age, but rather plain looking. Both seemed to be wearing smiles over a worried look. Deborah seemed to be completely self-contained. The more Jared watched her, the more he thought that she was a person intent on doing exactly the right things to make a good impression on her new boss.

After the salads, Helen Summerfield went into the kitchen and called a Hispanic lady named Maria to serve the rest of the meal. She served medallions of pork loin, potatoes au gratin, and a green bean casserole.

Joe Summerfield led the conversation, telling a little about each new person as a conversation starter. "Ed Osborne is coming to us from the Pennsylvania plant. There, he was manager of the compounding department. Apex sold that facility to another company, and we were able to get Ed to join us as assistant manager of the shipping department. We're lucky to have him with us."

Ed said, "Thank you. I feel lucky to be here. It's not easy for people my age to find jobs, and I appreciate your finding a place for me."

Joe said, "We feel fortunate that you were available just when we needed you and that you were willing to make the move. Have you found a place to live?"

Eileen answered, "We've rented a town house. We've leased our house in Philly to another family. We may go back there some day."

Helen said, "It's hard to leave a home you have loved, isn't it?"

"Yes, we had thought we would be there the rest of our lives. Now we'll just see where the future takes us. With all of the things that are going on in the world right now, it's hard to count on anything."

Michael Miller said, "Well, we hope it will be a happy journey, and we hope your time here will be a happy time."

Then Joe Summerfield turned to Deborah and said, "Deborah, I understand that you're a graduate of the University of Texas in Austin. Tell us more about yourself."

Deborah said, "Well, there's not much to tell. I grew up in a small town in central Texas. I went to the junior college that was in the next town and lived at home for my first two years. Then I finished at UT in Austin. I'm planning to study for my CPA examination."

Joe Summerfield said, "I've heard that examination is a tough one, but with the grades you made in college, I'm sure you won't have any trouble with it."

Deborah smiled ever so slightly and said, "Thank you. I actually stayed over in Austin and took the test. It was being offered right after the end of the semester. I just took it to see how I should study for taking it again. Hardly anyone passes it the first time through. But right now, I'm looking forward to seeing how the things I learned about accounting will apply to the operation of an oil refinery."

Michael Miller said, "You'll be surprised at how many ways accounting is used in a refinery."

Helen Summerfield asked, "What sorts of things do you like to do?"

Deborah answered, "I like to read. I like to listen to music, all kinds, from rock to the classics. I like to play tennis. Lots of things."

Joe said, "You'll find many opportunities to do interesting things in the Houston area. We hope you'll like it here." Then he turned to Jared and said, "Jared, I understand that you were in the navy before you went to college."

"Yes, I joined the navy to see the world. But, as they say, all I saw was the sea."

Michael asked, "Did you see any combat during your time?"

"Not really. I was on a missile cruiser in the Persian Gulf for a year, but during the time I was there we didn't have to shoot at anyone, and no one shot at us. We kept watching our backs, though. It was a scary part of the world."

"I'll bet that was interesting," Ann Miller said.

"Not really. In fact, it was pretty boring. I spent most of my time studying for advance placement tests so that I could cram a five-year engineering degree into four years."

Joe said, "I understand that you did it, and that you also played baseball while you were in college."

"I actually started college on a co-op scholarship with Star Petroleum, but when Star went into their merger, they discontinued their co-op program. After that, I was able to get a baseball scholarship. It helped."

Joe said, "I was glad to see that you had some experience through the co-op program. Apex discontinued our co-op program too. I was really sorry. I miss having the college students around. They were always excited about the future. They were good for us all."

Michael Miller asked, "Were you a good baseball player?"

"Good enough to keep my scholarship but not good enough to attract the attention of the pros."

Michael asked, "Had you hoped to play pro ball?"

Jared shook his head and said, "Not really. I just wanted some help getting through college. I really wanted to get on with my career. What I've always wanted to do is to work in an oil refinery." When he said that, Jared noticed just a little flicker of a smile passing over Deborah's face and maybe just a little bit of a wink. Jared thought that was curious. He went on, "I grew up around oil refineries. My father worked in a refinery."

Joe Summerfield asked, "Is he still in the refinery?"

Jared said, "No, he isn't, but I think his heart is. They offered him an early retirement, and he took it. Now he works as an inside salesman in an electrical supply house, but he still gets homesick for the refinery."

Ed Osborne volunteered, "I can understand that, but he did the right thing when he took the company's offer. Most older guys know that when you get that kind of an offer, you had better take it."

Michael said, "Jared, I'll bet our plant baseball team would like to sign you up."

Jared said, "I saw a poster about that on the bulletin board, but I didn't know if it would be okay for me to sign up."

Joe Summerfield said, "I don't know why it wouldn't."

Jared said, "Well, I know that some companies like to keep their management and technical people segregated from their hourly employees."

Joe Summerfield said, "I don't see it that way. You have a background in refinery work. I think it could be useful for you to build relationships on that. Of course, if there is ever a strike or anything, you may find yourself in an awkward position, but I hope that doesn't happen. I can't help thinking about one man who used to work for the company. His name was Elvis Kenney. He had grown up in a refinery family. His dad was a union man. The company eventually made Elvis their chief representative in negotiations with the union. He understood the union people and respected them, and they knew it. If they asked for something unreasonable, he explained to them why it was unreasonable, and they believed him. For sixteen years, while he was leading the negotiating team, Apex was the first to sign a contract with their union, and the rest of the industry just followed suit."

Ed Osborne said, "I think that's great."

Joe Summerfield said, "Yes, I always felt good about it. Some people up the ladder sometimes thought that Elvis gave away too much, but the company could afford it. It doesn't hurt to compensate people as well as you can. Besides, we didn't have any strikes for sixteen years. That helps to keep business moving."

Jared asked, "Is he still with the company?"

Joe Summerfield said, "No, they eventually promoted him to the position of a vice president. Two years later, they retired him. The year after that, we had a strike that shut us down for a month."

Michael Miller said, "The company is having to be a lot more careful about labor costs now because we're in competition on the world market with a lot of people who can get their labor cheap."

Eileen Osborne came to life when she heard that and said, "You know, I keep hearing that, but I wonder. If industry is reducing labor prices, and the cost of gasoline keeps going up, where is all of that extra money going? It can't all be going for more expensive crude."

Ed said, "Dear, we're not supposed to talk about that." Everyone laughed.

Eileen had a little more to say. "You know, I always used to have a feeling for the poor people in the rest of the world. I saw how some of them live when we took our Caribbean cruise. My heart hurts for them. I wished that they could have some industry so they could live a little more like we do. But what seems to be happening is that we're all going to be living like they do. Why can't things work so that everyone will have a better standard of living?"

Michael Miller said, "We always thought it would work that way, but I suppose that's as unrealistic as hoping that water will flow uphill."

Joe Summerfield got a mischievous grin on his face and said, "I don't know why we shouldn't expect water to flow uphill. Money seems to flow uphill, doesn't it, Eileen?"

Helen Summerfield interceded at that point and said, "Well, now it *is* time to change the subject." Everyone laughed. She turned to Deborah and said, "You're being awfully quiet. Tell us a little more about yourself. I'll bet you have a boyfriend."

Joe said, "Now, Helen, that is none of our business."

But Deborah laughed and said, "Oh, I don't mind. No, I don't have a boyfriend. I went with a guy while I was in college, but we always knew there was no future for us together. He wanted to be an air force officer, and I wanted a career of my own. After graduation, we shook hands and parted as friends."

Eileen volunteered, "I'll bet you'll find someone or someone will find you when the time comes."

Deborah said, "Well, I suppose so. Right now, I have my opportunity to move on into my career. I'm going to concentrate on that and let everything else just happen when it happens."

Michael said, "It sounds to me like we have two ambitious, career-oriented young professionals to work with."

With an expression on his face that was hard to interpret, Ed said, "I wish you both good luck."

At that time, Maria came back into the dining room and began to collect dishes from those who had finished eating. Ed said, "That food was delicious, Maria. You are a great cook."

Maria quickly answered, "Oh, don't thank me. I cook different from that. I'm just helping to serve. Mrs. Summerfield cooked everything."

Ed said, "Well, our hostess is not only a gracious lady, she's an artist in the kitchen."

Helen said, "Oh, I love to entertain."

Maria said, "Wait until you see what she's made for dessert: fresh peach cobbler with ice cream. Would anyone like coffee with it?"

For the rest of the time at the table, the conversation was about the dessert.

After that, everyone went into the living room and carried on some light conversation for a while. Jared noticed that Deborah was obviously paying attention to the conversation, but she spoke only when she was addressed directly. Jared thought she had intelligent but noncommittal things to say.

As the evening was winding down, Joe Summerfield made a short speech. "We're really glad to have all three of you on our staff. We are part of the greatest industrial nation in the history of the world, and the whole world benefits from our industrial advancement. But American industry is in a time of transition right now. We don't really know where it's going. I hope that all of us at Apex will be able to do our part to help it move ahead into an even greater era of creativity and productivity."

Jared said, "I'm excited about having an opportunity to be a part of that."

Deborah said, "Yes, I am too."

Ed said, "I'll do all that I can, as long as I am given an opportunity to be a part of it all."

Soon after that, the party broke up. Jared said to Deborah, "May I walk you to your car?"

She said, "Yes, thank you." Outside the door, Deborah seemed to relax a little bit.

On the way to the car, Jared said, "This was a really nice evening. I wonder how many plant managers actually invite their new staff people into their homes like that."

Deborah said, "I'll bet that not many do."

Jared walked with Deborah to the only car that was not there when he had arrived. It was a new, dark BMW convertible. Deborah punched the button on her key ring to unlock the door, and Jared opened it for her.

"Nice car," he said.

Deborah said, "I bought it as a graduation present for myself. I'm counting on Apex making me able to pay for it." She slipped into the front seat and said, "I'll see you at work." Jared noticed that she smiled at him in a way she had not smiled all evening.

On Thursday morning, Jared did not bother to go to work early. He had, at least temporarily, lost interest in meeting the girl he had seen in the cafeteria. There was someone else who had caught his interest—or at least his curiosity. After work, Jared got Deborah's phone number and gave her a call.

"Hello. Is this Deborah Olsen?"

"Who wants to know?" The reply was cautious without being unfriendly.

"This is Jared Philips. I met you at the Summerfields' house last night."

"Oh, hi Jared, I was hoping you'd call."

"You were?" Jared said, and then he wondered why he had said it.

"Sure I was. You are the only single guy I've met since I moved here, and I was hoping you would call." Deborah's voice sounded bright and cheerful, not like he had expected her to sound.

Jared paused a moment and said, "Are you sure this is Deborah Olsen from the accounting department at the Apex Refinery?"

Deborah broke into laughter, which sounded spontaneous and free. "Yes, this is Deborah Olsen from the accounting department at the Apex Refinery. Are you sure this is Jared Philips from the engineering department at Apex Refinery?"

"Well, I guess I messed that up. I was hoping that I could interest you in having dinner with me tomorrow evening and then going to a show or something."

"I would love to."

"Great. Is there a show you would like to see or is there something else you would like to do?"

"I like to bowl or play miniature golf."

"You didn't mention those things last night."

"I forgot."

"I will put my engineer's problem-solving techniques to work trying to locate a bowling alley or a miniature golf course and pick you up at six. Where do you live?"

Deborah gave directions to an apartment complex not far from his own and said she would be looking forward to the evening. Jared hung up and thought, *I'm still not sure that's the same girl I met last night. This is going to be interesting.*

At a little before six the following evening, Jared drove into Deborah's apartment complex and started the bewildering task of trying to find her apartment. He didn't have to. Deborah was waiting for him outside. When she recognized his car, she waved and came to meet him, half walking and half skipping like a little girl. She looked like a different person. Her hair was combed out and hung around her shoulders. She wore designer jeans and a brightly colored top. Jared noticed that she did have a figure, not spectacular like the girl he had seen in the cafeteria, but cute. When

Deborah reached the car, she opened the door for herself, got in, and said, "Hi."

Jared said, "Hi. How're you doin'?"

"I'm hungry," she said.

"You look different from the other night. I wondered what you would look like dressed like this."

"You know how it is. You have to be careful to make the right impression on your new boss."

"Yeah, I suppose so."

There was a pause, and Deborah said, "Well?"

Jared looked puzzled and said, "Well, what?"

"Well, how do I look dressed like this?"

"You look pretty. You look real pretty."

Deborah smiled broadly and said, "Thank you. Now where're you taking me to eat?"

Jared said, "I saw an Applebee's not far from here. How does that sound?"

"That's one of my favorites. Let's go for it."

Jared put the car into motion. When he had gotten out of the parking lot and into traffic, he asked, "How did your day go?"

"Just fine. There's a lot to learn, but I think I'm going to be able to do what's required. The people in the accounting department are real nice. They all seem helpful."

"That's good," Jared said.

She said, "You've been at things a little longer. Do you like what you're seein'?"

Jared began to tell Deborah about Al and the three old pipe fitters he had met, and about the things he was seeing and discovering.

Deborah said, "You really are for real, aren't you?"

Jared asked, "What do you mean by that?"

"When I heard you telling the Summerfields and the Millers how much you love engineering and working in the refinery, I thought you were really laying it on thick. But you really do love those things, don't you?"

"Yes, I suppose I do. I guess you must like refineries too. You took a job in one."

"Are you kidding? I took this job because it offered a higher salary than any of the other offers I got. And it put me near a place where I can study for my CPA exam and where I can go to night school. I could study for an MBA or a law degree if I have to do that to keep on moving up the ladder.

As soon as I finish my CPA exam, I'm going to start looking around. I hope to find something in a place that smells a little better."

"Ah, the lady is ambitious."

"You're darned right I am."

"I've got to admit that I kinda had my eye on a job with one of the big engineering firms on the west side of Houston. I hear that's where the real action is. But when that didn't come through, I told myself I'd better get interested in working in this refinery. That was really my first love."

Deborah said, "You're really something different."

"Well, what about accounting? I suppose you really like that, don't you?"

"I like it okay. But I chose it because it was something I could be good at, and it offered me the best chance to get a really good salary after finishing a four-year degree."

Again Jared laughed and said, "You have a BMW to pay for."

"Right!"

Soon they arrived at the restaurant. They went in and ordered. While they waited for the food to come, Deborah asked, "How'd you ever come to fall in love with oil refineries?"

"It's kind of a long story."

"I'd like to hear it."

Jared said, "It started a long time ago. My dad worked in a refinery, and one time when I was just a little guy, my mom had to go and pick him up after working the evening shift. She took my little brother and me along in the car. It was a rainy, dreary winter night, and the refinery was flaring off a lot of waste gas. We parked in front and waited. The flames were coming in spurts. And every time it happened, it lit up the whole sky and reflected in the mist and made everything look black on orange, like a Halloween horror show or something. It made a roaring sound like some big old animal panting, and it actually made the ground shake. I was scared. And when I saw my daddy come walking out of that place, I didn't know what to think. That night, I had a bad dream. I went into my mom and dad's bedroom and woke my dad up and told him that I thought there was a dragon hiding in that refinery, and I didn't want him to go in there any more. My dad laughed and picked me up and took me back to bed; he lay down with me and told me as much as he could tell a six-year-old about how a refinery works. A few weeks later, he managed to get permission to take me out to work with him to show me the plant—and,

I think, to show me to the guys he worked with. I have been fascinated by refineries ever since."

"That's a good story. I'll watch out for dragons."

"To tell the truth, I still like to think there's kind of a dragon hiding out there somewhere among the tanks and units. It adds a little bit of danger that makes work more interesting. And, as a matter of fact, a refinery is a dangerous place. There are lots of things that could happen. You have to stay on your toes. I told you it was a long story. I hope I didn't bore you too much."

"No, it was a good story. Thank you for telling it to me. I can see why the refinery feels like home to you. Do you think of yourself as a dragon slayer?"

"No, that has never occurred to me."

Then Deborah was quiet for a while.

Finally Jared asked, "What are you thinking?"

"I'm thinking I'm jealous of you for having a mom and a dad like you had. My dad left when I was a little girl. He found someone he liked better. My mom and I had to go it together without him."

Jared said, "Oh, I'm sorry. Don't you ever see him?"

"Just a couple of times a year, and that's more for his benefit than mine. He did make his child support payments like the judge required him to. He liked to remind us of that—as if he was doing a fine thing. Mom worked her rear off. She was a registered nurse in a hospital. I always had a part-time job. Mom put half of the money she got from my dad into a college account for me because she assumed that the payments would stop when I turned eighteen—and they did. We've been planning for years for me to get a good job and to make a good living."

"It sounds like you had a pretty rough time of it."

"It really wasn't all that bad. We always had enough. We just always knew we had to work hard to make it. There used to be a song, "You and Me Against the World." Mom used to sing it to me. Anyway, I'm always jealous of people who grew up in homes like yours."

Jared looked down at the water circles his glass was making on the table and said, "I suppose I had better tell you that I've been through one marriage that didn't work. The divorce was not my idea, and there were no children. But I suppose that still makes me a one-time loser."

Deborah looked a little embarrassed as if she had said the wrong thing, but Jared saved her from having to think of something to say by going on, "But, yeah, I did grow up in a good family." Then he said, "Oh, don't get me wrong. We were all very human. Every one of us sometimes acted like a jackass. But we all knew we loved each other. We were just an average, hardworking, churchgoing, blue-collar family. But it was a good life. I've learned that it was not to be taken for granted. I'm grateful for it."

"You're right. It was good. You said you were a churchgoing family. Are you religious?"

"Well, I guess I used to be. We went to church when I was at home. I even went to chapel sometimes when I was in the navy because there wasn't anything else to do. But in college, I got busy and dropped out. Besides, that was just after the marriage fell apart. I didn't blame God for that or anything, but I don't know, after it happened, everything was different. What about you?"

"That's just never been a part of my life. I say it's because we couldn't bring ourselves to put our faith in anyone they told us to call 'Father.' But the truth is that Mom always had to work so hard that she didn't have time or energy for anything but work."

"I think there are lots of people like that."

"I once took a Bible course in junior college for an easy elective."

"What did you think about it?"

"It was interesting. I can see how some people who really believe some of the things in the Bible could turn out to be really good people. But I could also see how bad people could use some of the other things in the Bible as an excuse to do some really bad things."

"I can see that." About that time, the waitress brought the food. Jared wrapped up the conversation by saying, "I'll probably go back to church some day. I really still believe almost everything I used to believe. I just got out of the habit of going."

They both began to eat. Deborah realized that she was eating like a hungry puppy. She laughed her happy laugh again and said, "I told you I was hungry."

"Eat up. You're going to need all of your energy to beat me in miniature golf."

After a while, Deborah began to eat more slowly and said, "Jared, does it bother you that you're making such a big commitment of your life to an industry that's sick?"

Jared looked up with a surprised look on his face and said, "What makes you say that?"

She said, "I guess we talked more about it in business school than you did in technology, but it has been in all of the papers and news magazines.

The rich and powerful are doing everything they can to squeeze all of the short-term profit they can out of the businesses and industries. They're neglecting maintenance and improvement of facilities, downsizing and outsourcing everything they can, moving all of the work they can offshore where labor is cheap, and putting the squeeze on workers at all levels. There is a limit to how much of that American industry can stand. Matter of fact, recently it seems that the exploitation of business and industry has just about pushed the whole world's economy over the edge."

"Yeah, I've been reading about that. But I guess it always sounded like something that was happening way off in another place. It seemed like a war that was being fought somewhere far away. I could read about it in the paper and care about it, but I didn't feel that I was involved in it. I suppose I just believed that there'll always be American industry and that they'll always need engineers."

"I guess most people think that way. But things are changing in big ways. I'll bet your dad felt intensely loyal to his company because he believed his company would be loyal to him. No one can count on that anymore."

"Yeah, he felt really let down when the company offered him that golden handshake."

"This really isn't something that is happening somewhere else. The conversation Wednesday night was saturated with it. Look at what happened to Ed Osborne. Heck, look at what happened to you. Industry has already let you down once in a big way when they discontinued your scholarship. I suppose they discontinued a job offer that went with it, didn't they?"

"Yeah, I guess you could look at it that way."

"How else could you look at it?"

"I don't know. You can't always choose what's going to happen to you, but you can choose what you're going to let it mean to you. I just never saw it that way."

"You're really something else!"

"But, yeah, I guess I've been bumping up against the reality you're talkin' about ever since I came here. I've been talking to some of the guys in blue coveralls, and they're feeling it too."

Deborah went on as if there were some things she had bottled up and needed to tell someone. "I don't think that we can take it for granted that there'll always be an oil industry and that there'll always be a need for engineers, or even accountants. American business and industry are on the ropes."

"They'll always need accountants, won't they?"

"Yes, but some lady in India with a computer connection can do it as well as I can, and cheaper."

"Is that the real reason you don't plan to stay with Apex very long?"

"That's part of it. I just think that, in today's business climate, you need to stay loose and ready to move and do what you have to do to survive and move up."

Jared smiled and said, "I suppose you plan to move on up into the ranks of those that are making the big profits out of all of this."

"Not really. Lots of my friends in college think that they can. They shout 'Hurrah' for what is going on in business right now because they like to see themselves as entrepreneurs. They think that management and professional people will be among those who profit. But they're dreaming. The people in power are crowding out the blue-collar workers, and they're making their management and technical people work twice as hard for what they get."

"Lean and mean."

"That's what they call it. And, really, the chances of anyone actually moving into that circle of the really rich and powerful are slim to none. That circle is getting smaller, not bigger. Those people are eating each other up."

Jared said, "But don't you think some of those rich and powerful people will eventually see what is happening and make some changes?"

"I don't think that's very likely. And, if some of them wanted to, I think they would have an awfully hard time doing it. They have something rolling that will be hard to stop."

"What about the government? Shouldn't they step in and set some limits?"

"As long as politicians need big bucks to get elected, big money will be able to buy the government they want."

"Of course I know you are right. What do you think about Joe Summerfield? He seems like a guy with some convictions and commitments."

"I think he's a man walking a tightrope."

"Why do you say that?"

"That wisecrack he made about money flowing uphill showed that he sees what's happening. But he's close enough to the people at the top that some of his convictions and commitments could get him into big trouble."

"Sounds like lots of things are in jeopardy."

"You know what grieves me most? The blue-collar good life that you grew up in is one of the things that's at risk. It's getting harder and harder to maintain. We've grown up thinking of that as the life of the average American. But it's not that way any more."

"Yeah, that's the real bottom line of this whole discussion, isn't it?"

Deborah looked at Jared for a long minute and said, "I'm sorry for dumping all of this on you. I've had to get this stuff off my chest. Most of my friends in the school of business administration didn't want to hear it."

"Well, you've made me look at some of the things I've been trying not to see. I suppose that was good for me."

Deborah took a deep breath and let it out and said, "Well, it was good for me. But that's enough of it. Now let's change the subject. Let's talk about nothing but miniature golf and funny stories for the rest of the evening."

They left the restaurant and went to the miniature golf course. On the way Jared wondered if he should go easy and let the lady win. He didn't have to worry about that. It soon became clear that they were both natural competitors. Deborah beat him two games out of three—and they both laughed a lot.

On the way home, Jared thought, *I can't believe how much this girl told me about herself—and about myself—on a first date. She is different. I have never known anyone like her before.*

When he walked her to the door, she said, "Thank you for this evening. It's been really special."

He said, "Thank you, too." Then, though he hadn't actually planned to, he bent over and kissed her lightly on the lips.

She smiled and said, "See you at work."

Chapter 3

On Saturday, Jared went to the first practice of the company baseball team. Practice was held at a private park that Apex maintained for their employees and for community activities. He had a good time getting acquainted with some of the younger men and playing ball—just for the sake of playing ball. He met Andy Evans, the coach, and thought he was someone he would like to have for a friend.

The next week, Jared went on with the job of learning the ropes and exploring the refinery. On Wednesday morning, he came into the office and found Al reading a *Sports Illustrated* magazine. Al looked up and said, "Hi, partner. Made any new discoveries about the refinery?"

Jared said, "Matter of fact, I have. Yesterday I walked around the compounding department and discovered that we're still mixing the heavy lubricants in batches in big vats. Doesn't it seem like it would be more efficient to be doing that in some continuous process, like almost everything else is done in the plant?"

"Say, you are good. It took Dietrich five years to see that. Of course, he had his mind on the steam generating project." Al got up and went to one of the large file cabinets where drawings were kept. He bent over, opened the bottom drawer, and took out a small stack of drawings. He put them on the table. "This is as far as we got in designing something better. This was the first suggestion that we got thrown back in our faces. At that time, Summerfield was assistant plant manager. He liked what we had done and piloted it through the channels to the people in power. We didn't hear anything back from them. After several months, he wrote them a letter asking what they were thinking. The answer was the one we have gotten to know so well. 'We will take the suggestion under advisement, and if we find merit in it, we will refer it to our engineering subcontractor.'"

Jared frowned. "What a bummer."

"It was just the first one. After getting that response several times, we quit trying."

"Do you think they'll ever take a different attitude toward innovation?"

"I have quit hoping for it. If you want to look at the plans we drew and see if you can come up with something better, you're welcome. But I'll give you a hint. If you want to interest the head office, you have to come up with something that'll reduce the cost of operation, probably by replacing people with computers. And it will have to be something you can build and install without any cost."

Jared spent a few minutes looking over the drawings that Al had taken out, and then he put them back into the bottom drawer and got to work going through his daily motions. He spent the day under a gloomy cloud.

Then that evening, Deborah called.

"Hey sailor. How'r ya doin'?"

"Until just now, not too hot. But now the day is looking up."

"What's your trouble?"

"Oh, nothing to talk about right now. How are you doin'?"

"Just fine. I've been exploring our environment, and now I'm thinking about taking an expedition into the big city to see what's there. I owe you a meal. How about riding along with me on Saturday and scoping out the Houston scene? I'll buy you lunch."

Jared was taken aback. He couldn't believe that Deborah had just called to ask him for a date. "That sounds great. I've been wanting to do that too. But I'm supposed to be at baseball practice in the morning. I can get away by eleven. Is that too late?"

"No, that'll be fine. I'll pick you up at your place. Wear a cap. We're going to ride with the top down."

"Great. I think you just salvaged my week." Jared gave Deborah his address. They chatted a little longer and then said goodbye. After he hung up, he caught himself smiling for no apparent reason.

On Saturday Jared left baseball practice early. He got cleaned up, put on his best casual clothes, and was waiting for Deborah in front of his apartment complex. Right on time, Deborah drove up in her BMW with the top down. She had pulled her hair back into a knot like she had worn it the first time he saw her, but she did not look severe this time. She looked like a young woman ready to have a good time. Jared climbed into the car and asked, "Are we going for a tour of the promised land?"

"I suppose you might say that. Are you ready?"

"Ready," he said.

The car wheeled out into the street and sped away. Deborah did not drive carelessly, but she obviously enjoyed the experience of driving. She pushed the speed limits a little bit. They were on freeways most of the time, and the traffic on a Saturday morning was not bad. Soon they were on Loop 610 circling south of town. In a few minutes, Jared saw a huge structure rising up on the right. "What in the world is that?" he asked.

"That's the Reliant Stadium, where the Texans play. I came this way because I suspect that you'll want to know how to get here."

Jared was impressed at the size of the stadium. All he could say was "Wow!" He asked, "Do they play baseball there?"

"No, they play that at another one of the wonders of the world downtown."

"How did you learn so much about Houston?"

"A bunch of us from school came down here one spring break. Some of them were Houston girls. They showed us around before we made the beach scene at Galveston. I was fascinated by Houston. It's a place where lots of important things happen. I didn't want to go on to the beach. Later one of the girls from Houston invited me to come home with her for a weekend."

Deborah turned off onto Westheimer in the middle of a cluster of big buildings that would have done any downtown proud. There were new and impressive office buildings, and prestigious-looking shopping centers. Traffic suddenly got congested. The cars were of a finer pedigree than those he had seen around Pasadena.

They were obviously in an affluent area.

Jared said, "It looks like we are in a really classy part of town."

"You got it." She waved toward a huge building and said, "Of course, that is the building that us girls think is the center of Houston, the Galleria, a multistory shopping mall built around a skating rink. All of the finest stores are represented there."

"I'll bet that's something to see," Jared said. But he was hoping she didn't plan to show it to him just then. He was getting hungry. He didn't have to worry. Deborah soon turned into the parking lot of a bistro. She found a parking space between a Mercedes and a Jaguar. Jared thought, *I suppose this really is the promised land.*

"This is a place my friend brought me when I stayed with her. I hope you like it."

As they were getting out of the car, they heard a woman's voice. "Deborah! Deborah Olsen. What are you doing here?" Deborah recognized an old friend from school. They ran to each other and embraced. It had actually been only a few weeks since they had seen each other, but both had been so involved in their new lives that it seemed longer. They were glad to make contact with someone whom they knew from their past. She was with a nice-looking older man. Deborah introduced her to Jared, "This is Melissa Morris, a fellow Longhorn. We had lots of classes together at the university."

Melissa introduced them both to Alan Wright, who worked for the company where she had been accepted into the executive training program. Alan grasped Jared's hand firmly and made eye contact in an act of practiced, friendly assertiveness. Jared guessed that the slacks and sport shirt that Alan wore must have cost more than Jared's best suit. "Hi, Jared," Alan said. "Say, I really like your car. You're brave to let Deborah drive it."

Jared said, "Oh, that's Deborah's car. My car is a real junker."

Melissa said, "Well, Deborah, you must be doing pretty well."

Deborah said, "I hope to do well. I got a good deal on the car. Some rich guy bought it for his son to drive. The kid was arrested twice in the same month for DWI. The dad thought he had better sell it before the kid wound up in jail."

Alan said, "Tough luck for the kid."

Jared thought that was a curious response.

Alan said, "If you're not meeting anyone, why don't you join us so the girls can catch up on their talking."

Jared said, "Sounds like a good idea to me."

They went inside and found a table. They passed up the customary detour by the bar. Jared was grateful. He was getting really hungry. The things on the menu were all unfamiliar to him. He asked Deborah what she recommended, and she made some suggestions for him. He made a selection. They all ordered. The men sat and listened as the girls got reacquainted and caught up on what they were doing with their lives.

When the food was served, there was a break in the conversation and Alan said, "So, Jared, who are you with?"

Jared said, "I'm with Apex Oil."

"Are you new here in the Houston office?"

Jared said, "No, I work in the refinery." Jared thought he saw Alan's eyebrows twitch just ever so slightly. He added, "I'm a process engineer."

"An engineer. That's good. It will probably be good for you to spend some time in a refinery. That will look good on a resume when you apply for your next job."

Jared caught the subtle implication of that comment, but he supposed it had been made with good intentions. "What do you do?"

"I'm with Gold Star Marketing. I do corporate sales."

"That sounds interesting."

"It is." He told a little about what he did, mentioning some rather glamorous travel. He ended by saying, "You might look into it someday when you're ready to do something else. We have some people with engineering backgrounds in our sales staff. Their training is a real asset in working with industrial clients."

Deborah mentioned that they were exploring Houston and that it was Jared's first trip into town. Alan said, "Then let me make a suggestion. After we eat, follow me downtown, and I'll take you for drinks at the Executive Club. You can see the whole city from there."

The rest of the conversation revolved around fluctuations in the stock market. There was no good news to be shared. Jared knew that he should be interested in that subject, but he had not yet really gotten into it. He listened and tried to learn. When the waiter came with the bills, Jared picked up their bill and paid it. They walked out into the parking lot and then followed Alan's Mercedes downtown.

When they were alone in the car again, Deborah said, "I was supposed to buy your lunch."

Jared smiled and said, "Yeah, but under the circumstances, I thought it would be better if I paid."

"Thanks."

"Now you owe me two. Was Melissa one of your best friends?"

"We had lots of classes together, and we liked each other. But I suppose she would have thought of her sorority sisters as her best friends."

"Were you in a sorority?"

"No. My mom tried to get me to pledge one. She said, 'You only go around once.' But it was expensive. I thought I could have plenty of friends and plenty of fun without it."

"Your friends look like they're quite successful."

"People in this part of the world are trained to look successful. You have to get to know them really well to find out if they actually are."

"Oh, are you saying there's a lot of phoniness?"

"They're just doing what they think they're supposed to do. They think that looking successful and acting successful can help them and their companies to actually be successful."

"Sounds like you have to be a little skeptical about everything you see or hear."

"You just have to learn to make some allowances for the differences between appearances and realities."

"I'm not sure I could ever be comfortable doing that."

"You'd better learn. It's necessary for survival."

"What about women who drive BMWs?"

"Be especially careful around women who drive BMWs."

About that time, Alan turned into a drive at the base of a tall building. A valet waited to park cars. Jared and Deborah followed them in. The valet took charge of their cars, and everyone followed Alan to the elevator, which took them to the top floor. Alan showed a membership card and said, "We just want drinks, but we'd like to sit at a table by the window." They were ushered into a large room with windows all around that opened onto a panorama of city scenery. The view was breathtaking. Alan said, "There are not many people here because it is Saturday. It would have been much more crowded on a weekday." Most of the people wore business suits, but a few wore casual clothes. Some carried briefcases. Some of the people seemed to be doing business, but many were enjoying a social afternoon.

At the table they placed orders for drinks. Then Alan suggested that they walk around and look out the windows while they waited for their drinks. He pointed out some of the biggest buildings. Then he walked them around to the west side of the building and said, "That cluster right there is the Galleria where we just came from. Some of the centers of major worldwide companies are right there, and others are downtown here. Out the Katy Freeway there are some of the research and development centers of major petrochemical and engineering companies. You will want to go out and explore those someday. Out that way and to the north and west are some of the finest residential developments in the city." Then he walked them back around to the other side of the building and said, "Do you see that smoky spot out there on the horizon? Those are the channel industries where you two work. They support all of the rest of the things you can see from here."

Deborah injected, "That great big thing over there is Minute Maid Park. That's where you will come for the baseball games."

Jared finally let himself say the word he had been repeating in his mind. "Wow!"

Eventually they returned to their table and enjoyed their drinks. Jared asked lots of questions. He thought this was a lot like being on top of the cracking unit with Sarge.

Eventually, Alan said, "Will you excuse us for a minute? I see a client that I need to speak to." They left Jared and Deborah alone for a few minutes.

Deborah said, "You're impressed, aren't you?"

"You're darned right I am. I've never seen such a display of business and industry in my life. It's fascinating."

"It is impressive. But you need to ask the same kinds of questions about companies that you ask about people. Are they as successful as they look?"

Jared said, "Oh, come on now. These big buildings don't just grow by themselves. There hasta be something dynamic makin' 'em grow."

"You mean like that tall building right there, the one that looks like it's silver plated?"

"Yeah, like that. That didn't just grow by accident."

"That used to be the Enron Building."

Jared stared at the building and finally said, "I see what you mean." He looked back at Deborah and said, "I get the impression that you don't like it down here."

Deborah said, "No. The truth is, I like it a lot. This is right where I want to be some day." Then she smiled and said, "I'm just practicing realism as a survival tactic."

Jared nodded.

After Alan and Melissa came back, the conversation lightened up. Alan asked, "How do you like downtown Houston?"

"I'm overwhelmed, but Deborah tells me this is right where she wants to be."

Alan said, "Oh, so the lady is ambitious."

Deborah smiled broadly and said, "You're darned right I am."

Alan said, "Well, I'll be on the lookout for an opening for an ambitious woman in our company."

Jared said, "You'd better think twice before doing that. I think she is planning to be the CEO of whatever company she works for."

When the bill came, Alan signed for it and suggested that they should get together again some time.

Back in the car again, Deborah said, "I want to take the long way home, so I can show you something Alan didn't mention, the Houston Medical Center. I think that is one of the most impressive things in this whole city."

They traveled out South Main, past the art museum and Herman Park, with its statue of Sam Houston on a horse. Deborah said, "He's pointing toward the Apex refinery—or maybe it's the San Jacinto Battleground he's pointing at. That's where he and his men won the independence of Texas."

Soon they were approaching an awesome complex of big hospital buildings, medical schools, and other medical facilities. Deborah said, "I don't know what all of those buildings are, but I understand that it is one of the most advanced and complete medical centers in the world."

Jared looked to his right and saw another assemblage of impressive buildings, all in a Mediterranean style and surrounded by oak trees. He asked, "What is that over there?"

She said, "That is Rice University. It's the Ivy League of the South. An engineer with a degree from Rice can get a job anywhere."

Jared gazed at the school for a long minute. Then he said, "You know, I was actually accepted there. But the tuition was too high and the scholarship was too low. I guess I didn't know how important that would be." Then after another minute, Jared said, "But what the heck. I'm satisfied with my education. There's no use in looking back." Then he changed the subject. "This really has been quite an adventure. Thanks for taking me."

"Oh, the pleasure was mine."

"Can we get together to do something next weekend?"

Deborah said, "No, not next weekend. It's time for me to go home and tell my mom about my new world. But any time after that."

"Say, do you ever eat in the company cafeteria?"

"I have a couple of times but thirty minutes does not allow for a leisurely lunch. I usually bring a sandwich from home and eat it at my desk. I'd be glad to meet you there some time."

"How about Friday?"

"It's a date."

Chapter 4

On Monday morning, Jared came to work early and stopped in the cafeteria for coffee. He had not finished filling his cup before he heard Mrs. O'Brien calling his name.

"Jared. Bring your coffee and come over here. There are some people I want you to meet."

Jared saw that the two young women he had wanted to meet were at the table with her. He smiled and went over. He put down his coffee cup at the empty space at the table but stood while he was introduced.

"Jared, this is Sally Williams and this is Angie Billings. Girls, this is Jared Philips. He's our new engineer and also the most eligible bachelor at Apex."

Sally was the redhead. Angie was the beauty that Jared had wanted to meet. Jared shook hands with both girls and said, "It's always a pleasure to meet pretty ladies." Then he sat down with them. Sally was a friendly, comfortable sort of person. Angie was something else. She was even prettier than Jared had remembered her. Her eyes were deep brown and focused on Jared's eyes. She smiled like someone posing for a photograph. Her figure was as he had remembered it, but it was hard for Jared to tear his eyes away from hers. He forced himself. Mrs. O'Brien was speaking and he needed to look at her.

"Sally is an operator in Section A. Angie works in the lab. They're a couple of the bright spots in this dreary old refinery."

Jared asked, "Where are you ladies from?"

Sally answered, "We both went to high school in Pasadena. We were best friends in high school, and we still are."

Jared said, "It must be nice to have friends that you have known for a long time. I'm a transplant. I've got to start all over making friends."

Angie said, "We have lots of friends that we've known all of our lives. But we like to meet new people."

Jared asked, "Do you like working for Apex?"

Sally answered, "I like it fine. Both of our dads work here and so does Angie's mom. It runs in the family. I feel like I belong here."

Jared said, "I can relate to that. I'm a refinery worker's kid. I suppose I always knew I'd work in a refinery. How about you, Angie? Do you like it?"

Angie, still smiling, said, "Well, I can imagine things I'd rather do, but Apex pays more than any of the other jobs I could get."

Mrs. O'Brien said, "Sally is still a school girl. She's going to college at night."

Jared said, "That's interesting. Where are you going?"

Sally said, "I'm going to San Jacinto Junior College right here at home. I'm working on an associate degree in process operation."

Jared said, "That sounds a little like what I'm doing. Do you plan to go on and study engineering?"

Sally said, "I've thought about it. They tell me I could. But I'm really just trying to learn how to do better what I'm doing right now. Maybe it will qualify me to move up to be a chief operator or something."

Jared turned back to Angie. She was still smiling. "Are you a chemist?" he asked.

"Not really. I almost flunked chemistry in high school. But I can run a viscosity test. I run tests on samples all day long. It's a quality control thing."

Jared said, "That's interesting."

Angie, still smiling, said, "No, it's not."

The conversation went on for a few minutes more. They talked about the things they liked to do. Angie liked country dancing. Sally liked to go fishing. Angie never took her eyes off of Jared and never stopped smiling. It made Jared just a little nervous but it left a suggestion that no man could miss—and, coming from someone that pretty, no man could ignore. Jared recognized the suggestion and played with it in his mind.

The conversation ended when it was time to go to work. Nothing very significant was said. When it was time to go, Jared said goodbye to the ladies, but the fantasies about going out with Angie stayed with him. He kept playing with them all day long. He imagined what it would be like to be with a woman that beautiful. The fantasies were practically irresistible. They followed him home and kept him up half the night. He thought about calling her and asking for a date. But he had become interested in what he had going with Deborah. But two dates don't exactly make an engagement. Besides that, Deborah was going to be gone this weekend. Jared remembered what Deborah had said about her relationship with the guy she dated in college. She probably wouldn't really be interested in any guy for long. But she seemed interested.

He spent a little more time playing with his fantasies about Angie. But by midnight, he had sifted his thoughts and decided that he was really interested in Deborah, and it would be best not to complicate things. If that didn't work out, he might give Angie a call. Then the thought occurred to him that he actually might like Sally better. He wondered how long he could enjoy that smile. Then he wondered how long the smile would last. A painful memory flitted across his mind. He brushed it away. By the time he fell asleep, he had decided to see where things would go with Deborah before he explored any other possibilities.

On Tuesday Joe Summerfield noticed that Michael had skipped his coffee and gone straight to his office. He didn't pay much attention to that. They did not follow the coffee ritual as regularly as the others did. About midmorning Michael came to Joe's door and said, "Can I come in?"

"Sure, come in and sit down. What do you have on your mind?"

Michael came in and closed the door behind him. He sat down and looked at Joe. Joe could tell that he had something heavy on his mind.

"Did you send your letter?"

"Yes, I took your advice and thought about it for a while. I rewrote it and put in a lot of assurances that I wanted to help make the company profitable. But I said I have a suggestion to make that I really believe they need to hear. Older employees are valuable. I felt like I had to say it."

"Well, I'm going to tell you something that you are not supposed to know. It's not good. I've been awake all night trying to decide what I should do about it, and I've decided that I have to talk with you about it."

The mood in the office suddenly became somber. "Okay, go on."

"When I got home yesterday, this letter was on my personal fax machine." He handed Joe a letter on Apex head office stationery. Joe read it silently.

It said, "You will understand that this correspondence is to be kept in the strictest confidence. Next week, you will be called to come to meet me at the Houston office to be briefed on some changes in company policy. I will meet you there. While you are there, I will want to talk with you about your future with Apex Oil and Refining Company. I would like for you to be ready to tell me how you would go about increasing the profitability of the Pasadena Refinery." The letter was signed by William Stone.

As Joe read, he turned white. He looked up at Michael, and the two looked at each other in silence for a long time. Then Joe said, "Sounds like I'm a dead man."

Michael said, "I want you to know that I'm not going to do anything to sell you out. I have great respect for you as a man and as a manager."

After another long pause, Joe said, "I can't tell you how much I appreciate that. But don't sell yourself out either. It sounds like my career may have already gone down the tube. Eventually, I'll handle that. You still have a career ahead of you—and if I can't manage this refinery, I hope that you will. Get ready to do what you have to do."

"If there is anything I can do for you, just let me know. Anything."

"Thank you, Michael. You are a real friend. If there's anything I can do for you, just ask."

Joe Summerfield stayed in his office most of the morning. Then he called Helen and told her he was coming home for lunch. He asked Michael to mind the store.

At home, Joe told Helen what had happened between bites of a sandwich. He soon abandoned the sandwich and started to walk back and forth, gesturing to vent his anger and to express his anxiety about the industry and the world and everything else that seemed to him to be going to hell. Helen listened intently. They had a good relationship. They had been partners for a long time. She knew it was time to listen. Finally, Joe ran out of steam and sat down. He said, "What do you think about that?" Then he took another bite of sandwich.

Helen answered, "Well, of course, I think someone in New York is crazy. I'm almost as angry at them as you are. And I agree with you that they are liable to scuttle the industry. But it's the industry I'm worried about and not you. If they decide to get rid of you, they'll probably make it profitable for you to go. You know it won't be long til retirement time anyhow. You will probably come out dollars ahead if they let you go early. I'd be glad to have you around the house—even at lunchtime. We could start taking all of those trips we've talked about. It's the industry that will be the loser."

"Yeah, and I really don't want that to happen. After all of these years I don't want to see it sink."

"I knew you were gonna say that."

"Do you think I should beat them to the punch and tell them what they can do with their job?"

"Why would you want to do that? You really don't know if this young squirt is talking for the company or if he just has some little agenda of his own that he's pushing. If you stay and fight, you can at least make someone listen to what you have to say. And, like I said, if they want to boot you out, they will probably make it profitable for you to retire. You'll come out ahead."

"It could get really unpleasant."

Helen said, "So? I'm up for it if you are."

Joe thought for a while and then said, "Okay. I'm gonna be a burr under their blanket, and they're going to have to contend with me until they get rid of me."

Helen smiled and said, "That's my man."

Joe smiled too and hugged his wife. Then he said, "Have we got any ice cream?"

On Wednesday Jared arrived at work early and went to the cafeteria for coffee. As he was filling his cup, he heard Deacon calling his name. He went over and sat down with the group that was gathered in the corner. Deacon said, "Jared, my two wicked friends have enticed me to meet them at the Ice House again after work today. Do you want to meet us there? I won't buy you a beer, but I'll remind Sarge that he owes you one." Jared wondered what that was all about, but he agreed to meet them there.

Then he sat for a while listening to Pop tell about his most recent fishing trip with his son. He was really hoping to avoid another encounter with Angie, or at least to shorten it if there had to be one. When he got up, he saw that Angie and Sally were sitting with Mrs. O'Brien again. He went by to speak to them. Again, he encountered Angie's adoring smile. It was hard to resist. But it was almost time to be at work so he visited for a couple of minutes without sitting down and went on to his office.

At quitting time Jared drove to the Ice House. He found Deacon and Sarge sitting on the porch. He joined them.

"Hey, how's it going?" he asked.

Sarge said, "We're just sitting here worrying."

"Worrying about what?"

"Our wives have gone shopping together, and we're wondering if we're gonna have to take out a bank loan to pay for what they'll buy."

Deacon said, "You wouldn't know about that since you are a single guy."

Jared said, "Oh yeah, I would. I was married once—to someone who really did like expensive clothes. You guys are probably in deep trouble."

Sarge and Deacon looked at each other and chuckled. Sarge said, "The truth is, my wife manages our finances. We would be in trouble all the time if I was handling the checkbook. I hope she does find something pretty. I can't ever get her to spend any money on herself."

Deacon said, "Yeah, the truth is we both married above ourselves. Say, I notice you finally got to meet that pretty lady you asked us about."

Jared got a shy look on his face and said, "Yeah, I did. But I've also gotten acquainted with another little lady that I'm kinda interested in."

Sarge said, "She must be something. Every single guy in the plant has his eye on Angie."

Deacon said, "Whaddaya mean, single guy? All of the guys grab a second look at her when she goes by."

Jared said, "Even you, Deacon?"

Deacon said, "Well, ahhh, strictly as a matter of appreciating beauty. Aesthetics, ya know."

While all of this was going on, Maggie Christopher and Jane Anderson were coming home from their shopping trip. Maggie drove her car into the driveway of the Andersons' neat brick home. The yard was well kept, and there were flowers blooming in the flower bed. It was not a pretentious place, but it gave the impression that it was important to the people who lived there.

Jane said, "This has been fun, even if we didn't find much that we liked. Would you like to come in and have a glass of tea?"

Maggie answered, "Sure, we have time. I understand that our men are meeting some other guys at that notorious den of iniquity, the Five O'Clock Ice House."

"Yeah, I got the impression that they were meeting for some reason. I wonder what that's all about."

"Who knows? Don't forget your package. It was hard enough to find something that looked nice for women our age. Don't the stores know that not all of their customers are cute young things?"

Inside, they sat down at the kitchen table, and Jane poured glasses of tea from a pitcher she took from the refrigerator. She sat down and said, "I miss Betty MacKinzie. I understand that she had lots of things to do before moving, but I wish she could have been with us."

"Yes, we are really going to miss them."

"You and Deacon are just about the only friends we are going to have left around here. Our kids have all moved to other cities, and all of our friends are retiring and moving away. We envy you. You have your daughter living in town, and you have all of your friends at church."

Maggie said, "You know we would be glad for you to come to church with us."

Jane said, "I would really like that, but you know Bill. He's not quite ready to do that yet."

"You can come on without him. Lots of women do."

Jane shook her head and said, "I don't want to do that. I think if I start goin' without Bill, he never will come. I want him to come with me. He's actually a whole lot closer to being ready to come than most people think. When we go with you, he always enjoys it. He really believes most of the same things you and George do. And he likes your preacher."

"Oh yeah, that's right. He met Tim when he went fishing with him and George."

"Yeah, I'll never forget that. When Bill found out that the other guy who was going along was the preacher, I thought he was going to rebel. I think he thought Tim would get him out in that boat and put the hard sell on him and not let him come back to shore until he had saved his soul. He'd have backed out if I'd have let him. He finally went, sayin' he was ready to swim back to shore if he had to. But when he came home he said the preacher turned out to be a regular guy. He enjoyed the trip."

"Then what keeps Sarge from being ready to come to church?"

"He says he has a reputation for bein' a hard-drinkin' old reprobate, and goin' to church would spoil his image."

"But he's not really an old reprobate. Everyone knows that. And I've never seen him drunk. How much does he really drink?"

"Never more than one beer a day. And he doesn't have one every day. Just when he has someone to drink with, or barbeque or fried catfish, or a hot day of mowing the yard."

Maggie said, "That is really not very much at all."

Jane said, "He used to drink a lot more when we were younger. In fact, when our children were little, he almost let it get out of hand. One

Saturday we went to a party with friends, and he made a real fool of himself. The next morning I convened a meeting of him and me. I told him that I loved him and that I would put up with a lot from him, but I wasn't going to be married to a drunk, and I wasn't going to put our children through having a drunk for a daddy. He knew I meant it. It took him about two minutes to make a decision. He hasn't had more than one beer a day since then. He is really a good guy."

"Good for you! Good for both of you! We know he's a good guy. He's really George's favorite friend."

Back at the Five O'Clock Ice House, Mac had finally arrived, and the four men had gone in and gotten their drinks. They chatted a little longer, and then Deacon said, "Jared, we had a special reason for asking you to come out here today. Mac wants to tell you something."

Jared looked at Mac and saw that he wore a somber expression too. He said, "Okay."

Mac said, "I'm a little worried about something, and I thought I'd better let someone know about it. You're the only one I know who works up in the head office. I thought if I told you, you could tell someone who could do some good.

"Go on."

"You know that I'm scheduled to retire at the end of the month. I've been training a guy to take my place supervising the maintenance work at Apex. He was a good guy, and he was taking things seriously. But about a week ago, someone made him a better offer, and he left Petrotech. Now they have me training another guy named Buddy O'Neil. He's one of the two guys you met when you were here with us before. I don't have as much confidence in him as I had in the other guy. Besides that, I really don't have enough time to train anyone before I leave. I just thought I'd better say something to someone so you can keep an eye on things."

Deacon chimed in and said, "You probably know that they're planning to do a maintenance shutdown on a cracking unit in Section C, and they'll be bringin' it up again right after Mac leaves. Some of us are not sure that the new guy will be ready to do that."

Jared said, "Is there any chance of you staying until after the shutdown?"

"I thought about that. Even made it okay with my wife. But my boss at Petrotech thinks the new guy will do just fine. He said, 'Since you're gonna go, just go on.'"

"Do you know what a turnaround is?" Deacon asked Jared.

"Yeah. You take the whole unit out of service, take it apart and clean everything and check everything, and then put it back together."

"Right. And there's just a whole hell of a lot of things that can go wrong in the process."

"What do you think we ought to do?"

"Just try to get a little more direct supervision. Maybe you could come around, or maybe someone else could pay a little more attention to what's goin' on."

"Who is supposed to supervise his work? That's got to be someone's job."

"It is," Sarge said. "It's the job of the maintenance supervisor, Marvin Elrod, the other guy you met when we were here before. Remember, he said he and Buddy were old beer-drinkin' pals. That gives you an idea of how O'Neil got the job. And like I told you, Elrod doesn't want to hear anything from me or, for that matter, from any of us. If I was ta go and try ta talk to him, he'd just bow his neck and show me that he is in charge and I ain't."

"I wish I'd had a chance to watch you do a turnaround so I'd have a better idea of what's supposed to happen. But it really isn't my job, and I expect, if I meddle too much with it, someone is gonna tell me that."

Mac said, "I wish you could just come around."

Jared gave a little laugh and said, "I know you guys are serious about this because I know how much you don't like to have an engineer lookin' over your shoulder."

Mac said, "You've got it."

Sarge said, "When you take your little late afternoon strolls for the next couple of weeks, why don't you stroll over to where the maintenance crew is working and let Mac get you acquainted with the new guy and the turnaround process."

"Would that be okay?"

Mac said, "I don't know how much good it can do, but I'd be glad to see you."

"Then I'll drop around."

The next morning, Jared told Al about his conversation with the pipe fitters. Al was surprised. "Those old guys never ask for supervision. They will probably raise forty different kinds of sand if we go around. Besides, that's the job of the maintenance supervisor. He and the operators are supposed to do regular inspections during the process. I am sure that he will keep an eye on the contractor."

"I know that. But they are actually asking us to keep an eye on things. I think we ought to take it seriously."

"So what can we do? Do you think you know how to spot anything that is going wrong in a turnaround? I've been around here a lot longer than you have, and I don't know what to look for. That's the job of the maintenance supervisor, the operators, and the maintenance contractors."

Jared was frustrated with Al for not taking the warning seriously, but he realized that he really didn't know what to do.

That afternoon, Jared headed over to where Mac and the maintenance crew were working. Mac was talking with Buddy O'Neil. Mac said, "Buddy, do you remember meeting Jared Philips at the Ice House?

Buddy said, "Yeah, I remember. Hi, kid."

Mac said, "Jared wants us to show him how a turnaround works. Maybe you can help me explain it to him."

Jared asked Mac to talk him through the checklist and the process for doing a turnaround just to give Mac a chance to go over it again for Buddy. Buddy guessed what was happening and walked away after the first few minutes of the explanation.

Jared mumbled, "I don't think we did any good."

Mac shook his head. "Probably not."

"If my co-op program hadn't fallen through on me, I probably would have had a chance to work a turnaround or two. I really wish I knew more about it right now."

Mac went on with the explanation for Jared's sake.

On Friday, Jared met Deborah in the cafeteria for lunch. They had both brought sandwiches so they did not have to go through the line. Jared noticed some of the people noticing that he and Deborah were eating together and he decided that was okay. They chated, mostly about Deborah's plans for her week end. Jared wished her a good trip back home. He invited her to go with him to the company barbeque the following Saturday. She said she would be glad to go.

Jared thought again about calling Angie for a date, but he decided that he'd go fishing instead. No use in complicating things unnecessarily. He asked Pop where he took his boy to fish from the bank and got directions to the Texas City jetty. He bought some inexpensive fishing tackle and set out fairly early Sunday morning. On the way, he crossed the high bridge over the Kemah Channel. The channel connects Clear Lake with Galveston Bay. He was awestruck by the view from the bridge. There was a yachting center there that he couldn't believe. Hundreds of sailboats and other pleasure boats of all kinds and sizes were tied up there. It was obvious that there was a recreational center too. He decided that when he got tired of fishing, he'd come back and explore this place.

After fishing for a while, he drove back to Kemah and began to look around. There were even more boats than he had imagined tied up in an elaborate complex of docks. Across the road from the docks was a street lined with shops selling arts and crafts, leading down to the banks of the Kemah Channel. There was a collection of restaurants and a hotel and other recreational facilities. Jared was impressed.

One sign caught his eye. It advertised sailboats for rent. Jared had once learned how to sail a small boat, but he hadn't sailed in a long time. He thought it would be fun to do it again. He asked directions and drove back up the road that led along the shores of Clear Lake toward the Space Center. There was a yacht club and lots of other boating facilities up that way. Finally, he found the boat rental place. They had several motorboats, jet skis, and other pleasure crafts. They had four nice small sailboats and one large one. He asked the price of renting a small one: one hundred and fifty dollars for half a day. Jared knew that he couldn't do that very often. But he made a reservation for half a day of sailing the Sunday after his next payday. He stood for a while watching the sailboats come and go on Clear Lake and anticipating the pleasure of sailing again.

On Monday morning, Michael Miller came into Joe's office and closed the door. He spoke softly. "I got my summons to meet William Stone at the Houston office."

Joe nodded. "When?"

"Tomorrow morning."

"Remember what I said. Tell him enough of what he wants to hear to keep him thinking of you as my successor."

"I've been thinking about it and I think I know what to say, but I really don't feel good about this."

"I know you don't, but it's what you need to do. It will be best for everyone."

"I'll let you know what happens."

On Monday afternoon, Jared walked around to where Mac and his maintenance crew had been working, but he found that they weren't there. The operator on the unit said Petrotech had sent them to work on a job in another refinery. They would be back just in time to start work on the shutdown on the cracking unit.

Before going back to his office, Jared went by the unit where Sarge worked. He got his attention by tapping on the control room window and beckoned him outside. He told Sarge that the Petrotech crew had been withdrawn until it was time for the shutdown. Sarge just shook his head and said, "Well, I guess we'll just have to play it by ear and hope for the best."

Tuesday afternoon, Michael came into Joe's office again and said, "Well, I had my meeting."

"How did it go?"

"Not as badly as I thought it might. He made some vague statements about me having a future with the company and said that I would probably be the next plant manager here in Pasadena. But he didn't say anything about when that might happen, and he didn't say anything at all about you. He asked me how I would go about increasing the profitability of the plant."

"Good. What did you tell him?"

"Well, I started by reciting some of the textbook rules for increasing profitability and mentioning some examples of things that we could do here to apply them. Pretty soon, he started telling me what he thinks we should do. There were no surprises there. I just listened and nodded and took notes, and where I could, I said something about how we might implement something he had said. I didn't have to make many commitments."

"Good. I hope you left him thinking that you're the man he would want in this job."

"It's hard to know what he was thinking, but I tried not to burn any bridges."

"Okay. Now we'll just wait and see what happens next."

Chapter 5

Saturday was a beautiful day for a picnic. Jared picked Deborah up about midmorning and drove to the Apex Company Park. On the way he asked, "How did your trip back home go?"

Deborah answered, "It went just fine. Mom was full of questions about everything. She's really happy about me havin' a good job."

Jared said, "Your mom must be quite a lady. I'd like to meet her sometime."

Deborah said, "I hope you can. I told her about you."

"Oh?"

"Yeah, she said it sounded like you might be a good guy."

"What made her think that?"

"I told her."

Jared laughed and said, "I'm glad I've still got you fooled."

It didn't take long to get to the Apex Park.

The park was all set up for a special occasion. Employees could use the park for their family outings or reserve it for their community organization's activities all during the year. It got lots of use. But the twice-a-year company barbeques were the primary function of the facility. Picnic tables, which were usually arranged in the pavilion, were placed in little groups under the trees to make room for a country and western dance that was to be held in the evening. The baseball field had been freshly chalked, and the barbeque pit had been smoking for twelve hours.

The program for these barbeques had become traditional. Things started at about ten in the morning. There were always games for children before lunch, sack races, three legged races, and a treasure hunt in which the kids scramble for coins hidden in a large pile of sand. Lunch was the big meal with barbequed brisket, chicken, hot links, and all of the traditional trimmings. Then there was a baseball game in the afternoon, more barbeque for supper, and a dance in the evening. Each employee bought a ticket for his or her family, but the cost of the affair was subsidized by the company. Joe Summerfield thought this kind of social gathering was good for the company.

The morning was bright and clear and not too hot. The smell of smoke and brisket that had been cooking slowly all night came to meet everyone who arrived. Everything was in place for everyone to have a really good time. Jared and Deborah were among the first to arrive. Deborah had never seen the park before. Jared was familiar with the baseball field but hadn't seen much else. They walked around to see what all was there. Deborah was impressed.

Eventually they found Deacon, Sarge, and Mac and their wives. They had set themselves up in a cluster of picnic tables under some trees. They had set up folding chairs and scattered their picnic supplies over a couple of tables. It was obvious that others were expected. When Jared saw them, he said to Deborah, "Hey, there are the guys that I've been telling you about. Those must be their wives. Come on, I want you to meet them."

When Sarge saw them, he shouted an invitation. "Hey, Jared, come on over here and meet some pretty ladies."

They joined the group. Jared said, "I always like to meet pretty ladies, and I have one to introduce to you."

The men stood as they were introduced to Deborah, and she shook each of their hands. Maggie Christopher, Jane Anderson, and Betty MacKinzie were pleasant and gracious. Jared and Deborah sat down and began to visit. Jared said, "It looks like you're expecting some more company."

Deacon said, "Just the same old bunch that we hang around with at the plant. They'll be bringin' their families. We enjoy this get-together."

Sarge added, "Stick around and you can meet them too."

Jared said, "We wouldn't want to intrude."

Jane assured them, "There ain't no such thing as an intrusion out here."

As they settled down, Jared said, "Mac, I see they have shipped you and your crew out for a while."

Mac nodded, "Yeah, Petrotech has us doing a little job over at Lubrizol, but we will be back in time for the shutdown."

"But just for a few days," Betty assured the group. "After that, he is mine all mine, and I am gonna keep him busy."

They sat and visited comfortably. Deborah seemed to fit right in. Other members of the group began to arrive.

The first ones to join them were John Slovacek, "Pop," and his wife, Amy, and their pride and joy, little Johnnie. Amy was a pleasant but rather plain little lady, several years younger than John. They arrived with each of them holding one of little Johnnie's hands. It was obvious that little Johnnie would not tolerate having his hands held for much longer, but for now he was going along with it. He was a typical boy. He looked a lot like his dad. They were obviously a very close family. They put down their things and met Jared and Deborah. Then they went off to find the place where the children's games were being played.

After they were gone, Jared commented, "Pop is a little bit older than most folks who have kids that young, isn't he?"

Sarge explained, "He got kind of a late start. He was in Vietnam, and I understand he had a pretty rough time. He doesn't ever talk about it, but he told me a little about it since I was there too, a little earlier. He saw some pretty bad stuff, and it took him awhile to get over it. I think he may even have spent some time in a mental hospital. But he's okay now, and he's making up for lost time."

Before long, the sound of a motorcycle announced that Hog had arrived. He came looking for the group, followed by his wife, Peggy. She was a chubby little lady, not too pretty. They were dressed alike in boots, blue jeans, and Harley-Davidson tee shirts. Hog spotted the group and said, "Hi, Sarge. Hi, folks. Is this where the gang's gathering?"

Sarge responded, "I suppose so. Come on and sit down. I expect you need to let your bodies relax after riding that motorcycle."

"Oh no, man. It's when we're on that motorcycle that we are relaxed."

Peggy said, "Speak for yourself."

Sarge said, "You don't know the MacKinzies, do you? And this is Jared Philips and Deborah Olsen." He introduced them all around. Peggy sat down on the bench of a picnic table near the group. Hog said, "I'm gonna get me a beer. Do you want me to bring you a beer, Sarge?"

"No, I'm gonna wait until lunchtime to start drinking."

Hog disappeared in the direction of the concession stand. Soft drinks and beer were included in the price of the ticket. One of the management people was always in charge of the drinks in the hope that he could discourage anyone from overindulging—but that didn't always work.

About eleven o'clock, Joe and Helen Summerfield and Michael and Ann Miller arrived. It was their custom to be there and to get around to speak personally to everyone present. As far as they were concerned, that personal contact was one of the important purposes of this event. The two couples usually moved around separately, so that they could be sure that everyone got a short visit with one of the big bosses. But this time they worked the crowd together. Joe and Michael saw the group gathering under the trees and came over to make their visit. Joe took the lead in the conversation. "Well, here's the coffee group gathering. How are you all doing?" The men all stood to shake hands with the visitors.

Deacon responded for the group, "Just fine. And the smell of that barbeque is about to drive us all crazy. I think you know Mac MacKinzie, but you may not know his wife, Betty. And this is Billy Bob Jacobs' wife, Peggy. And I'm sure you know Jared and Deborah. They're slumming with us for a little while today."

Mac volunteered, "I'm an old Petrotech guy who's crashin' the party."

Joe responded, "Oh, I remember you, Mac. You don't ever have to crash these parties. You're permanently invited. We have appreciated your work in keeping this refinery humming. But I've heard you're retiring. We're going to miss you."

Mac said, "Thank you for your invitation. We're moving away, but we may just come back for these barbeques."

Joe asked, "Does Petrotech have someone good to take your place?"

Mac responded, "Buddy O'Neil is replacing me. I'm sure he'll do fine after he learns his way around. I hope you will all give him some help until then."

Michael turned to Peggy and asked, "Where is Billy Bob? Doesn't he know he shouldn't leave a lady all alone?"

"He's gone to get something to drink. I expect he'll be back soon."

"Well, maybe we can see him later."

Joe tried to end the visit by saying, "Well, we'd better be getting along. We want to see the children's games."

But Deacon had a question to ask. "Before you go, I've been wondering if you ever got any response from the head office on those recommendations that the little lady from OSHA made."

"I have written to the head office four times requesting authorization to go ahead with the recommended improvements. Each time they responded that the additional sensors were on the list of planned improvements that were waiting for a place in the company budget."

"What about the recommendation that the computer systems on each unit be programmed to shut down the unit automatically under certain dangerous conditions? That really won't cost them much at all."

"For some reason they are acting as if they never heard that recommendation."

"Aren't they afraid that OSHA is gonna come back at them if they don't follow those recommendations?"

"I think they are hoping no one will notice."

"I hope they pay attention soon. I think the little lady's suggestions were good. Well, I don't want to get off on that on barbeque day. I will be interested in hearing if they ever pick up on those recommendations."

Joe said, "I'll sure let you know when I hear anything. You all have a good day."

After the bosses left, Mac asked, "What was that all about?"

"About two years ago, OSHA sent a little lady consultant down here to inspect our safety systems. I got to squire her around. That was a nice duty. She was a pretty little lady—and smart. She said that we need about three times as many sensors as we have to detect high levels of dangerous fumes and that some of them should be placed on top of the units as well as on the perimeter fences. And she recommended that the control systems in each unit be programmed to shut down the unit automatically if certain dangerous conditions were registered. Mr. Summerfield said he would request authorization to do both of those things. You see how he came out."

Mac said, "I wonder why they didn't pick up on the idea of programming the systems to shut down automatically."

Sarge offered, "I can guess. I'll bet they are afraid that some control system will shut a unit down in the middle of a process because of a computer glitch or a bone-headed operator, and then they would have to pay you Petrotech guys a lot of money to get it running again."

"It could save some lives."

"Yeah, but it would also cost some money. You can see what is important to the guys in New York."

Deacon said, "I'm sorry I brought it up. I just don't get many chances to ask the big boss a question. Let's go back to thinking about barbeque."

In a few minutes, Brown and his family joined the group. Deacon introduced Jared and Deborah to them. Armetha Brown was a large, pleasant woman with dark skin that seemed to glow. The Browns had two teenage daughters. Brown introduced them to everyone. The girls were very polite. They visited about as long as they thought was necessary, and then they asked, "Dad, can we go hang out with the other kids?" Brown said, "Yes, but come back when the lunch bell rings." The girls disappeared and went to find a group of people their own age. Brown and Armetha settled down and visited comfortably with the others.

Brown turned to Peggy, who had been sitting quietly, and said, "What do you reckon has happened to that man of yours?"

"I don't know. It sure is taking him a long time to get a beer."

Sarge offered a possible explanation. "There's another tradition at these barbeques. Some of the fellows always have a crap game going in a little grove behind the maintenance shed. I wonder if he got sidetracked into that."

Peggy nodded her head and said, "If there's a crap game, Hog has found it."

Armetha volunteered, "Honey, if that man is in a crap game, you had better go down there and get him by the ear and bring him back up here where he belongs. That's what I'd do."

Brown said, "Yeah, she means that too. Can't you see how my right ear is bigger than my left ear?"

Everyone had a laugh. But Peggy did not take the suggestion.

In a few minutes, another young man came up to the group. He was wearing jeans and a tee shirt with "Jesus Saves" printed on it. He asked, "Is one of you George Christopher, the one they call Deacon?"

"I'm guilty of that."

"I'm Dwight Madison. I just came to work at Apex last week. I've heard about you, and I've been wanting to meet you."

Deacon stood and shook hands with Dwight and introduced him to the others who were sitting there. He accepted the introductions politely and then went back to talking directly to Deacon.

"I understand that you're a Christian."

"Yes. I'm a Christian. I suppose that there are lots of Christians around here."

Mac volunteered, "Yeah, Betty and I go to church."

Sarge chimed in, "So do I, regularly—twice a year: Christmas and Easter."

Without smiling, Dwight said, "There is more to being a Christian than just going to church."

Sarge said, half under his breath but loud enough to be heard, "Well, I sure as heck believe that!"

Mac ducked his head so that Dwight couldn't see him stifling a laugh.

Dwight ignored the interchange and went on addressing Deacon directly. "Well, I'm a Christian too. I worship at Faith Tabernacle. Some of us who are Christians are planning to have a prayer and praise service at the lunch hour every Wednesday. We would like to invite you to come and join us. We haven't found a place to meet yet, but we're looking for one."

Deacon said, "That's nice. I'll try to see if I can come now and then. I'm usually busy at my lunch hours setting up my safety meetings."

"You know, you shouldn't let secular concerns get in the way of your service to the Lord."

"Oh, I don't think I do. I serve the Lord every day. I serve him in church on Sundays, and I serve him from Monday though Friday trying to keep this refinery a safe place to work."

"Don't you think you should spend some time praying that this plant doesn't just blow up some day?"

"Son, it would make you nervous if you knew just how much time I spend praying that prayer."

"Do you trust God to answer your prayers?"

"Oh, God always answers my prayers, but he usually answers with orders. I pray for a safe plant. He tells me to get busy and make it so."

Dwight looked a little surprised and said, "Well, I guess that could be an answer to prayers."

"I always took it for an answer. When you get your services started, let me know where they will be, and I'll try to drop in now and then."

"I hope that you'll decide to attend regularly." Dwight smiled, offered his hand to Deacon, nodded to the others in the group, and walked away.

Sarge asked, "Are you going to go to his services?"

"I'll probably visit now and then, but I'm not going to be a regular. Those folks at Tabernacle are good people and they mean well, but they see things a little differently from the way we see them at St. Paul's Church. I wouldn't really be comfortable at their service. And I have a notion that if I came regularly, they eventually wouldn't be comfortable with me."

About this time Pop and his family came back from the games. Amy was trying to brush the sand off little Johnnie. "Just look at you. After all the time I spent trying to get you to look nice, you're a mess."

Jane said, "Well, we saw him lookin' nice. Now we see him lookin' like a boy. We like him both ways."

Mac asked, "How did you do in the games?"

Johnnie took his hand out of his pocket and held it out, showing three coins. "I found two quarters and a nickel in the treasure hunt. And Dad and I came in second in the three-legged race."

Sarge gave a cheer. "I'm always glad to be in the company of winners."

Just then the lunch bell rang, announcing that the barbeque was ready. Everyone got up and moved toward the serving line. As they were going, Tex came ambling up. "Can an old bachelor join this happy family gathering?"

Maggie answered, "Of course you can, Tex. You know you're part of the family."

Hog joined the group on the way to the serving line. It was obvious that he had consumed more than one beer. He said, "Darn that dinner bell. I was in a crap game, and I was really on a roll, but when that bell rang, everyone quit."

Sarge jabbed at him and said, "So it's really true that you'd rather shoot craps than eat."

Jared said, "It's been great getting to know all of you, but we're supposed to meet Al and Maria Scardino for lunch. We'll see you all around later."

He and Deborah took their leave of the cafeteria crowd and started looking for Al and Maria. They found them just arriving from the parking lot. Jared called to them, "Hey Al. Are you just getting here? The party's already well under way."

Al laughed and said, "We like barbeque, but we don't like summer heat too much. We usually get here just in time to eat." Jared introduced Deborah and Al introduced Maria. Maria was a small woman with a pretty face and long dark hair. She seemed shy. They made small talk as they stood in line. Everyone got a big laugh when they got to the pavilion and saw a notice taped to the post where everyone would pass: "Lost in the area of the Apex picnic grounds: two large brown mules. Reward for return."

As they went through the serving line, their large paper plates were piled high with brisket that had been cooking slowly all night long, along with sausage and chicken. Everyone got whatever meat they wanted. There was also potato salad, beans, cole slaw, pickles, and thick slices of fresh onion, the traditional barbeque feast. They picked up drinks at the drink stand and found a table under a tree. When he had a chance, Jared said to Al, "You know, I told you about what Mac MacKinzie told me. He's here if you'd like to talk to him yourself."

Al looked a little miffed and said, "This is Saturday. I don't work on Saturday."

Just then, Mrs. Sanchez from the business office came up with her husband and asked, "May we join you?"

Then it was Deborah's turn to make introductions. Deborah was glad to see them. Mrs. Sanchez was quite talkative. Deborah was almost exhausted from trying to involve Maria Scardino in conversation.

Jared asked, "Are you all going to stay for the big baseball game?"

Al shook his head and said, "No, it's going to get pretty hot before that game is over. We usually just eat and run."

Mrs. Sanchez said, "We usually stay for the whole program, but we have another appointment. Grandparent duty calls."

Jared put on an exaggerated long face and said, "What? Here I've been practicing in the hot sun for close to a month so we can represent dear old Apex and beat the team from Shell, and you're not going to stay and watch."

Mrs. Sanchez said, "Oh, I'm really sorry. I promise we'll come next time and stay for the game."

Jared accepted the apology and the chatting went on as they finished their plates of food.

Jared groaned, "I don't see how I'm going to play baseball after that, but I guess it's time for me to report for duty." He jogged to the car to get his mitt and cap and his company tee shirt. Then he came back to the table for Deborah. They went to the baseball field, stopping at the men's room on the way so that Jared could change shirts. At the field, they met Andy Evans and his wife, Adele. Adele was very cordial. As the coach's wife, she felt that it was her job to make everyone feel at home. She invited Deborah to sit with her in the bleachers during the game. The two women hit it off immediately. They sat and cheered for the team as if they were watching the last game of the World Series. The Apex team won. Jared got a couple of hits and made several good plays.

As the game was winding down, Adele asked Deborah, "Are you and Jared planning to meet anyone for supper?"

"Jared didn't say anything about meeting anyone. We plan to eat and stay for the dance tonight."

"Good. Why don't we sit together? We can listen to the boys brag about the game."

After the game, they informed Jared and Andy of their plans. They were glad to hear of it. The guys went back to the men's room to wash up a little and change shirts again. Then they rejoined the girls.

After that they headed for the drink booth. Sitting in the sun and cheering can generate a mighty thirst. But when they arrived, they found drama in progress. A confrontation was happening that seemed very out of place in the festivities. An argument was well under way when Jared and Deborah and Andy and Adele Evans arrived. People were gathering around.

Hog was standing at the concession stand, arguing with Barney Myers. Barney was supervisor of the compounding department, and he had been put in charge of the drink booth for the afternoon so that he could monitor the distribution of beer. He was doing his job.

"No, you can't have any more beer. We want this picnic to be a place where people can bring their families, and we don't want people getting drunk and making things unpleasant for everyone else. I've been put in charge of seeing to that, and I think you've had enough beer for today."

"What do you mean? You know I've just been up here two times today. The ticket I bought said it was good for all of the food and drink I want. Now I want some more beer."

"Well, I don't know where you got it, but you've had more than two beers. I know that several people came from behind the shed and asked for beer to take to their friends. And I know that someone may have brought something besides beer with them, and I know that you have had too much to drink, and I really think you ought to go on home now. I can't tell you to do that, but I can tell you that you can't have any more beer."

"I ain't drunk. I'm feeling just fine." Hog was beginning to shout. "I don't care if you are a boss. You ain't my boss. If you don't give me another beer, I'm gonna come back there and take it."

At this point, Peggy and the others from the coffee group arrived and saw what was happening. Peggy took Hog's arm and said, "Come on, Hog, let's go." Hog pushed her away.

Then Sarge joined the conversation and tried to persuade Hog to come away from the stand. Finally Hog turned back to Barney and said, "Well, if I can't have a beer, can I have a Coke?"

"Yes, you can have a Coke." Barney handed Hog a cold can of Coke.

Hog popped the opener on the can, took a drink, and laughed at Barney. "You wouldn't let me have another beer, but I've got something out in my saddle bag that will make this Coke even better than beer." He turned and headed for the parking lot, staggering a little as he went. He almost fell but managed to right himself. He turned to the others who had gathered around him and laughed.

Peggy took him by the arm and begged, "Please, Hog. Please don't drink any more."

He shouted, "Shut up, woman. You ain't my mama."

"Please, all of your friends have their children here. They don't want to see you drunk."

"If they don't want to see me having a good time, they ain't my real friends. My real friends are the people in the motorcycle club."

"But, Hog, just last week the people in the motorcycle club told you not to come back until you get your drinking under control."

Hog shouted, "Shut up, woman!" and slapped Peggy hard in the face.

Sarge stepped in and put his arm around Hog. He tried to persuade Hog that it was time to go home. He led him away and sat down to talk with him privately.

Hog enjoyed the attention. His speech was slurred as he said, "Sarge, I'm gonna tell you sumthin' I ain't never told nobody before. I never knew who my daddy was. And none of my mama's boyfriends ever gave a rip about me. I've had to scrounge for everything I've ever gotten in my life. I've always wished I could have a friend like you, Sarge. I'd like to be a man like you." In a few minutes, Hog began to weep.

Sarge came over to Peggy and said, "Hog is ready to go home now. Can you ride your bike and lead us there?"

"Oh yes. Thank you. I didn't know how I was going to get him home."

Mac and Deacon came closer. Deacon asked, "Do you want me to go along?"

"No, I think it will be best for me to do it. But Mac, I'll need you to drive us."

"Sure."

"You girls can keep each other company. We'll be back in time for the dance."

Peggy shook her head and said, "Dance. It would have been nice to go to the dance."

Jane and Maggie suddenly felt the deep unhappiness that was there in Peggy's life. They looked at each other on the verge of tears.

Jared and his friends were standing by watching. Jared felt that since they had spent the first hour of the day with this group, it would not be right just to walk away until they could see that things were going to be okay. Finally he said, "Let's go get something to drink and relax a little."

They went to the drink stand and all asked for soft drinks. They found a picnic table and sat down. Deborah said, "I hate to see things like that."

Adele said, "I do too. But there's a lot of abuse out there. As I told you, I'm a teacher. In teaching, we see a lot of the results of it."

Jared asked, "What do you mean, a lot of alcohol abuse?"

Adele said, "Well, yes, lots of that and lots of spouse abuse and lots of child abuse, and just lots of all sorts of things being messed up in peoples' lives. The children always seem to come out the big losers."

Andy said, "There's a lot more of it than you think. Most people think abuse and things like that just happen somewhere else. But it's everywhere. When you work with kids like I do with the Little League, you learn to kind of see it back there behind a lot of the kid's problems."

Deborah said, "That must really break your heart."

Adele said, "It really does. It keeps me remembering how lucky I am to have a good man and a good marriage."

Andy said, "Yeah, she doesn't beat me up more than two or three times a week." Adele made a face and swatted at him.

Jared asked, "What makes a person an abuser?"

Adele answered, "I think it's mostly stress and frustration. Of course, we don't get into the psychotherapy of things, but I think most of the abusers are not really bad people; they don't like what they're doing, but they get so frustrated with things going on in their lives that they take their frustrations out on the people nearest to them."

Jared asked, "What kinds of things?"

Adele said, "Anything that can cause stress. Lots of people are out of work right now and lots of others are working harder than they should have to and still just hanging on, especially single parents. That generates lots of frustrations."

Deborah said, "I know about that."

"Then there are others who seem to have everything going for them, but they put stress on themselves because they're living with some kind of a sick value system that keeps putting pressure on them. That's my idea of what causes it. The children usually come out hurting in one way or another. We try to spot that pain and to do what little we can about it."

Deborah said, "Adele, you must really love being a teacher."

"I really do. It's hard work. There are lots of down sides to it. I know I'll never get rich. But I feel like I'm making my life count for something."

Andy said, "Even if I can't be involved in teaching myself, I feel like I'm helping by backing her up."

Deborah asked, "What kind of future is there for you in education?"

Adele said, "I expect that I'll be able to take a couple of steps up in school administration. Andy can probably hope to get a couple of promotions too if something doesn't go wrong. None of that will change our lifestyle very much. I guess that we already are pretty much where we're going, but that's okay with us. We're happy with the life we have got. We just hope that we can hang on to it. No one can take anything for granted any more."

Jared asked, "You feel okay about that?"

Andy and Adele both nodded and said, "Yeah, we really do."

Andy said, "Say, they're serving barbeque again. Let's go get supper."

Deborah said, "If that hadn't been so good, I might not want any more than I had for lunch, but I at least want another sandwich."

They all went back through the line again and had supper.

As darkness began to fall, other people came in dressed for the country dance. Barbeque and drinks would be served all evening. A western band had set up at one end of the pavilion. Jared noticed that Sarge and Deacon and Mac were back and were dancing with their wives. Then they watched little Johnnie so that Pop and Amy could dance. The Browns danced too, and their daughters found partners and danced on another part of the pavilion floor, pretending that their parents were nowhere around.

Deborah said, "Hey, let's dance."

Jared said, "I just realized that I don't know how to dance that way."

"Well, come on, I'll teach you."

They joined the crowd on the floor. So did Andy and Adele. Jared learned quickly.

They danced several dances, and then, in the pause between dance numbers, Jared heard someone calling his name. He turned and saw Angie standing there, dressed in boots, stretch pants, and a western shirt that wasn't buttoned all of the way to the top. She had looked good in company coveralls, but in this outfit she was a real knock-out. She was with one of the guys Jared knew from the ball team. He had gone home and changed into western clothes before picking her up. Angie was giving Jared that same smile she had given him before. He felt awkward about that since she was with another guy. He introduced her and her partner to Deborah.

Jared felt like he needed to make some conversation so he asked, "Did you get some of that great barbeque?"

Angie said, "Oh yes, I wouldn't miss that. Did you have good barbeque where you came from?"

"No. Nothing like this."

"There are lots of good things in Texas that you need to discover."

Angie kept smiling at Jared. Her partner couldn't help noticing. When the music began to play again, he said, "Come on, let's dance," and he danced her away.

Deborah said, "She's pretty."

"Yeah, she is."

"She is really pretty."

"Yeah, she is."

"And she's got her eye on you."

"Oh, what makes you think that?"

"Come on now. Any fool can see that."

Jared looked at her while he tried to decide what he should say next.

Deborah broke the silence. "Do you want to change partners? It's okay if you do."

Jared said, "Nah."

"Are you sure?" Jared looked at Deborah. Her face did not beg for any particular response. She wore a quizzical half smile. But he knew she wanted an answer. Jared really hadn't been sure when Deborah asked, but he knew that he had a decision to make, and he made it.

"Yeah, I'm sure."

Deborah smiled and said, "Then let's dance."

About eleven o'clock, the band played a tune for a slow dance. Jared and Deborah stopped talking and danced together in silence. Deborah's head was against Jared's chest. Jared found himself thinking, *This is the first time I have been really close to this girl. I'll bet that if I had been dancing with Angie all evening, we would have been close. But, I would have had to settle for that smile instead of intelligent conversation. Seems like a person could have both. I wonder if the conversation is sometimes meant to keep me at a distance. Well, whatever—she is close now.* Jared held her just a little closer, and she seemed to like it.

Then the music stopped, and Deborah said, "You know something, sailor; it's been a really good day, but it's been a long day, and I'm tired. How about calling it a night."

"Let's go."

On the way to the car, Deborah said, "I've really had a good time today. We've met lots of interesting characters. And most of them are real."

Jared said, "Real?"

"Yeah, they are who they are. You don't have to wonder. I liked most of them. I really like Adele and Andy. They're nice people."

In the car going home, Deborah got quiet. Jared wondered if she had fallen asleep. But she finally spoke and said, "You know, I've been thinkin', I really enjoyed the day, but I feel kinda like I've been at a party on the deck of the *Titanic*."

Jared asked, "What do you mean?"

"Well, it all seems like something that can't last."

"Is that because you think American industry is doomed to disappear and to take this whole lifestyle with it?"

"I do kinda feel that way."

"You're being kinda negative, aren't you?"

"I don't mean to be."

"Could it be because you've decided just to be a visitor and not to become a part of it? Are you what is temporary?"

"That is a good question. I'll think about it."

She thought for a moment and then said, "I would really like for some things to be permanent and dependable."

"Each moment of life lasts at least as long as it lasts. If we make the most of it, we'll have it to remember forever."

"Thanks. I like that thought."

After another pause, Jared asked, "Do you like to go sailing?"

"I've never been."

"Would you like to go?"

"Yeah, sure."

Jared said, "Well, I've got a sailboat reserved for next Sunday afternoon. Would you like to go with me?"

Deborah got excited and said, "That sounds great. I guess I've always wanted to try sailing. I'll be looking forward to it."

Then they were at Deborah's apartment. Jared walked her to the door and kissed her good night. It seemed to Jared that she kissed him back a little more intensely than she had before.

Chapter 6

On Monday morning, Mac MacKinzie met with Buddy O'Neil. "Okay, Buddy, this is my last day with Petrotech. You're about to be in charge of the work at Apex. Is there anything you want us to go over again before I leave it with you?"

"There's one thing I've been wanting to ask you. How much has Petrotech been paying you to do this job?"

"Oh, well, that's not exactly what I meant."

"I know, but I think I know all of that other stuff. I've been a pipe fitter out here for three years. I've worked dozens of turnarounds."

"Yeah, but this is the first one you've had to work as a supervisor."

"I can handle it. Now back to my question. How much have they been paying you? I figure that if I'm gonna do your job, I oughtta get your salary."

"You know that the company has told us that we're not to discuss salaries. That could get a guy fired."

"What do you care? They can't fire you. They're plannin' to pay me fifteen dollars an hour to work as a supervisor. That's less than you're gettin', ain't it?"

"Well, I'll say this. After you get them thinking they can't live without you, you might talk to them about a raise."

"Yeah, I may have to just not show up some day or maybe sabotage something so they'll know to appreciate me."

"Man, don't even joke about that. You know how dangerous all of these contraptions are."

"I'm just jokin'. I know what to do."

"It bothers me that after doing this job for twelve years, I'm still worried about it, and you aren't worried even though you have never done it yet."

"Everyone has always said you're too uptight about everything."

"Well, my being 'uptight' has kept me and you and a lot of other people alive. I think it's good to always be just a little bit scared."

"Relax."

"I'm about to. But now you've got to take this unit apart and put it back together again. Are you sure that you know how to get it running again?"

"I'm sure."

"And there's nothing you need for us to talk about?"

"Yes, there is. How much are they paying you? Someone told me that they're paying one of the other supervisors twenty-five dollars an hour. I've seen that new SUV of yours. I want one of those too."

"You're hopeless. Let's get to work."

Late in the afternoon, Jared came around to talk to Mac. Buddy saw him coming and avoided him. Mac looked at Jared and shook his head. He said, "Do what you can."

The next morning, Jared reported the conversation to Al. Al just shrugged and said, "There's nothing we can do. That is the job of the maintenance supervisor. He wouldn't want us telling him how to do his job."

Jared said, "Could we at least tell the technical manager that we are hearing some people expressing some anxiety about the new guy?"

Al said, "I'll tell you what. It will be stepping way out of line, but I'll call Ken Allison up and tell him what you have been hearing, just for what it's worth."

Jared said, "Thanks. That will make me feel better."

Al said, "Okay now, just relax. It's all gonna be okay."

On Monday, after work, Jared's phone rang. It was Deborah. "Hey, sailor, I need a favor."

"What can I do for you?"

"I've been invited to a cocktail party, and I need an escort."

"My pleasure. When and where?"

"It will be Friday evening at a home in the Memorial Drive area over on the other side of Houston. Do you remember that I told you about staying with my friend, Ginger Rayburn, during spring break? Well, Melissa told her that I am living here now. She has found out that several of her college friends are living in the Houston area now, and she has invited us all to come to a party her dad is giving for some of his business associates."

"Sounds like fun."

"It will also be a chance to meet some people we may eventually want to know."

"Ah, a little networking going on here," Jared said. "What should I wear?"

"Do you have a really nice suit?"

"Just one. The one that I wore to the Summerfields'."

"That will be just fine. Pick me up as soon as you can after work. It will take a long time to get through the traffic."

As Jared hung up the phone, he smiled at how excited Deborah was about the party.

On Wednesday, Jared was especially restless. After work, he went to the Ice House for a drink just in the hope that he might run into someone to talk to. He had not been there long when Sarge came sauntering in. He got his beer and looked around. He saw Jared and came over. "Hey, young feller. Whatcha doing here in this wicked place without a chaperone?"

Jared was glad to see him. "Come on over and sit down."

When Sarge was settled Jared asked, "Where are your sidekicks?"

Sarge said, "Well, Mac is gone. His moving van pulled out yesterday. And old Deacon really doesn't usually come around here unless he has some special reason."

"He's real religious, isn't he?"

"Yeah, he is."

"Does that bother you?"

Sarge shook his head. "Naw. It don't bother me because he *is* real religious and not phony religious like so many people. He really believes what he says he believes, and he tries his best to live it. The truth is, I admire him for it."

"And yet, you're not religious."

"Nah, I guess I'm not. But I may be some day. I really believe most of what he believes, except about the beer, of course. I even understand why he feels the way he does about that. Are you religious?"

"I used to be. I grew up going to church, but I've gotten out of the habit. I'll probably get back into it sometime. I guess the believing is still there."

"If you hang around with the Deacon long enough, he'll invite you to church. He always does. And he'll talk with you about religion if you want him to, but he won't push it on you."

"I just may get around to goin' with him."

Sarge said, "But there are some religious folks I'm not comfortable with. Do you remember that little guy, Dwight Madison, that came around at the picnic to talk to Deacon?"

"Yeah, I remember."

"Well, he came around to see me Sunday afternoon. I don't know where he got my address. I'd gone over to check up on Hog and Peggy first thing in the morning. Then I came home and mowed my yard. After lunch I finished the trimmin', and I sat down under a tree in the front yard and had a beer. I had just started to relax when this car pulled up, and this guy, Dwight Madison, and another guy from his church got out. They asked if they could talk to me, and I said sure. I offered them a beer. They said they didn't drink beer, and I shouldn't either. Pretty soon they got around to telling me that they figured that I'm goin' to hell, and they had a simple solution for that. They preached at me for a few minutes about Jesus dyin' for my sins, and they said if I would let them say one little prayer for me, everything would be all right, and I would go to heaven."

Jared smiled and said, "What did you do?"

"Well, I told them it seemed to me that there ought to be more to it than that. They said, 'No, that's all it takes.' I was tempted just to let them say their little prayer so they would go away, but I got to feelin' ornery. I decided I didn't want them carvin' another notch on their gun butt and telling everyone that they'd saved my soul. So I told them that I had a friend that I was planning to let attend to my salvation. They asked what would happen if a truck ran over me before that happened. I said I figured God would have sense enough to know what to do. That made 'em mad. They started preaching again, and I said I heard my wife calling me, thanked them for coming, and went in."

Jared laughed and said, "Sounds to me like you handled that pretty well."

Sarge said, "Yeah, but you know, I didn't feel good about it. Like Deacon said, they meant well. But that just wasn't what felt right to me."

Jared said, "I guess there are different ways of being religious. By the way, you mentioned seeing Hog and Peggy. How are they?"

"I went over there because I was afraid Hog would wake up feeling mean and take it out on Peggy. I talked to him some about his drinking and told him that he really ought to get some help with it. That made him mad. He said I was just another hypocrite like the Deacon, and he didn't want anything more to do with me. He hasn't showed up for coffee since."

"That sounds bad to me."

"Did you have a chance to drop in on Mac and his crew?"

"Yeah, but just once. Mac tried to explain a shutdown to me, but it all came out like book knowledge. I already knew that. I really needed to see it done, and that wasn't possible. Buddy O'Neil wasn't interested in helping me. The next time I went around, the Petrotech crew had been moved to a job in another plant. I tormented Al until he said he would say something to the technical manager, but I don't know if he's done it yet."

Sarge shook his head and said, "I hope Deacon keeps on sayin' those prayers."

Jared couldn't sleep well on Wednesday night. He kept thinking about Section C. Finally he decided to bring it up one more time. When he went to work on Thursday, he asked Al how he came out in his conversation with Ken Allison.

"I never was able to get to him. I called right after I promised you I would, but Allison wasn't in his office. I left a message with the secretary that I had heard some of the men were anxious about the turnaround going forward with an inexperienced foreman and asked him to watch it."

"Did you get a response?"

"No."

"Did you try to get through to him again?"

"No. He is my boss. I am not going to try to jerk him around."

"Damn it, Al, I just don't think we should just sit on our hands while something really dangerous is about to happen."

"Forget it. Everything is gonna be okay."

"I can't forget it. If you won't talk to Allison about this, can I go in and talk to him? When I first met him, he said I could come and talk to him if I need to."

"No, you'd be even more out of line than I would."

"I don't mind bein' out of line now and then if there is a good reason to."

"Oh hell. Go on in and talk to him if you've got to. But be sure he knows I didn't send you."

"All right."

Jared walked out of the office and down the hall to the technical manager's office; he knocked on Allison's door.

He heard a voice from inside say, "Come in." but it sounded like it came from someone who was preoccupied.

Ken Allison looked up. "Oh, Jared. What can I do for you?" He did not invite Jared to sit down, so Jared stood as he talked. He told Allison about the anxiety some of the men were feeling about the turnaround and Buddy O'Neil's inexperience.

Ken Allison punched a button on his intercom and called Marvin Elrod into his office. He came immediately.

Allison said, "Marvin, Jared is telling me that some people don't have much confidence in the new Petrotech foreman, and they are worried about the turnaround on Section C. Jared, tell Marvin what you told me."

Jared began to repeat what he had heard.

Marvin listened to about the first two sentences and then interrupted. "Kid, you've been drinking with old Sarge too much. You haven't been around here long. After you've been here a while, you are going to realize that Sarge thinks he ought to be the plant manager. My advice to you is to tend to your own job and let me tend to mine. If you let old Sarge tell you what to do, you are going to get a reputation for being a troublemaker. And you don't want that to happen."

Jared felt hot anger rising inside of him. He felt his hand tremble, and he knew he must be turning red in the face.

Marvin Elrod saw that and moved toward the door, smiling. "Take my advice, kid."

Ken Allison said, "Stay on top of this, will ya?"

Marvin said, "You know I will." Then he left.

Ken Allison said, "Thanks for coming in."

Jared said, "Thanks for listening," as he walked out the door.

In the hall again, Jared found himself doing a slow burn. He felt he had to get away. He went back to his office and put on his Nomex and hard hat. Al guessed what had happened so he said nothing. Jared went out and walked around the plant until he cooled off. He decided that it would be best for him not to tell anyone about what had happened.

On Friday, Jared left work as soon as he could and got dressed for the cocktail party. As he drove to Deborah's apartment, he wondered if she would have on that same drab suit that she had worn to the Summerfields'. He didn't have to worry. Deborah had been shopping. When she came to the door, she wore a brand new cocktail dress that looked like something out of a fashion magazine. Suddenly he wondered if he should have brought her a corsage like he did when he took Judy to the senior prom. But it was too late to think about that. He said, "Wow! I knew you were a pretty woman, but I didn't know how pretty you could be."

Deborah was obviously pleased. She smiled warmly and said, "Thank you." Then her expression changed to one of mild anxiety, and she said, "Jared, would you mind if we took my car?"

"No, I wouldn't mind."

"And would you mind driving?"

"I've been wishing you would let me drive it."

Deborah handed Jared the car keys. Jared gave her his arm as they went down the apartment steps and held the door for her as gallantly as he could. Then he got behind the wheel of the car. He looked over the dashboard for a minute and then started the engine. He backed out and then shifted into drive. He accelerated a little too fast, and the tires squealed. They both laughed. That let them both relax a little. Jared soon got the feel of the car. He said, "I'd better not drive this car too often. I could get to liking it."

Deborah said, "We are going to want to take the loop to Interstate 10 West. After we get closer I will give you some more directions."

Jared said, "I think I can get us on I-10 West. Tell me something about where we are going and what will be happening."

Deborah began to explain. "Well, Ginger's dad is one of those self-made businessmen. He built up a successful business from nothing. It's Rayburn Supply Company. I understand that it is out in the LaPorte area somewhere. They have a house that you just won't believe. They have a tennis court and a swimming pool out in back. But they are real nice people. When we came and stayed with them that time, they treated us like honored guests."

"I'm afraid I may be a little out of place in that company. I'll try not to embarrass you."

"I'm not the least bit worried about that. I really don't know who all will be there. I expect to see some old friends. But I also think I may meet some people I may need to know someday. You may meet some people you may need to know, too."

"Isn't that kinda like exploiting a friendship?"

"That is what these parties are for."

"You know, I just never think about making business contacts. Maybe I should."

"Yes, you should. Possibilities often open up when you have made strategic acquaintances."

Houston traffic is bad between five and six o'clock, but Jared and Deborah moved along smoothly since they were going against the flow. Once they turned onto Interstate 10 West, they were in stop-and-start traffic. Deborah told Jared about the friends from college that she expected to see at the party.

When they finally arrived at the Rayburns' house, Jared was overwhelmed. He said, "I've never been in a house this big before. And I see that the other houses on the street are just as big. And look at all of the cars! I sure hope I will know how to act."

"Relax. You'll do fine."

At the door, they were met by Ginger Rayburn and her parents, Ben and Sheila. Ginger was a pretty young woman, but her mother was strikingly beautiful. She looked more like Ginger's sister than her mother. Jared thought she was dressed like a movie star. In her high heels, she was just a little taller than Ben, who was rather unspectacular by comparison. He was short, balding, and a little heavy. But he wore a nice suit and wore it well. All three had a way of being completely comfortable with themselves that made them able to make others comfortable with them, too. Ben and Sheila remembered Deborah from her earlier visit. Deborah introduced Jared, and all three welcomed him cordially.

Sheila said, "Deborah, I'm so glad you could come. We had such a good time when you and the other girls from the university stayed with us. We have been looking forward to seeing you again."

Ginger took charge of them and said, "Come on, let me introduce you around."

Introducing them around was no small undertaking. There were about forty people in the house. The party was a gala affair. Everyone was all dressed up. Jared thought they were all beautiful. A pianist was playing popular music. Drinks and snacks were being served. Most people were standing, but some were sitting in small groups, talking and laughing. Jared had the idea that no one was talking about anything very significant. The objective seemed to be to move around and visit for a few minutes with everyone who was there. He was surprised how well Deborah fit into the situation. She was outgoing, almost flamboyant, a sharp contrast to the cautious and reserved person he had met at the Summerfields'. Jared thought again that she was a person doing what was expected. Jared tried to follow her lead and to act as a foil for whatever she seemed to be doing.

Ginger did not just introduce her guests to the other college friends as if they were junior members of the gathering. She introduced them to everyone. There were purchasing agents from several of the petrochemical industries in the Pasadena-Baytown area, the sales manager for the Rayburn Company, Rayburn's accountant, their stockbroker, and several other people who seemed to be just friends and neighbors. One man, who owned a business in another field, explained that he was Ben's golfing buddy.

Soon they encountered Melissa and Alan, whom they had met at the bistro on Westheimer. They greeted Deborah and Jared like old friends. Alan said, "Jared, are you still enjoying engineering?"

"I sure am."

"And Deborah, are you still enjoying accounting?"

"Oh yes."

Then Alan said, "There is someone here you need to meet. He came with Emily, whom you know from UT." Alan led them to the other side of the room. Deborah and Emily had not yet seen each other, and they exchanged greetings and hugs. As soon as it seemed appropriate, Alan introduced Emily's escort. "This is Rick Rogers. He is one of the accountants with Logan and Harley." Logan and Harley was one of the biggest accounting firms in Houston. This was obviously the kind of contact that Deborah wanted to make. Alan told Rogers that Deborah was in accounting.

Alan went on with his introduction. "Rick has been with Logan and Harley for six years now, and he was just telling me that they have tapped him to start a new subsidiary to deal with some specialized accounting needs of big companies."

Deborah said, "That sounds exciting. I would love to be able to do something like that some day."

Rick said, "Are you an accountant?"

Deborah said, "Not quite yet. I am still studying for my CPA examination. I've heard that it's pretty hard."

Emily said, "It's hard but on the basis of what I remember about how you did in class at the university, it won't be a problem for you. I'm betting that you ace it on your first try."

Rick asked, "Are you looking for employment?"

Deborah said, "I've got a job that I like right now, but maybe sometime in the future I may look for one I would like better."

Rick said, "It's good to have a job that you like and still look for one you might like better. Would you call yourself an ambitious person?"

"Yes, I suppose I would."

Jared added, "She is the most ambitious person I have ever met. She is going to wind up moving up a ladder somewhere."

Rick smiled and said, "Keep your eyes open. Your opportunity will come along." He and Emily moved on to the next little circle of people.

Jared mumbled in Deborah's ear, "I suppose that is what you call networking." Deborah smiled and nodded.

Ginger came over to Deborah and Jared and said, "Jared, I understand you are an engineer. There is someone else here that I would like for you to meet." She beckoned for a young man who was standing with a small group of people, and he came over. Ginger said, "This is one of my oldest friends, Herschel Rosenberg. We went through school together. He has just gone to work for Brown and Daniels. Herschel, this is Jared Philips. He is an engineer at the Apex Refinery."

Jared flinched inwardly just a little bit. He thought, *I wonder if this is the guy who got the job I wanted.* He put the thought away and smiled broadly and shook hands with Herschel "Are you another University of Texas graduate?"

"No, Ginger and I went through high school together, and then she went off to Austin, but I stayed here and went to Rice. I have never gone anywhere—except on vacations. I grew up right down the street. I went to a university in my home town. And now I work for a company whose head office is about three miles from here. As a matter of fact, I envy your experience working in a refinery. We design refineries and other petrochemical plants for companies all over the world. But most of us have never worked in a refinery."

Jared said, "Well, I guess it kind of came naturally for me. I have lived around refineries all of my life."

"Do you like what you are doing?" Herschel asked.

Jared said, "Yes, I do, but I've sometimes thought that I would like to do what you are doing some day."

Herschel said, "What you are doing now is good preparation. There are about a half-dozen engineers in our company who have had experience in the field, and their experience is really valuable to us. Matter of fact, one of them just came to us from Apex. Do you know Dietrich Schmidt?"

Jared said, "No, I've never met him, but I've heard a lot about him. Actually, I think I am probably sitting at his old desk."

"Now there is a coincidence. Dietrich is really a smart guy."

"That's what I've heard."

Herschel said, "Maybe some day you will come our way too."

Jared said, "Maybe so."

Just then Herschel saw someone else he needed to speak to and moved on.

Deborah whispered, "Networking."

Immediately, Ginger was back with a tall, middle-aged man who had an air of importance about him. She introduced Jared and Deborah and said, "This is Dr. Ainsworth; he and my dad went to college together, and he taught me my sophomore government class at the university. Deborah, I was just wondering if you had any of his classes."

Deborah said, "No, I took my government class in junior college, but I remember seeing him on campus."

Dr. Ainsworth was very friendly. "I am sorry that I missed that opportunity. I understand that you both work for Apex Oil."

Deborah answered, "Yes, we do. We are both new in the Pasadena Refinery."

"I hope you will both work real hard because I own some stock in that company. I am counting on you to make me rich."

Jared said, "We will do our best. The refinery seems like a great place to work. Mr. Summerfield, the plant manager, has made us feel really welcomed. We feel good about being there."

"I'm glad to hear it. I hope your jobs live up to your best expectations." Dr. Ainsworth smiled and moved on.

Ginger whispered, "It won't really be necessary for you to make him rich. You have just met a member of the board of directors of Apex Oil."

Jared and Deborah looked at each other and said in unison, "Ooh!"

Ginger moved on to another group of guests. Deborah said to Jared, "Will you excuse me for a few minutes. I need to go freshen my makeup."

"Sure," he said. As Deborah went to the ladies' room, Jared decided to take advantage of the respite to catch his breath. He walked outside and stood by the pool for a few minutes. Not many people were there because the night was a little too warm and humid for comfort. Jared didn't mind. As he stood by the pool, he noticed a little flicker of lightning in the distance, and a minute later he heard a low rumble of thunder. He wondered if there was about to be a thunderstorm. In a few minutes, he turned to go back inside, but he could see through the door that Deborah was in a huddle with her college friends, so he decided to sit in one of the lawn chairs and let her find him when she was ready. He enjoyed listening to the music. The pianist evidently liked Andrew Lloyd Webber. So did Jared.

In a little while, Jared heard someone moving a chair next to him. It was Ben Rayburn. He said, "I've got to come out here to smoke. My wife doesn't let me smoke in the house."

Jared smiled and said, "Half of the people in there are smoking."

"Yeah, but the rules are different for company. Now, your name is Jared, and you are an engineer with Apex Refinery. Is that right?"

"That's right." He was impressed that his host had gone to the trouble to know that he was an engineer. He didn't remember telling him that.

Ben went on, "I started out as an engineer. I worked for Exxon in Baytown. I liked what I was doing, but I could see that I would never be able to make enough at it to keep my wife happy, so I started my own business."

Jared said, "I understand that you have Rayburn Supply. I've seen your building out on Southmore near the airport. Just what do you do?"

"We sell fittings and valves and gages for the petroleum industry, and we supply them fast. When I was at Exxon, I sometimes saw units shut down for as much as a week waiting for some part to come in. I knew that was costing the company big bucks in terms of lost production. I went to my boss and asked what the company would be willing to pay for parts if they could get them within twenty-four hours. He said they would pay a whole lot. That was all I needed to know. I borrowed some money, rented a warehouse, put my wife to work as a secretary, and went into business. I called on all of the refinery maintenance engineers and asked what parts they had the most trouble getting when they needed them. I stocked as many of those as I could afford. And I found out where to get the rest of them in a hurry. I love to fly an airplane. I have had a pilot's license since I was a kid. I flew cargo planes in the air force. When someone needed a part in a hurry, I would rent a small plane and go get it. It gave me an excuse to support my hobby. Well, to make a long story short, the companies appreciated our attention to their needs, and the business grew. Now we have service centers in six different industrial areas across the Southeast. We still give twenty-four-hour service when we can, for a price. Do you do any purchasing for Apex?"

"No, I'm a process engineer. And I've only been with the company for about a month."

Ben said, "I sometimes deal with a man out there named Elmore. And there is a fellow named MacKinzie who is with one of their maintenance contractors who sometimes calls me."

"I know both of those men. But MacKinzie has just retired."

"I'm impressed. You've only been there for a month. You must have gone to some trouble to get acquainted."

"It seemed like the right thing to do."

"Do you like living in the Pasadena area?"

"Yes, I like it just fine. I grew up living in an industrial area. It seems natural to me."

"We used to live in LaPorte. I liked it fine out there, but my wife wanted to live over here. So we moved. Now I spend an extra forty-five minutes each way going and coming to work. But we've got to keep the ladies happy."

Just then there was another flash of lightning, closer this time, and another low rumble of thunder. Jared said, "It looks like we are going to have a thunderstorm."

Ben said, "Yeah, we need the rain, but I don't like thunderstorms much."

"I expect it is hard to fly an airplane through one of them."

"It sure is. I tried doing that once when I was young and stupid. It was the scariest experience I ever had. I am not going to risk my life or anyone else's doing something that foolish."

"Not even to make the big bucks?"

"Not even to make big bucks. It usually only takes a little longer to fly around a storm. You know, trying to see how much money I can make is a game I play, like some guys play golf. I do it just for fun. Lots of people I know make a religion out of it. The whole meaning of their lives depends on it. Sure, I'm an aggressive businessman, but I'm not going to sacrifice anything more important for a little money."

"Then there are some things that are more important than making the big bucks?"

"Yeah, there are. Lots of things. And you will be a healthier and happier person if you remember that."

"I'll remember."

Ben stood up and said, "Well, I'd better get back inside. Besides, I see a pretty girl coming to look for you."

Deborah came up to them and said, "There you are. Did you think I had abandoned you?"

"No, I just saw that you were visiting with your friends so I decided to stay out of the way. I got to have a nice conversation with Mr. Rayburn."

"Call me Ben. Come on in and have some more snacks and drinks."

Just then it thundered again. Deborah said, "Oh, I hope we don't have to drive home through a thunderstorm. I really don't like thunderstorms. But the party is breaking up. It's about time to head back across town."

They spoke to a few more people, and then they found their hostesses and thanked them for the evening. Ginger reminded Deborah that the four college friends were planning to meet for dinner and a longer visit on Thursday. Then she and Jared walked to the car.

As they walked, Jared noticed that the thunder was coming more frequently and the sky seemed to be flickering almost constantly. He said, "Thunderstorms always seem like something symbolic to me. They make me think of bombs exploding in some war that is happening just over the horizon and moving toward us."

"That's an ominous idea."

"Sometimes when I am sitting alone in the dark and listening to the thunder, a picture comes to my mind like a sequence out of an old war movie. I don't really know where it came from. I see an RAF fighter pilot walking out onto the runway in the rain. The drops of water stand out on his leather flight jacket and aviator's cap. He stands and looks toward the horizon where he can see the flashes of bombs exploding. Then he gets into his Spitfire and flies off alone to do battle with the enemy."

"That sounds like another version of the knight riding off to slay the dragon. Does the pilot come back safely?"

"I don't know. That is not part of the picture that comes to my mind. Maybe that is part of the significance of the picture—that I don't know."

Deborah said, "You know, you are more of a philosopher than you think you are."

Jared said, "First time anyone has ever accused me of being that." He opened the car door and let Deborah slide into the passenger's seat. Then he got in and started the engine. He purposely changed the subject. He felt a need to lighten up. "That was really some party. This was the first time I have ever been to anything like that. The Rayburns seem to be really nice people. They seem to have been successful in a good way."

"Do you think they have?"

"Yeah, but of course, it's too soon to know. I was amused at him talking about being henpecked."

"If he really were, he wouldn't be talking about it. I think they really like each other."

Jared said, "That's nice, isn't it? He talks about buying the big house to keep his wife happy, but he seems to be enjoying it too."

"Yeah, they both enjoy it. But I think they enjoy it in a good way. If they didn't have so much, I'll bet they would still enjoy life."

"Do you reckon so?"

By the time Jared turned onto the freeway, it was beginning to rain. The lightning was flickering constantly. He turned on the windshield wipers and stopped talking. It was raining hard, and he wanted to concentrate on driving. Trucks on the highway were tossing up spray that made visibility even worse. Jared slowed down. He was following a big truck that had slowed to a safe speed. It was raining so hard that Jared couldn't see anything but the lights on the truck. The truck pulled off onto the shoulder to stop.

Jared followed the truck off the highway and said, "This guy has a good idea. I am going to park right here behind him until the rain lets up. Where are the emergency flashers on this car?"

Deborah reached over and pressed the button on the top of the steering column. Jared could see that her hand was shaking.

Jared said, "Now we will just sit here and visit until the storm is past."

Deborah did not feel like chatting. The rain was falling in sheets so that nothing was visible outside of the car. Gusts of wind rocked the car, and the thunder and lightning were almost constant. Deborah said, "Jared, I really, really don't like thunderstorms. Would you do me a favor and put your arm around me?"

Jared said, "With great pleasure." He put his arm around her shoulders, and she moved as close as the car's bucket seats would allow. But Jared knew there was nothing romantic about what was happening. Deborah was scared. She was trembling.

Then suddenly there was a bright flash of lightning and a huge clap of thunder that seemed to be right on top of them. It happened so suddenly that both of them jumped, and Deborah let out a scream. As soon as they could see that they were both still alive, they both began to laugh. The tension was broken. The storm lasted about fifteen minutes and then moved past. They spent the time alternating between screaming and laughing. Once the storm had passed, the rain stopped completely. It was hard to believe that it had been so fierce. Jared pulled back into the traffic and drove home.

Deborah was quiet. Jared supposed that she needed to be, so he didn't try to make conversation.

Finally she said, "I'm sorry I was such a sissy during the storm."

"That's all right. It's kinda good to know that there is at least one thing you are afraid of."

"There are lots of things I'm afraid of."

"What sorts of things?"

"Things that are too big or too dangerous for me to control."

"There are lots of things like that."

"Yeah, there are." Then she went quiet again.

When they reached Deborah's apartment, Jared walked her to the door and gave her keys back to her. He said, "Thank you for letting me be your escort for a very special evening. You are helping this old blue-collar boy learn a lot about a part of the world I've never seen before. I hope I did all of the things I was supposed to."

Deborah was herself again. She said, "You did just great. Thanks for going. And—thanks for everything you did." She stood on tiptoes and planted an appreciative kiss on his lips.

Chapter 7

Sunday was a bright, clear day with a brisk breeze, just the right kind of day to go sailing. Jared and Deborah arrived at the boat rental dock a little before one o'clock, the time for which he had reserved the boat. Jared said that, at that price, he didn't want to waste a minute. The man on the dock showed them to a neat little boat, about twenty feet long. He explained the sails and the rigging. It was a sloop-rigged boat with a mainsail and a jib. It was equipped with an outboard motor for emergencies, but Jared was determined not to use it unless he had to; he had come to sail. He assigned Deborah a couple of tasks and explained how to do them so that she could be the crew. Then he cast off from the dock, pushed out a few yards, and raised the jib. With the jib, he navigated out into the lake and then raised the mainsail. The breeze filled it immediately, and the boat moved gracefully forward. It moved quickly and almost silently. Jared couldn't help smiling. This felt good. It felt good to Deborah, too. She let out a girlish, "Whee!"

"Do you like this?" Jared asked.

"This is really great."

For an hour they just sailed around Clear Lake, getting accustomed to the boat and enjoying sailing. Occasionally they noticed things around them: a luxury hotel with a lighthouse in front of it, lakeside condominiums and apartments, and the yacht club where someone was having a wedding reception on the deck of one of the larger boats. There were lots of other boats around too: sailboats, motorboats pulling water skiers, and daredevils on jet skis. It was fun to be in the middle of all of that, but Jared thought it would be better to have a little more space. He set his course to go under the high bridge between the communities of Kemah and Seabrook and through the Kemah Channel out into Galveston Bay.

It was difficult to navigate the channel under sail. Most people would have dropped the sails and started the outboard motor. But Jared was determined. It was especially tricky because there was a procession of boats of different kinds and sizes going through the channel. They fell into line behind a magnificent, ketch-rigged yacht that must have been eighty feet long. A group of people all dressed in white sailing clothes were having a cocktail party on the deck. As they passed by the line of seafood restaurants, the people on the yacht waved at the people having lunch on the outdoor dining decks of the restaurants. They were like the royalty in a Mardi Gras parade waving to their subjects as they passed.

Deborah said "Boy, look at that yacht."

"Yeah, isn't that a beauty. I can't wait to see her with her sails up and underway. I'll bet that'll be a sight to remember."

"How much do you think a boat like that would cost?"

"Probably well over a million dollars. Do you want me to buy it for you?"

"Nah. Wait until I get rich and I'll buy one for myself. I may want a bigger one."

Just then, a low rumbling sound came from behind them. Deborah said, "What in the world is that? It sounds like the big bad wolf."

Jared said, "Look behind us."

She looked and saw a large, streamlined speedboat of the Baha class. Two huge engines were rumbling, quietly boasting their power as they worked to restrain themselves to stay under the channel speed limit and to keep from running over any little sailboats.

"My gosh. What *is* that thing?"

Jared smiled and said, "Just wait and you'll see."

In a few minutes, they came out of the channel into Galveston Bay. The yacht continued on its way. Jared bore slightly to the starboard to get out from behind it. The Baha, still rumbling, pulled past them. Two guys whose bare, suntanned chests and shoulders made it obvious that they had been lifting weights, waved at Deborah, and then pulled ahead of the sloop and accelerated to full speed. The engines roared, and the boat lurched forward, spraying eagle's wings of water to both sides, and in two minutes, the boat was out of sight.

Deborah said, "I guess I was right. It was the big bad wolf."

Jared laughed and said, "That is another kind of awesome boat. You wouldn't believe the amount of horsepower one of those babies has or the amount of gasoline those two guys are going to burn in one afternoon. And, in case you're wondering, they don't sell those boats cheap either. Start thinking about a quarter of a million."

A little later they saw a large cabin cruiser with a bridge for steering built above the cabin. It was equipped for deep sea fishing. It was evidently coming in from a morning out in the gulf. The person piloting the boat reduced speed as a courtesy to keep from swamping the sailboat with their wake. Some of the fishermen gave a friendly wave as they passed. Eventually Jared piloted the boat into a place where there were no boats around and they could enjoy the experience of sailing. Unlike the Baha, the sailboat slipped quietly through the water. It seemed to participate in the natural forces that were around it rather than fighting them. Jared and Deborah kept watching the yacht to see it put up its sails—but it never did. Evidently the plan for that day was a cocktail party, not sailing. Eventually they were able to see two other really big yachts under full sail. They were beautiful.

Jared said, "You know, it's amazing to me that anyone could have so much money that they could spend a million dollars or more on a boat that's strictly for recreation. That's an awfully expensive toy. Half of the world's population is living in poverty. Thousands of Americans are unemployed. The economy as a whole is moving downhill. And yet there are apparently still a lot of people who can afford million-dollar toys."

Deborah said, "You've just gotten the picture of how the world's economy works. Somewhere on the economic ladder, there is a line that separates those to whom money flows and those from whom it flows away. The gap between those two groups of people is getting wider. That's why I'm determined to find some way to move across that line into the winner's circle."

"How do you plan to do that?"

"I really don't know yet. Maybe I'll form my own accounting firm. Maybe I'll retrain and move into another field like law. Maybe I'll build some other kind of a business."

"You are an ambitious woman."

"Not really. I'm just being realistic about how things are and about what a person has to do to survive."

"Doesn't it seem that something could be done to change the way things are so more people could have a chance to survive and maybe even thrive?"

"Now that's what I call an ambitious idea. Change the world."

"Yeah, but doesn't it seem that someone ought to try to do it?"

"Well, maybe. But if you decide to take it on, be careful. Those people who have it going their way have power. They truly believe that they have a God-given right to their million-dollar toys, and they'll come down hard on anyone who tries to take them away."

"Well, I wasn't exactly planning to start a movement, but I'll remember that in case I ever do."

"Okay, and when I get my big boat, I'll take you for a ride on it—and we will put up the sails."

"I'll remember that and hold you to it. But right now I calculate that we have just about an hour and a half left with this little boat before my present resources run out. Let's make the most of it." With that, Jared brought the boat about so that the breeze filled the sails; the boat rose and fell as it rode over the waves in a rhythm that has thrilled sailors for thousands of years. Both Jared and Deborah smiled spontaneously. They looked at each other and caught each other smiling. They both broke into laughter in their enjoyment of the moment.

The sun began to drop toward the horizon, and the hands on Jared's watch showed him it was time to bring the boat back to the rental dock. Jared steered the boat back toward the channel that would take them back into Clear Lake. They followed a commercial shrimp boat with an escort of hungry seagulls.

As they passed the line of restaurants, the smell of frying fish overpowered all of the other smells that hover around a waterfront. Deborah asked, "Do you like seafood?"

"I love it."

"Well, after we check the boat in, I'll buy us some. I haven't forgotten that I owe you a meal or two."

"You're on."

Later, as they sat on the deck of the restaurant, eating fried shrimp from a basket, Deborah commented, "This is a really nice recreational area. I'd like to come back and explore the shops some time."

"Yeah, it's quite a place. It's hard to believe that all of this was under water not long ago. When I came down here prowling around, a fellow told me that Hurricane Ike, back in '08, had a storm surge that put most of this under ten or twelve feet of sea water. He said that in Galveston, the storm surge was up to twenty feet."

"Oh, that's scary. I don't want to think about that."

"Yeah, it's scary. But this just shows that communities have a capacity for coming back."

Just then they noticed the same yacht that they had followed into Galveston Bay coming back in. They still had not put up the sails, but the cocktail party was still going on. Other boats of all types and sizes were coming back in from their day on the bay. Lots of them were big expensive boats. Jared again commented, "I just can't get over how many million-dollar boats we're seeing in one day."

"Yeah, and do you get the idea that we're watching some kind of a fashion parade, that lots of those people are more interested in showing off their boats than in sailing?"

Jared shrugged and said, "Oh well, they are something to see." Then he dropped into silence as he watched the boats passing.

Deborah watched Jared for a while and said, "What's bothering you, sailor?"

"What do you mean?"

"I've been watching you all day. Most of the time you've been having a good time, but every now and then, it's like a cloud comes over you and you drop into some kind of a pensive gloom. You were doing it just now."

"I didn't know it showed."

"I have a notion that it's something other than the inequity of the world economic system that's bothering you."

Jared said, "You have a spooky way of reading my thoughts. The truth is I'm worried about something that is going on back at the plant right now. Mac MacKinzie has retired from Petrotech. He left on Monday. Right now his replacement is just finishing a turnaround on a unit in Section C. Mac doesn't have much confidence in the guy who's replacing him. I've met him, and I don't either. At every level of things, it seems that there are some people who are committed to trying to make things work and other people who just want a paycheck. Mac was the first kind. I think the new guy is the other kind. Mac asked me to see that the company gives him some more supervision. I tried to talk to Al about it, but he just blew it off. I even barged into the office of the technical manager and told him about the things I have been hearing. I didn't get anywhere with that—except maybe in trouble. I really don't know the unit well enough to give it close supervision. Besides that, it really isn't my job. But I'm worried about it, and I don't know anything that I can do about it."

"Mister Responsibility. I can see why that bothers you."

"If I stay around here long enough, I'm eventually going to know those units well enough to give supervision to things like that. It seems to me that's what an engineer ought to be able to do."

"Then you're thinking about staying around here for a long time."

"I don't know. But while I'm here I'm going to be here, and I'm going to try to do my job and make things run better."

Deborah said, "Good for you, sailor. I'll bet you'll feel a lot better tomorrow when that unit is up and running again."

"I sure will."

"Well, let's change the subject. Look, there's a little sailboat coming by. I'll bet even a process engineer could eventually afford to buy one of those."

"Well, maybe. But as expensive as it is to rent a boat, it's still a lot cheaper than owning one."

"What about the pride of ownership?"

"That's just something the salesmen talk about." Jared smiled and stuffed another french fry into his mouth.

They watched the boats pass in silence for a while longer, and then Deborah said, "Jared, what happened to your marriage?"

Jared was surprised to hear Deborah ask that. As a matter of fact, the subject had been hovering just behind his consciousness for a couple of hours. It always seemed to be there when he was worried or depressed about anything. He hesitated before responding.

"If you don't want to talk about it, just forget I asked."

"No, I don't mind. I suppose I need to talk about it more. I hardly ever do. And you have a funny way of knowing what is on my mind."

Jared gazed at the water for a long minute, and then he began. "The truth is, we were both too young. We didn't know what we wanted out of life. We were high school sweethearts. We were just naturally matched up in high school. I was the big jock, the captain of the football team. She was the school beauty. She was voted homecoming queen twice. Our romance was kind of a tradition in the school. Everyone in town talked about it. We were kind of carried along by our popularity as a couple.

"We talked about my plans to go into the navy and then to go to college. That sounded great to her. We got engaged at the senior prom, and we got married just after I finished basic training. The first whole year was a honeymoon. Leaving home together was a romantic adventure. We were stationed in San Francisco, and that was glamorous. She liked being married to a sailor, and I liked being married to the prettiest girl in every gathering we went into. No kidding, everywhere we went, I could see everyone looking at her, especially the guys but the girls too. We were having a great time, and we thought we were really in love.

"But after about a year, she began to get dissatisfied. She was getting tired of waiting for some of the things that couldn't come for a few years."

"Was she wanting to have children?"

"No, not children. She was wanting other things, nice clothes, a nice house, a nice car. She saw other people with those things, and she wanted them too. I told her that those things would come, but there was no way I could get them for her quickly; we had to follow the plan we had made.

"During our second year, I was still in love with Judy, but she was restless. I think she started to fall out of love with me. I tried to get her to register for some college courses. She took a nine-month business class instead. Then the time came for me to deploy. Judy took a secretarial job in a big office building. I'm sure she caught the attention of every guy in the building the moment she walked into the place.

"She wrote, but I noticed the change in her letters. At first they were full of memories of the days we had spent together—and the nights, and of the plans we had made for the future. But eventually they changed. At first she stopped talking about the memories. Then she stopped talking about the plans. Eventually she was just telling me about the things she had done each day. Finally, just a few weeks before I came home, she wrote that she had found another guy. Reading between the lines, I could tell that it was someone who could give her the things she wanted without making her wait another four years."

Jared took another sip of his iced tea, gazed down into his empty shrimp basket, and went on. "After I was discharged, I drove home and my family helped me to get my head together. When it was time to start college, I was ready to throw myself into it because that was all there was left for me. I concentrated on my books and on baseball. I had a few dates the last year in college, but I really wasn't ready for another relationship. When I finished college, I had a long talk with myself and told myself that it was time to get on with my life."

Jared had finished his story. He looked at Deborah and saw that she was still listening. She asked, "Do you ever hear from Judy?"

Jared shook his head and said, "No, I haven't heard a word from her or about her since the divorce was final. I suppose she is still living the glamorous life out in California."

Deborah looked as if she wanted to ask another question, but she didn't. She looked away. Finally she said, "I feel like I intruded where I shouldn't have, but thanks for telling me that."

"Thanks for listening. It seems that there is an awful lot of trouble in the world."

"Yes, but there is also sailing and that makes everything better."

"Yes, there is also sailing. But now I suppose it's time to go home and get ready for tomorrow."

"Oh yes, tomorrow." Deborah paid the check, and they went home feeling that the day had been special in lots of ways.

Chapter 8

On Monday morning, Jared was restless. He couldn't forget about Mac's misgivings about his replacement. He went to work early and wore his Nomex coveralls. Before going into the office, he walked down to Section C and looked at it from the road. The day shift crew was just coming on. He could see nothing that looked out of the ordinary to him. He hadn't really expected to. If anything was wrong, it would not be conspicuous. As he stood looking at the unit, he heard a voice beside him saying, "Can you see anything wrong?" It was Deacon.

Jared was startled. "No, but I'm not smart enough to recognize it if there is."

"Me neither. I've been climbing around on the unit for an hour, and I can't see anything. But there are all kinds of things that could go wrong that no one could see, a pipe not screwed in where it belongs, a gasket left out of a flange, something hooked up wrong inside. There's no way of telling. Let's just hope that Buddy is a better man than Mac thinks he is."

"Are you still sayin' that prayer?"

"Yeah. Always."

They parted and went to their jobs. Jared walked back to the engineering office and waited for Al.

Al came in just before the whistle blew. He was as cheerful as ever. But he could read Jared's feelings on his face. "Hey, partner, what's got you all down in the dumps this morning? Did your girlfriend say 'No' to you?"

Jared tried to smile, but he was glad for the invitation to tell Al what was on his mind. "To tell you the truth, I'm still worried about Section C. They're supposed to be bringing it back online today after the shutdown. Mac MacKinzie sure doesn't have much confidence in the guy he left in charge of the Petrotech operation."

"Don't let old Mac worry you. He's been doing that job so long that he thinks he owns it. If he didn't want to turn it over, he just shouldn't of retired." Al went into his office and picked up a paper that had been left on his desk. He looked it over and then handed it to Jared.

"Here's the report from Petrotech. It's just like the ones that old Mac turned in after a turnaround. It says the unit is ready to bring back online."

Jared said, "Is that all we do? Just look at the report? Shouldn't we go down there and give them some more direct supervision?"

Al said, "That's the job of the maintenance supervisor. You can just guess how well our goin' down there would go over with him and the subcontractors. Besides, do you think you know every bolt and fitting on that unit well enough to check their work?"

Jared said, "I guess not." He tried to get busy with the Monday routines.

Deacon came early to set up for a safety meeting that was scheduled for Section F. He wanted to touch base with Sarge.

Sarge came out and said, "Here is Mr. Do Right. Are you going to give us the last word on safety?"

Deacon said, "Yeah. It's time for the regularly scheduled safety meeting. There is nothing special on the agenda. I am just going to review the evacuation plan one more time and ask the people if they have noticed any hazardous conditions."

"How about you? Have you noticed any hazardous conditions, like maybe around Section C?"

Deacon said, "I went by there this morning and climbed around on the unit. I couldn't see anything out of the ordinary, but of course, you know it would have been unusual if I had, even if something had been wrong. Jared was there. We managed to get him worried about it, but I don't think he was able to get anyone else to pay attention to him. I wish everyone cared as much as that kid does. How is everything else going?"

"Aw, okay I guess. Say, have you seen anything of Hog? I haven't seen him since the picnic."

"I saw him yesterday. He's been at work, but I think he is avoiding you. What happened between you two?"

Sarge said, "Well, I guess I got over into your territory and did a little preaching. On Sunday morning after I took him home, I went to see him and talked to him about his drinking. I was worried about him—and about Peggy too. I tried to help him see that it might be gettin' outta hand. He didn't like it much. I think I disillusioned him."

Deacon chuckled and said, "Well, that explains it. I asked him why he hadn't been coming for coffee, and he said he didn't want to see you. He said you are a worse hypocrite than I am. For your information, I am an honest hypocrite, and you are a dishonest hypocrite."

"Oh!" Sarge said. "Well, maybe I can get back on his good side sometime. Well, I'll get back inside and tend to my rat killing and let you set up your chairs."

About two hours into the morning, Jared turned on his computer and brought up the technical reports on Section C. The pressures did not look right to him, but then, he really didn't know what the pressures should have been while a unit was being brought up. He decided to risk looking like a worry wart one more time and called to Al, "Hey, Al, take a look at the pressures on Section C and see if they look right to you."

Al said, "Okay, if it'll make you happy." A few minutes passed and Al said, "As a matter of fact, they don't look quite right."

"Should we tell them to shut it down and check it out?"

"Not yet. Do you have any idea how much it would cost to shut a unit down again at this point in the process? I'm going to call the unit and ask what's going on."

Jared could hear half of the conversation through the glass partition between the two cubicles. He got up and went to the door of Al's cubicle. In a few minutes, he hung up the phone and said, "Sure enough, something isn't right. They think it may be a computer malfunction. The unit isn't responding to their controls. The pressure built up like it was supposed to when they started the unit up, but then it started to drop. They said the chief operator has gone out to do a visual inspection to see what's goin' on. I'm gonna to call Ken Allison and give him a heads-up that something may be haywire."

"Do you think I ought to walk over there to see what's goin' on?"

"That might not be a bad idea. Call me on your cell as soon as you know anything."

Jared put on his hard hat and went out of the building. The smell of the refinery seemed a little stronger than usual to him, and his eyes were burning just a little, but he thought it was probably just his imagination.

He walked past Section A and began to trot. He didn't know what he could do if there was a malfunction, but he felt somehow that it was urgent for him to try. Section C was almost a mile from the front office. He began to run. He noticed that some of the workers were coming out and looking around as if they had a notion that something was wrong.

In the front office, Ken Allison, the technical manager, walked over to Joe Summerfield's office and rapped on the door. Then he opened it without waiting for a response. Summerfield was talking on the phone, but he turned to face Allison and raised his eyebrows as an invitation to speak. Ken said, "I just got a call from Al saying there seems to be a problem with Section C."

Summerfield interrupted the person on the phone, saying, "Excuse me, something has just come up that needs my attention. Can I call you back?" Then he hung up and said to Allison, "What seems to be the problem?"

Allison said, "Either there's a computer malfunction or the pressure in the unit is dropping."

At just that moment the phone rang again. The secretary answered it and, in a moment, half shouted through the door, saying, "Safety's on the line. They say it's urgent!"

Summerfield answered and heard the person from the safety department saying, "We're getting some readings from the sensors that say there's a dangerous level of combustible gas in several parts of the refinery. We recommend that we shut down and evacuate."

Joe Summerfield said, "Do it!" Then he hung up and said, "We're going to evacuate. Get everyone out of the office suite and moving toward the front gate. Hurry!" Within a minute, the plant alarm began to blast a long, loud moan that no one for miles around could fail to hear. Within a few minutes, everyone in the office suite was outside and running toward the gate.

Joe Summerfield hesitated and looked back at the plant. Michael Miller saw him doing that and read his thoughts: *There is nothing you can do back there. The people know what to do. You're going to be needed on the outside.* Summerfield nodded and began to run with the others. Miller noticed one of the secretaries heading for her car in the parking lot. He ran after her and took her by the arm. He shouted, "You can't use your car. The ignition might cause an explosion. Come on and run." She nodded and ran with him toward the gate.

As Deborah Olsen was leaving the plant, she looked around to see if she could see Jared. She couldn't.

As the alarm began to sound, Deacon was still preparing for his safety meeting. Sarge came running from the control room and said, "Is this a drill?"

Deacon said, "Not that I know of."

The two ran outside and looked up. They saw a cloud of iridescence shimmering around the tops of some of the units. Deacon said, "Great goodness. This place is liable to blow up. I've got to get everybody out of here."

Sarge said, "You've already done all you can about that. We've got to see if we can fix it."

Deacon said, "Do you think you know how?"

Sarge said, "I'd bet on the old manual cut-off valve on Section C."

Deacon thought for just a second and said, "I'll bet you're right. I've got some pipe wrenches in the truck."

Sarge said, "Let's get 'em and go." They ran to the safety department truck, got two pipe wrenches that Deacon used for safety demonstrations, and started to run toward Section C. They had not gone far before they realized that they could not run as fast as they once could. Their eyes were burning. They felt their noses and throats burning, and they tried to hold their breaths, but they couldn't do that while they ran.

At an intersection in a plant street, they met several men running together in the direction that the evacuation plan had taught them to run. When they saw Deacon and Sarge running toward them, they broke their pace as if they would go with them. Deacon shouted, "Get out of here!" The men started running again.

A few yards farther, Deacon shouted to Sarge, "You know we are liable to get ourselves killed, don't you?"

Sarge yelled back, "Yeah, I know."

It seemed important for them both to know that they both understood what they were doing. They said no more. They saved their breath for running. Their minds were racing ahead, remembering all that they knew about Section C and trying to imagine what they might be able to do.

A few miles away, at the home of the Andersons, Jane Anderson was pouring coffee for herself and Maggie Christopher. She had called Maggie to come over because she had been feeling depressed and needed company. When they heard the alarm siren, she stopped abruptly. "Did George say anything about a safety drill today?"

Maggie said, "He didn't mention one to me—and he usually does."

Jane said, "I've got a bad feeling. I'd better turn off the air-conditioner and go through the other safety drills. George has convinced us all that we ought to take these things seriously." She got up and busied herself checking to see that all windows and doors were firmly shut. Maggie helped. Then they sat down again and looked at each other in worried silence.

When Jared heard the alarm siren, he was running toward Section C. He stopped and looked up toward what he thought was the source of the sound. Only then did he notice that the tops of the units around him seemed to be dancing in a translucent cloud of gas. He stood still for a moment, trying to decide what he should do. Then he remembered the line from the brief safety manual Deacon had written: "When you hear the alarm, there is nothing more that you can do. Shut down whatever you are working with and evacuate." All around him, Jared saw people doing that. He tried to remember which way people in this part of the plant were supposed to run. Then he decided just to assume that the people around him would remember and to run the way they were running. It was soon obvious that they were running toward the side of the plant where the tank farm was. Jared ran that way too.

Jared soon saw that the major barrier between the people who were running and safety was a seven-foot chain link fence. He saw a few people climbing over the fence. Then he saw some people farther down the fence waving and beckoning people to come that way. As Jared ran that way, he suddenly realized that he was really scared. So was everybody who had sense enough to understand the situation.

Jared arrived at the place where the fence was only six feet high. About the same time, two women in company coveralls got there. One was Sally, Angie's friend, whom he had met in the cafeteria. The other was a badly overweight middle-aged woman. They were obviously having a hard time deciding how to get over the fence. Sally was trying to help the older woman. Jared stopped to help them. Part of him wanted to just get out of there—but he knew he would not be able to live with himself if he escaped and these women didn't.

Jared remembered a tip from his navy physical training. He waved to the women, turned his back to the fence, bent his knees, and made a stirrup of his two hands. Sally got the idea immediately. She tried to shout to the older woman and tell her what to do, but the older woman couldn't hear because of the siren. Sally decided to show her by going over the fence first. She ran toward Jared, put her foot in his hand, and jumped up as Jared boosted her toward the top of the fence. She got both hands and one foot on top of the fence, and then she went on over and landed on her feet on the other side. Jared waved for the older woman to do the same thing, but she didn't understand. She walked up to Jared, put her foot in his hands, and waited for him to lift her over the fence. Jared tried. He strained every muscle in his body, but she was really heavy. Finally, the woman began to climb Jared like a ladder. When she took her foot out of his hands and climbed onto his shoulders, he grabbed the fence to keep from falling under her weight. She then stepped on his head, jamming his hard hat down so that he could hardly see. She finally got to the top of the fence. While this was going on, two other men came and scrambled over the fence, but they didn't offer to help. When Jared felt the woman's weight off of his head and shoulders, he turned to face the fence, only to see that the woman was losing her balance and was about to fall back on him. He put both of his hands on her bottom and pushed. The woman went on over the fence and landed in a heap on the other side. Sally helped her up, and they began to run.

Jared felt like he had been beaten up. Every muscle in his body hurt. He pulled off his hard hat and threw it down. He was not sure that he had enough strength to get over the fence—but he realized that not getting over was not an option. He reached up and grabbed the bar at the top of the fence, pulled himself up, swung his right foot up to the top of the fence, and rolled over—but his pants leg caught on a wire twist on top of the fence, and he swung down head first. For a moment he thought, *Oh no! I'm gonna hang here and barbeque.* But then his pants tore loose, and he fell in a heap. He got up quickly and started running as hard as he could.

Jared had gone only about thirty or forty yards when he heard an awful sound behind him, a voom, and the concussion threw him forward so that he landed face down on the ground. He was grateful for the grass to break his fall. Before he tried to stand, he rolled over on his side and looked back. All he could see was a massive wall of flame. He could not see the fence. He felt the searing heat on his face. He tried to get up and run, but he found himself fighting a hurricane-force wind drawing him back toward the flame. He realized that the flame was consuming all of the oxygen around it and pulling all of the surrounding air toward it. Suddenly Jared remembered the dream he had the night after his first day at Apex. He thought, *Oh, so this is what that was about.* He didn't spend much time thinking about it. He fell on his knees and crawled as fast as he could until he felt that he could stand and run again. As he went, he heard several other explosions as other units and storage tanks burst into flame. Finally, Jared came to a plant road and followed it toward a gate that he could see in the fence around the tank farm. The gate was open. When he felt he had reached a safe distance, he collapsed beside the road to rest. He looked back. It seemed that the whole refinery was in flames and that the sky was hidden by black smoke. He sat there until he felt his strength returning.

The sound of the explosion was heard for miles. The people who had evacuated and were gathered in different places around the plant turned and stared in silent awe and horror. They saw a great fireball rolling up toward the sky, and they felt buildings shake and heard windows breaking around them. The sound of the alarm stopped and was replaced by the roar of the flames, punctuated by other explosions. After the shocked silence, the people watching began to mumble softly spoken prayers, and curse words, all at the same time, and both seemed appropriate. A short distance outside the front gate of the refinery, the people from the front office were gathered. Deborah had learned from Al that Jared had gone into the plant just before the explosion. She was worried sick. She realized that she cared deeply about what had happened to him.

In the kitchen of the Andersons' home, Jane and Maggie heard the explosion and both stared at each other in horror. They stood up and embraced. Maggie kept saying, "Maybe they got out. Maybe they got out." They had every reason to believe that their husbands would have escaped. After all, Deacon had designed the evacuation plan. But there was something they both knew about their men that made them feel that something bad had happened to them.

Chapter 9

As Jared sat beside the road, two fire trucks came through the gate, one from the Deer Park Volunteer Fire Department and another from LaPorte. Following them were the cars of some volunteer firemen who had not gotten to the station before the truck left. The driver of one of the cars saw Jared and pulled over. He shouted, "You okay?" Jared nodded his head and held up his thumb. The fireman went on his way, and Jared started walking toward the fence. He realized then that he was going to be okay—and he was very grateful.

Once he was out of the tank farm, Jared crossed the highway to a convenience store. The Pakistani man who ran the store stood out in front, watching. Jared came to the store. The man asked, "Were you in the plant?"

Jared nodded and asked for a soda. He felt a desperate need for it. The man took Jared inside and got him a soda. Jared fumbled for some money to pay for it, but the man said, "Oh no, man, just take it. You need it. You look like you have had a bad time. Why don't you go back to the bathroom and clean up, and then I will put something on your wounds?"

Jared thanked the man and went to the bathroom. He caught his first look at himself in the mirror. He was filthy, and there was blood caked on his hands and face from the scratches he had accumulated. His face looked like it had been sunburned. He took advantage of the opportunity to clean himself up. He was glad to see that all of his wounds were superficial. He looked much better after washing. He even combed his hair. He noticed that he still had his plant security badge, and he was glad he hadn't lost it.

When he finally came out, the man said, "You look a lot better now." He took some antiseptic and Band-Aids from the store shelf and dressed Jared's wounds.

Jared thanked him. He rested awhile and drank his soda.

"Can I get you something more?"

"No, thanks. I couldn't handle anything else right now. Have there been any others coming out this way?"

"Oh yes. Lots. A highway patrolman picked some of them up to take them to report in somewhere. He said he would come back in case any others came this way."

"Good. I'll just wait right here for him."

Both men stepped outside so that they could watch for the highway patrol. Jared sat down on the sidewalk and leaned back against the wall of the store and dozed off.

The man from the store stood by him and watched for the highway patrolman to return. When he saw the patrol car, he ran out waving and shouting to get the patrolman's attention. The car pulled into the parking lot. Jared woke up and stood to go with him. There were two other men in blue coveralls in the car.

The patrolman asked, "Are you with Apex?" Jared answered that he was. The officer asked if he needed to be taken to the first aid station or to the command center where the employees were to report in.

Jared managed a smile and said, "I've already had treatment by the good doctor here. I had better go check in."

Once in the car, Jared introduced himself, "I'm Jared Philips. I'm an engineer, but I was almost just a roasted wiener." All three men told their stories as they were driven back to the command center.

The patrolman asked Jared, "Are you a company official?"

"I'm an assistant process engineer."

"Do you know about the whole plant?"

"Well, I suppose so. I'm pretty new, but I've been trying to learn all about it."

"The Channel Six reporter asked us to find some company official who can interpret the extent of the damage to take a ride with him in the news helicopter and explain things to the people who're watching."

"I suppose I could do that."

The patrolman made contact with someone by radio and then took Jared to a school ground where he could meet the helicopter. Then he took the other men to the command center. Jared was not sure that he was the right one to be the interpreter, but he was the one who had been asked, and he knew that lots of people in the community would need to know what was happening.

In a few minutes the news helicopter landed. Jared bent over to avoid the turning rotors and ran to the door that had been opened for him. The reporter inside said, "Thanks for coming. Lots of people need to know what's happening."

As the helicopter was lifting off, Jared heard himself being introduced to a live television audience. "We have Jared Philips, the assistant process engineer from the Apex Refinery, riding with us. We're going to ask him to describe what we are able to see from the air."

Jared knew that it would be important for him to say enough but not too much. He did not want to cause any anxiety or to say anything that the company would have to explain away later.

The reporter turned and started interviewing Jared as the cameraman transmitted live pictures of the plant, which was burning below them. The helicopter flew in a circle around the flames and smoke, just far enough away to keep them safe.

"Mr. Philips, I understand that you were in the plant when the explosion occurred."

Jared saw a good opportunity to say an encouraging word to the viewers. "I was in the plant when the alarm began to sound, and I followed the plant's plan for evacuation. I'm sure that most of the people in the plant did the same thing. We hope that they were all able to get out before the explosion happened."

"Have there been any reports of casualties?"

"I haven't yet been to the company's temporary headquarters, so I don't know about that. I suspect that it's too soon to know."

"Mr. Philips, as we fly around the plant, can you just tell us what you are seeing and what is burning and what is not?"

Jared did just that through the rest of the trip. He was aghast at what he was seeing below him. A third of the central part of the refinery seemed to be burning. He tried to keep his emotions to himself and to be cool as he described what the people were seeing on television.

Eventually, the inevitable question came. "What was the cause of the explosion?"

"It's much too soon to know the answer to that question. I'm sure that a thorough investigation will be made as soon as it's possible."

"I know that our viewers are all wondering about one thing. Is there any chance that this was the result of an act of terrorism?"

Jared composed his answer carefully and then said, "As I said, it's too soon to know the cause of this explosion, but speaking for myself, the things that I saw just before the explosion did not suggest an act of terrorism to me. I'm sure that the company officials will explain the cause of the explosion to the community as soon as an investigation has been made."

Jared shook his head, suggesting to the reporter that he didn't want to say anything more about that, and the reporter followed his lead and asked him about something else. After two trips around the burning refinery, the helicopter took Jared back to the schoolyard. The reporter thanked him for his interpretation, and the television station's truck picked him up and took him to the command center so that he could report in.

The couple of hours after the explosion were full of motion. Many community law enforcement and firefighting agencies immediately mobilized to do things they had been instructed to do in emergencies. The sheriff's department set up a command post in a small park just a short distance outside the Apex front gate. They were in touch by radio with observers closer to the scene. Fire departments from several surrounding communities and other industries immediately came to the scene and were dispatched by the sheriff's department. Ambulances and paramedics came to stand by and rush injured people to the hospital. Soon a "company office" was established in a tent near the command center. Within an hour, a group of chaplains and counselors trained in trauma response came to stand by and to talk to anyone who had need of them. Tim Mathis, the pastor of the Christophers' church, was one of them.

An uninitiated person might have thought he was witnessing mass confusion, but things were actually going pretty well according to plans that had been made and perfected months before.

Most of the people who had escaped from the plant were in some degree of shock. Some wandered around for a while trying to collect themselves. The evacuation plan had instructed the employees to first try to contact a family member to let their families know that they were safe. Then they were to find the command center and the company office to report in so that the company could know who was and who was not accounted for. Most of the people who escaped did that almost instinctively.

Soon the Red Cross came and set up a portable coffee bar near the command center. Many of the people who had come out of the plant did not go home immediately but tarried around the command center to see what they could hear. Joe Summerfield and Michael Miller wandered around among them. People kept asking, "What happened?" They could only answer, "We don't know. It was something that wasn't supposed to happen."

There was a bar near the command center that had a large-screen television. When the televised pictures of the plant came on with Jared's commentary, someone shouted that the plant was on television. As many people as could crowded into the bar. Joe Summerfield came, and everyone made way for him to come in and watch. When Deborah heard that Jared was being interviewed, she groaned and said, "Oh thank God." Everyone in the bar and around the door watched the pictures on the screen in shocked silence.

Eventually, a company personnel officer with a clipboard came walking around among the survivors asking if anyone could give him any information about who got out and who didn't. He wrote down everything that he was told. Eventually, two of the men who had met Sarge and Deacon as they were running spoke up and told him what they had seen, adding, "We probably lost those two."

The personnel officer said, "You saw them running toward Section C? Do you suppose they were confused?"

"Naw, not those two. If anyone knew the way out, they did. There's only one explanation for what they did. They were carrying wrenches and running in toward Section C. They were gonna try to fix the problem and save the refinery."

Pop was sitting on the ground nearby in a daze. He overheard the conversation. He spoke up and said, "I can't be sure, but I thought I saw them running into Section C just before the explosion." A group of people gathered around to hear this piece of news. Someone said, "I could never figure those two out. They were so different, but they were friends."

Brown was standing nearby. He said, "I think they were really two of a kind."

Someone said, "Who'd have known it?"

Brown volunteered, "They knew it."

After that, Pop stood up and began to mumble something. He seemed unaware that his hair had been singed and that there were blisters on his face and that he was bleeding from scratches he got climbing over the fence. He started to wander off. One of the chaplains saw him and went to him. He asked, "How're you doing?" Pop's answer was not very clear. He began to wander away.

The chaplain asked, "Do any of you know that fellow?"

Brown said, "I know him."

The chaplain said, "Maybe you had better go with him. He may need some help."

Brown followed for a while and then said, "Pop, this is Brown. How are you doing?"

"Not so good. I'm having some of those same feelings that I had in Nam."

"Can I help?"

"Help me get to Amy and Johnnie. I'm going to have to call my doctor."

Brown took Pop to the ambulance station and went with him to Southmore Hospital. He called Amy to meet them there.

The story about Sarge and the Deacon running toward Section C traveled quickly through the crowd of people gathered around the command center. Each person who heard it seemed to respond in the same way, with a moment of reverent silence. When Tim Mathis heard the story, he knew he had a sad duty to perform. He went to the company office to check the authenticity of the story. When he found that no one had seen or heard from Bill or George since the explosion, he told the chaplain coordinator that he was going to have to go and see the families.

About two o'clock Jared Philips found his way to the command center and sought out Joe Summerfield. Joe said, "Jared, I'm glad to see you. I saw part of the television coverage and heard your explanations."

"Yeah, the reporter asked me to go with him and interpret. It seemed like something I should do. I tried not to say anything you would have to deal with later."

Joe said, "You're a good man. Tell us again what you saw." Michael and several others gathered around to hear. Before Jared was finished, he was in the center of a crowd of people who wanted to hear what they could.

"Well, Sections C and D are engulfed in flame. We can pretty well assume that they're gone. Sections A, B, E, and F are not burning now, but it will be hard to know what effect that intense heat is having on them. One or more of them could still explode. Of course, you see that the front office is not burning. The community fire departments have moved in and are keeping it cooled down with water. There's no way of telling what damage that's doing. The tank farm seems to be safe. The fire departments are keeping the tanks nearest to the fire cooled down by spraying water on them."

Joe nodded, "That's good. What about the compounding department?"

"The compounding building was not burning at that time, but it's awfully close to Section D. The fire departments probably can't get to it. I think it's still in danger. The same is true of the shipping sheds. And there were two ships tied up at the dock. One was a tanker."

Joe nodded, "The *P. T. Bailey.*"

"And one was a container freighter."

"Yes, the *Enterprise.*"

"Well, the tanker captain was evidently able to cut loose and to get a tug to pull his ship out of harm's way. But the freighter evidently couldn't get free of the gantries. I saw the crew and maybe some longshoremen or others in a lifeboat headed for safety. The harbor fireboat was spraying water on the freighter and on the shipping sheds. I think they may be okay."

Joe hugged Jared in an act of appreciation and said, "Thanks a lot for doing that. Now we know a lot more than we did. Stick around. We have an appointment to meet some people from the head office at the airport. I have a helicopter standing by to take them for a tour, and I want you to go with us."

Jared found a place to sit down and rest for a while. In a few minutes, Al came around with a sheepish look on his face. He said, "Well, I guess you were right. We should have checked up on the turnaround."

Jared nodded and said, "Yeah, but you were right too. There was nothing we could have done other than what we did." He held out his hand, and Al gladly took it and shook it.

Jared said, "Do you reckon the big boys would pay attention now if we sent them a plan for monitoring maintenance contractors?"

Al shrugged and said, "I don't know. Probably."

Jared began to walk around among the people who were waiting to hear what they could about their coworkers. Some family members who had not heard from their loved ones who worked at the refinery began to come and ask around, "Has anyone seen so-and-so?" It was heartbreaking to see the anxiety on their faces. A tiny little Hispanic woman in blue jeans and a faded tee shirt came carrying a baby almost as big as she was and leading another child, a little boy. She kept saying something in Spanish.

Finally, one of the company officials shouted, "Hey, does anyone here speak Spanish?"

A Hispanic man came and said, "I do." He talked with the little woman in Spanish for a few minutes and then turned to the group, which had gotten quiet, and asked, "Has anyone seen Lupe Salazar?"

A man said, "I know Lupe. He was at work today, but I haven't seen him since the explosion."

The interpreter told the little woman what the man had said. She began to cry. The man tried to comfort her. He took her baby and led her off toward the company office. Jared watched that with a lump in his throat.

Sally Williams saw Jared and came over to him. "I sure want to thank you for helping me and Mrs. Atkins over that fence. I just couldn't bring myself to go off and leave her."

Jared said, "I felt the same way."

"Well, if you hadn't helped us, we wouldn't have made it."

"I hope everyone made it. But I know that's too much to hope for."

Then Sally asked, "Have you seen Angie?"

"No. I suppose that she was in the lab near the front of the plant. Surely she must have been one of the first ones out."

"I thought that too. But when I didn't see her, I asked one of the guys from the lab. He said she had gone to collect samples down at Section E."

"Maybe she got out through the other side of the plant and just hasn't made it by here yet."

"I sure hope so."

Suddenly it occurred to Jared that he had not seen either Sarge or Deacon. He would have expected to see them there. He asked Sally about them. She told him what, by then, everyone around the command center knew. Jared couldn't believe what he heard. He wandered off by himself and sat down.

Deborah had been walking around with a clipboard, helping with the registration of survivors. She saw Jared sitting alone, and she came over to him. "You've heard, haven't you?"

Jared nodded.

She sat down beside him.

In a short while, Michael Miller came looking for Jared. He said the car was ready to leave for the airport, and Joe wanted him to come along. He rode the short distance to Ellington Field in silence. When they arrived at the airport, they found the helicopter that Michael had ordered standing by near the runway where the company jet was supposed to land. Michael parked the car. They all got out to watch for the plane. Joe and Michael stood near a hanger.

Jared thought the proper thing to do would be to give them some privacy. He went and stood by the chain link fence beside the runway and watched the smoke rising in the distance. Now and then, he could see a tongue of flame, even from this distance. His body was aching with fatigue. His head was spinning as he tried to take in the meaning of all that was happening. He began to feel a pain in his hands, and he realized that he was clutching the chain link fence so hard that he was hurting himself. He intentionally loosened his grip. He knew he was standing in a historical place, an airbase built during the Second World War, the place where George W. Bush flew his National Guard missions, the place from which the astronauts flew to Florida for space flights. But he had a sense that he was seeing something happen that would be another turning point in history. The thought came to him, *I knew if that damned dragon ever got out, all hell would break loose.* He chuckled at himself. Then he caught a mental vision of Sarge and Deacon running toward the trouble with a pair of pipe wrenches. A great sob started to come up from deep inside him—but he stifled it. Jared wondered what would come of the things he was seeing—and what they would require of him.

After a while, Joe Summerfield went into the hanger to look for a restroom, and Michael came over to Jared. He said, "It really looks bad, doesn't it?"

Jared was startled when he spoke, but he recovered quickly and said, "Yes, sir."

Miller went on to say, "I need to give you a heads-up about something. Joe Summerfield has been at odds with the head office about some things for several months. It may erupt in the middle of the conversations we're about to have."

Jared turned to face him and said, "I didn't know that."

Michael said, "It's not the kind of thing you want known. Joe is an old-timer in the refining business. He remembers when all of the major oil companies were like big families. Even the unions and the management had developed a basic respect for each other. Everyone worked together to get the job done."

"Sounds like a good way to work to me."

"It is. But recently a lot of factors, like foreign competition and stockholder demands, have caused top management to think they have to do things to enhance the value of stocks and attract investors, things like cutting costs, cutting staff, and maybe going easy on maintenance and safety to increase profitability. I'm sure you've seen the symptoms of that."

Jared nodded.

"New York has been pushing us to reduce staff and especially to get rid of older employees and replace them with people we can pay less."

Jared said, "They call that getting lean and mean, don't they?" Then he immediately wished he hadn't said it.

Michael said, "Yeah, that's what they call it. But Summerfield has been arguing that we need to take a long-term approach to keeping Apex healthy. He wants to invest more in maintenance and improvements, and he thinks that more experienced employees are worth the extra money."

"I hope he's winning his argument. But it looks like it is too late now."

Michael shook his head. "Just between us, he's in trouble with the head office and especially with William Stone, who is probably one of the people who is coming. I wanted you to know that so we can try to avoid saying anything that could provoke a confrontation. And if anything like that happens, we should try to stay out of the way of it and keep it to ourselves after it happens."

Jared said, "I understand. Thanks for telling me."

Miller saw that Summerfield was coming out of the hanger and went back to join him.

When the Apex jet landed, Joe, Michael, and Jared went out to meet the people who were getting off. Joe and Michael had managed to get ties and jackets to dress for the occasion. Two men in three-piece business suits got off the plane. The first was William Stone, an energetic little man who immediately took charge of the situation. The other was the company's chief executive officer, Frederick Alexander. He was a tall grey-haired man. He seemed strong but quiet. He gave the impression that he was hearing and seeing everything that was going on around him and assimilating and processing it. Joe and Michael had met Frederick Alexander on several occasions before. Stone was new to the top echelon of the company, but he took charge and introduced himself and Alexander to Joe and Michael. Joe introduced Jared and explained that he had seen the plant from a news helicopter and could help them to understand the extent of the damages. When Stone shook hands with Jared, Jared was not sure that he had been recognized as a live person. He had the distinct impression that Stone was looking at the rip in his pants leg.

Stone said, "We saw the smoke as we were flying in. It looks catastrophic."

Michael answered, "I'm afraid it is. We have a helicopter standing by to take us for a closer look. We're going to ask Jared to explain what we're seeing and to compare it with what he saw on his earlier trip around the site."

Jared thought it was significant that Stone and Miller were doing most of the talking. He thought it was probably Alexander's disposition to be reserved, but Summerfield, who was naturally outgoing, seemed to be holding back on purpose. He thought he noticed his hand trembling.

The helicopter took the men to the site and flew around it at a distance, to insure safety. Jared explained that the two sections, C and D, were composed of the kinds of units that perform the main function of the refinery, breaking crude oil down into its component parts for its various uses. These were still burning. He observed that Sections A, B, E, and F had not exploded as he was afraid they might have, but there was no way of knowing what damage the intense heat might have done. As Jared had feared, the compounding building was burning. That was the building where all of the lubricants that the refinery produced were mixed with their additives and packaged for shipping. The tank farm still seemed to be safe. The dockside shipping facilities and the front office building were still standing. The captain of the freighter had managed to get his ship free from the dock and moved to safety. The harbor fireboat was spraying water over the dockside buildings.

Alexander asked a few questions, which the three local men tried to answer. Finally William Stone asked the big question: "What was the cause of this explosion?"

Michael answered, "We have no way of knowing until a complete investigation can be made. None of the people who have come out of the plant have been able to give us anything but speculations. In fact, we may never know because, as you can see, the things that we would have to look at are being destroyed."

"But certainly you must have some suspicions. Is there any evidence that this may be the result of an act of terrorism?"

"All we know is that the trouble seems to have originated in a unit in Section C, which had just been shut down for periodic maintenance and was just being brought back up online. As you know, our maintenance work is done by Petrotech, one of our contractors."

Stone was insistent. "To whom or to what do you attribute the blame for all of this?"

Miller stood his ground. "It's too soon to know that."

"Well, eventually someone will have to accept the responsibility."

Jared didn't like where that conversation was going so he interrupted it by pointing out how the local fire departments had responded to the emergency.

Stone asked, "What about our own firefighting units?"

"They were unable to respond because they were too near the center of the trouble. To start their engines would have risked an explosion."

Stone asked, "I don't suppose you have yet made any estimate of the extent of the damages or of what it will cost to rebuild."

Miller answered, "This is the first time we've had this opportunity to look at the plant from this vantage point."

Stone said, "Mr. Philips, you are an engineer. What do you think?"

"I really wouldn't want to guess. It does look to me like close to one third of the refinery's central facilities will have to be rebuilt or extensively repaired."

Stone commented, "We will need to know that as soon as we can. We will have to evaluate whether we should make our investment in rebuilding here or in expanding facilities in some other places where we've been wanting to locate refining operations."

Summerfield said, "I certainly hope we can rebuild here. The loss of this refinery would have a devastating effect upon the economy of this area." It was Joe's first major contribution to the conversation, and he spoke with a tightness in his voice.

Immediately Stone said, "If that's so, do you think the community would be willing to participate in the cost of rebuilding through some tax advantages or through the investment of community development funds?"

Joe said, "I hadn't thought about that yet."

Stone said, "Well, those are questions we'll have to ask and answer in the near future."

Jared thought that William Stone was not much older than himself, but he had so internalized the current "wisdom" of the business community that he was sure he knew what was the right thing to do in every situation. Jared did not see in William Stone any of the feeling of a need to learn that he felt so strongly within himself. He thought that was remarkable—and troubling.

After flying around the burning refinery twice, the helicopter landed. Summerfield said, "We've set up a temporary office in the conference room of our bank. It's close to the command center where the employees are reporting in and where the disaster response work is being coordinated. Would you like to go back there to talk?"

Stone said, "We have seen all we need to see here. We can just go back into the company plane and talk there."

Jared thought, *No, you haven't seen all that you need to see. You need to see the people gathered around the command center waiting to hear news about their friends.* But he didn't say anything. He only asked, "Do you think you'll need me for this meeting?"

William Stone said, "Probably not, but come on in and stand by just in case we need something from you."

Jared thought, *Yeah, you might want to send me out to get coffee for you.*

The company jet was equipped with a conference table, around which four people could sit to work together. Jared found a seat further back in the plane, and the other four men sat around the table.

The first thing that Stone said was, "You know, with the climate of anxiety that exists in the country today, everyone would be more than ready to believe that this was the result of an act of terrorism."

Joe was about to answer, but Michael spoke first. "We see no evidence that any terrorism was involved, and I really wouldn't want any rumor to that effect to get started. Things like that cause armies to start marching and bombs to start falling and people to start dying."

Stone said, "But someone is going to have to be found responsible. There will have to be a company investigation. And, of course, there will be an OSHA investigation. We will need to be prepared to influence the outcome of that."

Alexander broke in, "I think Mr. Miller is right. We really should wait for the results of a thorough investigation."

Stone shrugged and opened his briefcase. He said, "We had better get down to business. We'll need for you to give us complete information about all of the employees who were either killed or injured. We'll want information about lost earning potential and other statistics that will enable us to know how much money to offer their survivors so that they will not bring suit against the company. We need to get to them and get them to sign releases before the lawyers get to them."

Joe seemed taken aback by that. "Isn't it a little too soon for that? Those people are still in shock."

"The lawyers won't think it's too soon. You can bet they're already working at lining up their suits."

Joe spoke with a tremble in his voice. "Forgive me, but these are people we know. I have a hard time trying to fix a dollar value on someone's life."

"It needs to be done. Otherwise those people will take the company to the cleaners."

"But can't we wait a little while for that?"

"Whose side are you on anyhow, the company's or the employees?"

"I didn't realize that we were not on the same side."

"What planet have you been living on?"

Michael said, "I have a suggestion. Mr. Summerfield and I will be calling on the families of all of the employees who were killed or injured in the explosion. Why can't we just say to each of them that you have asked us to express your deepest sympathy and to assure them that the company is planning to make some generous provision for them?"

Alexander said, "That sounds like a good way to go. Then we can get around to the settlements as soon as it seems appropriate. By the way, how many people have you lost?"

Michael responded, "As best we can tell, there are eighteen who have not been accounted for. Some of them may still turn up. There are thirty-seven in hospitals. Six of those are in critical condition. Some of them may not make it."

"And how many people did you have in the plant at the time?"

"There were 1,263, including contract workers."

"If I may say so, it seems to me that you've had a rather low level of loss considering the number of people who were at risk and the short time in which you had to evacuate the plant."

Miller answered, "Yes, we were fortunate. I give the credit for that to an evacuation plan that one of our safety technicians had developed just recently. He called it the 'Which Way to Run' plan. Everyone knew what to do, and they did it."

"That's really good," Alexander said. "We should give some recognition to the person who developed that plan."

Joe replied, with his voice quivering, "He's one of those who are not accounted for. He and one of his friends were seen running toward Section C carrying pipe wrenches just before the explosion. They evidently thought they might be able to do something to save the plant."

Alexander was visibly moved. He said, "That's one of the most heroic things I have ever heard."

Then Joe turned to Stone and said, almost in a shout, "Well, at least it solves another problem. Those were a couple of the older guys that you wanted us to get rid of so we can hire cheaper employees."

Stone stood and replied angrily, "See here. You must certainly know what we have to do to survive in today's competitive business environment."

Joe shot back, "I know what you think we have to do. But just how well is that working for us right now?" The two men were standing, leaning across the conference table under the plane's low ceiling, shouting in each other's face. It looked as if they might start throwing punches any time.

Stone was about to reply when Alexander interrupted, "Gentlemen, I think we have done about all we can right now. William, I think we should let these men get on with all of the important things they have to do." Then he said to Joe and Michael, "We'll be in touch with you daily. We'll want your complete damage reports as soon as possible."

Soon after the company jet was airborne on the way back to New York, William Stone took advantage of the private time with his CEO to advance some of his agendas. "Doesn't it seem that Joe Summerfield is living in the past? He's out of touch with the new paradigms of business."

Alexander replied, "That may be so, but he has something we need right now."

"What?"

"Experience."

Stone said, "A person who is preoccupied with his past experiences may not be the forward-looking kind of person that we need in top management."

Alexander said, "I know that's sometimes true, but he does know the refining industry. The board of directors hired me as CEO because of my success in increasing the profitability of a company in another industry. I hired you because of your success at Harvard. Neither of us knows the refining business very well yet. We may need Summerfield before the Pasadena Plant is up and running again."

"How can that help us?"

"I think we ought to at least give some thought to some of the things that can be learned from him and from what happened today."

"Like what?"

"Well, for one thing, maybe we ought to rethink the practice of outsourcing our maintenance functions."

Stone looked surprised. "That practice has proven to increase the profitability of a plant by reducing the cost of employee salaries and benefits. You've seen the studies on that."

"But would that practice still prove profitable if we figure in the cost of rebuilding half of the Pasadena Refinery?"

Stone was insistent. "Outsourcing as many functions as possible has become standard practice in all industries."

"I know. But that doesn't mean that we shouldn't take another look at it. Those paradigms you are talking about were not created in heaven or at Harvard. They came from the experiences of people running businesses in the real world. And they're not unchanging laws. They need to be constantly reexamined and reformulated. If they aren't, they can become the graves that industries are buried in."

Stone thought about that for a minute and then said, "I just know that we need to keep the bottom line in view. The board of directors hired you and recommended me to do one thing, and it is not to build up miserable little communities like Pasadena, Texas, or to provide employment for rednecks or to maintain a healthy industry or even to produce petroleum products. We were hired for one purpose and that is to generate a profit for the stockholders."

Frederick Alexander was careful not to let his facial expression change. Stone's subtle suggestion that he had been hired by the board of directors and not by the CEO caused Alexander to see something that he had been missing for months. He realized that the man sitting next to him did not see himself as a young protégée who wanted the CEO as his mentor. He saw himself as his successor and competitor. Alexander realized that Stone might very well become his assassin. He wondered if the ideas Stone was reciting were his own or if they came from some members of the board of directors, and if so, which ones of them. Frederick Alexander felt like a camper who had just discovered a rattlesnake in his tent. He knew that the next few things he did would have to be done very carefully. Experience in the executive suite had taught Alexander how to think thoughts like that without letting them show. He responded quickly to Stone's last statement by saying, "Yes, to generate a profit for the stockholders and for ourselves too. Right?" He smiled at Stone.

Stone smiled and said, "Right!"

Alexander changed the subject and began to discuss the procedures for assessing the feasibility of rebuilding at the Pasadena location, but his mind was on something else.

Very little was said in the car traveling back to the command center. But the silence was charged with emotion. The things that were not being said were weighty. Everyone seemed to be digesting the things that had just happened and thinking about where they would go from there.

Jared had the awkward feeling that he had heard things he should not have heard—but he was glad he had heard them. He thought he had learned some things that he would need to know if he was to be a part of the future of the refining industry.

After a while, Joe shared one of his thoughts. "A lot of our people are going to be unemployed."

Michael said, "'Fraid so."

After another pause, Joe said, "We had better meet with the union officers as soon as we can and tell them about what is going on. We don't want them to be out of the loop."

Then there was another silence. After a while, Joe said, "Jared, the company is going to need you to help with the rebuilding. I really don't know if I'll still be here, but if I am, I really want you to be here too."

Jared said, "Thank you, sir. I hope we'll both be here."

Michael and Joe dropped Jared off at his apartment. He picked up his mail from the mailbox, but he didn't read it. He made a phone call to his parents to let them know he was okay. He cleaned up and went to bed. He fell asleep quickly and slept hard until around midnight. Then he dreamed about the explosion. He woke up with a start and slept only fitfully after that. At one time he dreamed that he could see Sarge and Deacon trying to close a valve on a feeder line. He woke up yelling at them to get out of there. He didn't sleep any more.

Chapter 10

On Tuesday morning, the refinery was still burning. There was no way to extinguish the fires but to let them burn themselves out. Announcements on local radio and television stations had told most of the refinery employees not to report for work. During the week they would be contacted and told what to do. Al and Jared and a few others were contacted and told to report to work. They were to begin the process of inventorying the damages. They would begin by making an inspection of the parts of the plant that could be entered safely and then work their way through the rest of the plant when it was safe to do so. Jared spent the day doing that.

Late in the afternoon he came to Section F, the part of the plant where Sarge had worked. It occurred to him that he could get a good view of several parts of the refinery if he climbed to the top of the tower where Sarge had taken him his first day. At first he planned to do that for purely practical reasons. But about halfway up the ladder he realized that he was making some kind of a spiritual journey. He was remembering Sarge. When he reached the top of the ladder, he remembered Sarge standing there looking at him with that little grin, watching to see if he was man enough to make the climb. He climbed out onto the platform and looked around. His mind began to replay all of his memories of Sarge and Deacon and of everything that had gone on between them. He began to feel weak. There was an empty feeling in the pit of his stomach. He grasped the rail around the platform and began to cry. He stood and cried for half an hour. He let himself do it. He realized that it was something he needed to do. When he finished, he felt better.

Then he remembered what he had come up there to do. He looked around, made some notes, and then climbed down and walked back to the front of the plant. At the front of the plant he found that the parking lot had been cleared and that he could get his car. He drove back to the temporary company office. He spent a little time talking to Al and began to put a report together. Then he went home. He was feeling exhausted. He knew that he was experiencing emotional fatigue as well as physical fatigue. He threw himself down on his bed and let himself rest. He thought he could have just stayed there until morning, but in a few minutes, the phone rang. It was Deborah.

"Hey, sailor. I still owe you another meal. I've heard of a place close by that they say has good seafood. Do you feel up to going?"

Jared was glad to hear from her. He realized that he really needed someone to talk to more than he needed to crash in bed. Deborah was just about the only person he felt he could talk to. He said he would need a little time to clean up. She said she would pick him up in an hour. He wondered how she knew that he needed to talk and that he needed for her to pick him up. He thought, *She's quite a lady.*

The sun was setting when Deborah came. She had the top down on her car, and the moving air felt good after the heat of the day.

Deborah started the conversation. "How'r ya doin'?"

Jared said, "Well, aside from feeling like I've been through a mulching machine, I feel just fine." They both laughed a little. Then Jared went quiet. Deborah let him be until he was ready to talk.

Eventually, Jared said, "I've learned a lot of things in the last couple of days. There are some things that I can't tell you about. But I can say that I understand some more about what's happening in American business and industry. And you're right, it's not happening somewhere else. It's happening right here." Then he went quiet again.

Deborah drove out to the highway that ran in front of the plant and turned onto the road that ran by the San Jacinto monument. The huge obelisk rivals the Washington Monument. It was built to commemorate the battle in which Texas won its independence from Mexico. As they drove between the monument on their right and the USS *Texas,* an old Second World War battleship, on the left, Jared said, "You know, it seems like there's always some kind of a battle going on somewhere. There may not be any shooting going on, but the conflicts are being fought, and the history of the world is being shaped by them."

Deborah said, "Is that what you think is happening in business and industry?"

He said, "Yeah. I guess I do."

After a while, Jared said, "You know, it's funny. I went through three years of military service without having to see any of my friends die in action. But now I feel like I've lost two friends in battle right here in the refinery, where I always thought I would feel at home."

Deborah said, "Sarge and Deacon really did die heroic deaths."

Jared said, "Yeah, they did."

Deborah drove into the parking lot of a two-story seafood restaurant that was built right by a ferry landing on the ship channel. Before they went in, Jared looked behind him and saw the black smoke still rising. He looked at it for a long moment and then very purposefully turned his back on it and went into the restaurant. They walked upstairs and were given a table by a window. They ordered bowls of gumbo and sat and ate them slowly. They watched the Lynchburg ferry make a trip across the channel. Soon after that, a freighter flying a Panamanian flag came by. The channel was opened again. Lots of ships that had been standing offshore, waiting until it was safe, were coming into the Port of Houston. Jared and Deborah tried to relax. They sat in silence and watched the ships for a while.

Eventually Jared said, "You'll never guess who I just got a letter from."

Deborah said, "Who?"

"Mr. Chung, the guy who interviewed me from Brown and Daniels Engineering. It came Monday, but I didn't open it until just before you picked me up."

"Well, what did he say?"

"He wrote to say that one of the Aggies they hired instead of me has already gotten another offer and left. He wants me to apply again. He said he is sure that Brown and Daniels would hire me this time."

"You're going to do it, aren't you?"

"I don't know. I'll have to think about it. It really is the job I wanted. But now I feel like I have a responsibility here. Joe Summerfield said that he wanted me to stay on and that there would be an important job for me to do here. When I think about what Deacon and Sarge did, I think I'd feel like a deserter if I left now."

She said, "But you really don't know what things are going to be like here at Apex. You don't know whether they'll have a job for you long term."

"That's true," he said. "I don't know whether Joe Summerfield will still be here. Heck, I don't really know whether there will be an Apex refinery here. But I feel a loyalty to Mr. Summerfield and the others."

"You're dealing with some of that stuff you can't talk about, aren't you?"

"Yeah, I guess I am. Don't say anything about any of that. Anyway, I'll have to do a lot of thinking about a lot of things before I make a decision. Like I said, I wouldn't want to be a deserter."

They watched the ferry shuttle back across the channel again and then watched a tanker outbound for who knows where. Deborah broke the silence.

"If you had a wife and kids, you'd never desert them either, would you?"

Jared was surprised by that. He said, "Why, of course not. Why in the world …" He was about to ask why she would ask that, but suddenly he knew the answer.

He reached across the table, took Deborah's hand, and said, "Deborah, most men would never desert their wives and kids."

She said, "I really want to believe that. But heck, you have been deserted too. And I don't suppose you have come out believing that all women will desert their husbands the first time they get a better offer."

Jared said, "I never thought of it that way. But then, I was grown when it happened to me. I had some other role models to look at. I suppose my mom knew that she would never be anything but a working man's wife, but I doubt if she ever thought of leaving. No, losing Judy hurt me a lot, but it didn't change my whole understanding of the shape of reality."

Deborah said, "I've got to learn that. If a person can't trust the commitment of others, she is crippled for life."

There was another long silence. Then Jared said, "I have to tell you about something really strange." He told her about the dream that he had on the first night after coming to work at Apex. Then he said, "Right after the explosion, I realized that I had just had exactly the experience I had dreamed about. It was really weird."

Deborah said, "I have heard about things like that before. What do you think about that?"

"I really don't know what to make of it."

"Does that mean that the future is all planned out and the things that just happened were predestined to happen?"

"I don't want to believe that."

"Me neither."

"I guess what I make of it is that there are just a whole lot of things I don't understand and probably never will."

Deborah looked out the window and watched the ferry loading for a few minutes. Then she looked at Jared, smiled, and said, "I understand that

Sarge and Deacon were not the only ones who performed acts of heroism yesterday."

Jared said, "Oh?"

She said, "Yes, while I was standing around the company headquarters helping with the survivor registration, I met a middle-aged lady who told a story about a handsome young man who boostd her over a fence."

Jared immediately blushed and felt flustered and said, "Oh, did she tell you about that?"

Deborah smiled. "She sure did."

Jared said, "As I was about to climb over the fence, I met these two women who couldn't get over it. I helped the younger woman over pretty easily. But that other lady didn't seem to know what to do. She wound up climbing all over me. When she got through, I wasn't sure I would be able to get over myself. And if she decides to blame me for the bumps she took when she fell on the other side or to take offense at some of the places I had to put my hands to get her over, she might bring a lawsuit against me or the company." Jared looked at Deborah in wide-eyed anxiety.

She laughed and said, "Well, you can stop worrying. She thinks you're her hero."

Jared relaxed visibly, and Deborah laughed at him. Eventually he laughed too. Then they began to exchange funny stories about things that had happened during the disaster. It was really just what Jared needed.

On the way home they passed the San Jacinto monument again. Jared said, "You know, one afternoon a couple of weeks ago, I came out here and read the inscriptions around the base of the monument. It said old Sam Houston and his little bunch of fighters had been running away from the Mexican army for weeks. They had run halfway across Texas because the Mexicans had them badly outnumbered. Then, finally, they decided to turn around and fight. They caught the Mexicans napping and attacked them and beat them before they had a chance to get organized. It was quite a story. Of course, I couldn't help wondering how it would have sounded if a Mexican had written it. But anyway, I got to thinking, we always do a lot of running when we seem to be outnumbered and outgunned. But if there needs to be a battle we can sometimes find the right time to fight it, and we can come out better than we think."

Deborah said, "That's interesting. I have a notion you're thinking about something besides Texas history, but I'll wait until you're ready to tell me about that."

Jared thought for a minute, looked at Deborah, and said, "Yeah, you're right."

The day after the explosion, Joe Summerfield and Michael Miller began working at putting things back together. They found empty space in a new shopping center that could be used for a temporary front office. They worked together to come up with a design for a basic organizational structure and contacted an office furniture rental firm to set up temporary partitions and basic furnishings. They assumed that anything that could be salvaged from the old front office would have to be extensively reconditioned. They called in someone from the company's Houston office to set up a temporary computer system and connect it to the New York office. They were grateful for the computer age, because everything from engineering documents and personnel records to the most recent payroll records had been copied to the New York office and was readily available to them. They contacted each of the department heads and had them call back the people they would need to carry on the basic functions that would be needed in an interim structure. Late Wednesday afternoon, Joe found Michael and said, "Michael, we need to get together in a quiet place and think ahead. Come over to my house tonight and plan to stay late."

After supper, Michael arrived at the Summerfields' door. Joe greeted him, "Come on in, Michael. Let's go into my study and talk."

Helen appeared and asked, "Would you like coffee, Michael?"

"That would be nice."

Joe said, "Make a big pot. We'll be needing it."

Once they were settled, Joe started the conversation by saying, "I've been thinking full time about where we should go from here and how we should plan to get there, and I know you have too. We need to bounce our thoughts off of each other and put together a plan."

Michael asked, "Do you think New York is going to let us make the plan?"

"I don't know, but we'll have a better chance of staying in control of things if we're the first to present a plan."

"Right. Tell me what you're thinking."

"Well, the first thing we have to do after the inventory of damages is complete is to try to get some parts of the plant back into partial production. The engineers are telling us that, at first look, all of the units in Sections A and F and most of Sections E and B are intact and probably could be brought back into production fairly soon. However, all of those units would need a complete inspection and maybe an overhaul, much like a turnaround, just to be sure they haven't been damaged or just plugged up by the process of the emergency evacuation. Then we would have to rebuild some of the infrastructure that connects the sections so that they can work together around the parts of the plant that have been destroyed."

Michael nodded, "Yeah, that's what I've been thinking too. Who are you thinking about to do that work?"

Joe said, "I'm not thinking about Petrotech."

Michael said, "I hear you. But the folks in New York are going to wonder why. Petrotech would look to them like the logical choice."

Joe said, "Yeah, I can just hear some of the head office people saying, 'If it ain't broke, don't fix it.' But I'm ready to argue that something is quite obviously broke and in need of fixing."

Michael asked, "Then who can we get to do the work?"

Joe said, "How many of our own people have had experience as pipe fitters or boilermakers or electricians or in other skills that we need? Couldn't we organize something ourselves using them and our maintenance people and operators, and bring in some other people?"

Michael said, "I hadn't thought of that. I doubt that they could do the heavy construction on the units that were destroyed, but they might be able to work with the operators to check out the units that weren't damaged too badly."

Joe said, "Right. Sections C and D are going to have to be redesigned by an engineering firm and built by a major construction company. We might even get some needed updating of processes out of that. Right now I'm just talking about the inspection and renovation."

Helen arrived at the door with coffee and served it.

Michael stared into his coffee cup and said, "It would take some organizing to put together a team that could get that done."

"It's going to take some organizing to get the job done no matter who we use. I think our own people would be easier to organize than some people who've never set foot in the plant before. And it would give us a chance to put some of our people back to work instead of laying them off."

"If we can make it work, that would be the real beauty of the plan."

"I'm stuck on one thing. Someone would need to organize all of that. I think our engineers would need to be involved, but I'm not sure they would be the ones to supervise the work. Marvin Elrod will have to be in on the job, but I have a feeling I can't trust him to do it alone. I wish that Bill Anderson and George Christopher were still around. They could do it."

Michael said, "How about Mac MacKinzie? He could do it."

Joe's face brightened. "Yes, he could. I hadn't thought of him. Do you think he would? He hasn't had time to get tired of his retirement yet."

"How would we do that, by hiring him on as a consultant?"

"I don't see why not. Head office is always ready to hire engineers and other technical people as contract consultants. Why not a pipe fitter?"

"We should probably feel him out about this before we make any proposals to head office. Do you know how to get in touch with him?"

"I'll bet we'll see him within the next few days. He is sure to be here for his friends' funerals. Let's try to get an appointment with him while he's here and run the idea by him."

"We should be ready to make it well worth his while to come out of retirement so soon."

"I would want to do that, but I suspect that if he is receptive to the idea, it will be because of some other motivations."

"I'll bet you're right."

Joe said, "Well, let's brood on that and get together tomorrow with a little more information to see if this can work. I really don't know if we can sell that to New York."

Michael said, "What's next on the agenda?"

"We're going to have to reckon with Stone's question about who is to blame."

"Yeah, we will. He's really pushing that."

"I think almost everyone here is thinking that, when the investigation is finished, we'll find that Petrotech is to blame, and Petrotech will probably blame Buddy O'Neil. That will wrap it up in a nice neat package, and everyone else can claim to be innocent. They are sure not going to want to talk about those safety improvements that OSHA recommended and they ignored."

Michael said, "But you don't think that's really the right answer, do you?"

"No, not really. I think it's the whole system that's to blame. We've been so preoccupied with short-term profit that we've skimped on maintenance and lots of other things that have contributed to this disaster. We've all participated in creating the conditions that caused this."

"Some, like you, have gone along kicking and screaming."

"That's true, but we've all gone along."

Michael said, "No one is going to like that answer. William Stone is really not going to like that answer."

Joe said, "I know it. And he sees that answer coming, but he doesn't want to deal with it. That's why he's so eager to find someone to blame."

"What're you thinking?"

"I'm thinking I want to use this situation to push the company to look at the bigger problems in the industry. I don't want to excuse Petrotech or anyone else, but I want us all to take another look at the basic values we're working with and our standard way of doing things."

"How do you plan to do that?"

"I plan to write the report of the cause in a way that will push everyone to look at the bigger issues."

"How're you going to get that past Stone?"

Joe said, "I don't know, but I'm going to have to get it to Alexander and, if I can, to the stockholders."

"You know you're probably going to get shot down. Everyone likes to think their systems are all okay and wants to blame one person for the problems. They may wind up blaming you."

"I know that. And here's something I want us both to keep in mind. I'm going to be the point man on this. And I'm going to be expendable. We both know I'm already on shaky ground. We need for you to stay out of it so that, if I get shot down, you can still be acceptable as my replacement. You understand that, don't you?"

Michael frowned, "I would hate to let you go out on a limb without backing you up."

"Michael, I know that. I know where your heart is. But this is necessary for the long-term good of the company and the industry. Do you understand what I'm saying to you?"

"I guess so."

Jared felt better after his date with Deborah. He went to work each day and helped to complete the inventory of damages. Most of the front office people and some of the plant workers were called back and put to work at different tasks. No one talked about the layoffs, but everyone knew they were coming.

For the first few days, the damages Jared could report were minimal, but that was because they were working in the parts of the refinery that were considered safe. As the fires began to burn out, they were allowed to move closer and closer to the center of the explosion. The damages there were more conspicuous. He knew that he would eventually be seeing scenes of total devastation.

After work on Wednesday, Jared was hot and tired, but he really didn't want to go home. He thought about going to the Ice House for a beer. He hesitated because he knew it would be sad to go to the place where he had met with Sarge and the Deacon. But he decided that he couldn't let his grief rule him. He went to the Ice House.

After getting his drink, he looked around to see if he knew anyone there. At a table in the corner, he saw Pop and Tex and Brown. He went over to them and spoke to them. "Hey, what're you guys doing here?"

Brown said, "Just reminiscing."

"Thinkin' about Sarge and the Deacon?"

They all nodded their heads, and someone said, "Yeah."

Jared asked, "Can I sit with you?"

Pop said, "Oh yeah, sure. Sit down."

Jared said, "We're all going to miss those two, aren't we?"

Tex said, "Yeah, and we ain't never gonna forget what they did."

Jared said, "I know I won't. I didn't get to know them as long as you did, but I will never forget them."

The men were all quiet for a few minutes. Then Jared said, "Where's Hog? I would've thought he would've been here with you."

Tex said, "He's in a mental hospital being treated for post-traumatic stress syndrome."

Jared said, "That kinda surprises me. This thing must have hit him pretty hard."

Tex ducked his head and said, "Nah. It didn't hit him any harder than it hit the rest of us. He called me just before he went in; some lawyer had contacted him and told him that if he would go to a certain hospital and be treated for post-traumatic stress, the doctor would testify that he couldn't work any more, and the lawyer could get him a settlement big enough to retire on."

Pop said, "Yeah, and the lawyer could get a big piece of the pie for himself."

Jared said, "Wouldn't he have to prove that he couldn't work any more?"

Tex said, "The lawyer told him that the company wouldn't fight it because it would be cheaper for them to pay him off than to go to court. Hog said the lawyer asked him to see if any of his friends wanted to try the same thing. He gave me his name and number and told me I should call him."

Pop said, "I know about post-traumatic stress syndrome. That's something real. I had to spend time in a hospital with that right after I came home from Nam. It was bad. And when I heard that explosion and saw all of those flames on Monday, some of it came back on me. I spent the night in a hospital. The doctor gave me some medicine and made some appointments for me to come in to see him. But I'm goin' to the doctor so I can get ready to go back to work, not so I can get out of work. I don't think much of what Hog is doin'."

Brown said, "I don't either. A lawyer contacted me about doin' something like that. He was one of our people. He started giving me a bunch of stuff about remembering how our people have been mistreated down through the years and how this was my chance to get something back. I just told him I didn't want to hear any of that line of stuff. When I think of how bad our people have had it, I just realize how good I've got it. All I want is a chance to go back to work at the refinery and earn a good livin' for my family. Then you know what he said? He said I should give him a chance to get something back. I told him that with his law degree and his big car and nice suit, he didn't exactly look like he was being oppressed, and as far as I was concerned, he could go take a leap."

Tex looked at the water rings on the table and said, "I have to admit, I thought about it. I know I don't have much seniority, and there are gonna be layoffs; I don't have any education or any skills. I know that the way things are out there right now, I may not be able to find a job. I was tempted. But then, when I thought about what Sarge and the Deacon did, I knew I could never respect myself again if I gave in to that kind of crookedness."

Just then, two men in company coveralls and hard hats came into the Ice House. They picked up their beers from the bar and looked around. One of them recognized the men from Apex and came over to their table. He had some news.

"They think they have found Sarge and Deacon."

The four at the table stared at the man in coveralls for a minute. He recognized the pain in their expression and realized that they must have been friends.

"There wasn't much left of them, but they found them right where they expected to. They were by an old cut-off valve in Section C. Each of them had a pipe wrench in his hands. They are going to check the dental records, but they don't think they are going to have to wait for a DNA test."

Jared asked, "I don't suppose you heard anything about funeral arrangements."

The man said, "The families were expecting it so they had the arrangements all made. Sarge will be buried after work on Friday, Deacon on Saturday morning, and there will be family visitation for both of 'em tomorrow night."

Everyone went silent. The man said, "Sorry, fellows." Then he moved on to another table where some other Apex people were sitting.

All four friends stared at the table for a while. Jared said, "Damn!" Everyone nodded.

In a few minutes, Pop said, "I think I need to go home."

Brown said, "I'll go with you."

Pop said, "Thanks."

The group dispersed.

On an impulse, Jared went to the table where the men in coveralls were sitting and asked, "Have they found any of the others?"

"Yeah, four others."

"Do they know who they are?"

"Not really. But they are fairly sure about one of them. It was a woman. And the only woman that they haven't accounted for is Angie Billings."

That news came like a kick in the gut for Jared. He suddenly realized that he hadn't even thought about Angie since the explosion. He had assumed that, since he had heard nothing to the contrary, she was safe. A wave of guilt feelings washed over him because he had not asked about her.

One of the men saw the shocked look on Jared's face and said, "Yeah, pretty Angie."

"Where did they find her?"

"Near the fence between Section C and the tank farm."

"What was she doing there? I heard she had gone to the other side of the plant to collect samples."

"That is quite a story. Her friend Betty said she saw Angie coming back on her bicycle with a basket full of samples and shouted to her. She stopped to talk. They were fussing about the fumes when Angie looked down toward the crossroad and saw some guy. She said she wanted to go say hi to him and so she started riding in his direction. Then Betty said the guy did a funny thing. For no apparent reason, he started to run. Angie rode after him. A couple of minutes later, the siren started to blow. That is the last anyone saw of her."

Jared suddenly felt like he was about to faint. Without saying anything else, he walked out into the parking lot, leaned against his car, and vomited. He got into the car and sat awhile. Had Angie been coming after him when the plant blew up? Jared tried to imagine what chain of events might have followed from her coming after him—but he couldn't.

One of the men from inside the Ice House came and tapped on Jared's window and asked if he was okay. Jared said, "Yes." He thanked the man for asking, started his car, and drove home.

Immediately, Jared began to be tormented by feelings of deep guilt.

He thought, *Any time a woman turns to a man, the man ought to be able to rescue her. But that's crazy. I didn't even see her. I had no idea that she was there. But if she was coming to see me, I am responsible for her death. But no. That's a crazy thought too. Maybe a part of me was secretly in love with Angie. Maybe those fantasies have not really died. Why am I feeling that I should have been able to save Angie? It doesn't make sense.*

Eventually Jared was able to sort out his thoughts and his feelings. There was no real guilt there. He was not really responsible for Angie's death. But the feelings of guilt were there—and they were really deep. The more he thought about it, the more he realized that he was dealing with lots of other guilt feelings too. He was feeling guilty for the deaths of Deacon and Sarge. They had come and asked him for help, and he hadn't done anything. He thought he had done all he could do, but had he really? Why didn't he put his job on the line, march into Summerfield's office, and tell the boss to fire Buddy? *I'm the guy who wanted to save the oil industry. Why couldn't I have saved this plant?* Again, it eventually became clear to him that he really had done all that he could. But still the feeling of guilt was there. He realized that he was feeling what lots of sailors felt in wartime, the guilt for still being alive when some of their shipmates were dead. In his head he knew there was no real guilt—but in his gut there was a load of guilt so heavy that he felt he would not be able to swim without sinking. He flopped on his bed, but his thoughts kept tormenting him. He knew that he would never sleep.

Eventually he began to think about Angie, beautiful Angie. He remembered the fantasies he had played with through the night after he met her. He knew that he could have turned those fantasies into realities if he had chosen to. But now he imagined that beautiful face, that beautiful body blackened beyond recognition. It came to him that all of life is like that. No matter how beautiful it is, it's only temporary. It will eventually be turned into something like a charred carcass—or worse. He realized that, for the first time in his life, he was dealing honestly with the reality of death.

By now, darkness had come. He thought, *Is this what it's like? Does it all end in darkness? Is this what it's like now for Sarge and Deacon and Angie—and eventually for me?* He reminded himself that he had always been a religious person. He didn't really believe that life ends in darkness. At least he never had believed that. But what if the things he had always believed were not true? By this time, it was completely dark. The darkness had closed in around him. He realized that doubts and fears and feelings of guilt were tumbling in on him from all of the dark corners of his mind, from places where he had been pushing them away for a lifetime. He tried to pray. But somehow he felt that his prayers were not reaching past the darkness that had wrapped itself around him.

After wrestling with all of those demons for several hours, Jared told himself that he knew he was reckoning with a lot of things he had needed to deal with for a long time and that, in time, he would whip them. Since he knew that he was not going to sleep, he got up and turned the light on. He dug around among his things and found his Bible. He spent some time reading favorite passages that he had learned in his younger days. He assured himself that there would come a time when he would be able to believe them again. Then he turned the television on and tried to escape into an old western. About three in the morning, he fell asleep in his reclining chair.

When the first rays of morning came through the window and woke him up, he remembered the night. He thought about all of the things he had felt. He knew something important had happened to him. But he was not yet able to say what.

Thursday evening, Jared called Deborah. He asked, "Would you like to go with me to Sarge's funeral tomorrow afternoon?"

Deborah said, "Yeah. I think we really should go."

"I'll pick you up after work, and we can go straight from there. After that, I thought we might go down to Galveston for some seafood."

"That is sounding better and better. But won't we need to go home and dress for the funeral?"

"No. Sarge's family decided he would have wanted it right after work, at the time when most of his friends might go to the Ice House, and that it should be a graveside service so everyone could come as they are."

"Sarge was a really unique character. When did they find them?"

"Just yesterday. That was the first time anyone could get into the area to look. They were both found beside the old manual shutoff valve on the main supply line to Section C. They were evidently trying to shut it off just like we all thought. There really wasn't much left of them. The caskets will stay closed."

"What about the Deacon's funeral?"

"It will be Saturday morning at his church. Both families had the plans all made so they could go on with the funerals as soon as they found the bodies. And, by the way, they think they have found Angie Billings too."

"Yeah, I heard."

Nothing else was said.

After talking to Deborah, Jared went to the funeral home for the family visitation. He wanted to go alone to speak to Jane Anderson and Maggie Christopher. He felt that this was something he needed to do alone. When he arrived at the funeral home, he found the parking lot full. He had to park on the street two blocks away. When he walked up to the door, he saw that there were two lines extending out into the yard, one leading to the room where Deacon's casket was and the other leading to Sarge's. Their families were there to speak to visitors. Jared got into one of the lines and discovered it was the one for Deacon's family. It didn't matter. He wanted to see both.

The line moved slowly. Each of the wives was spending a little time talking to each visitor instead of just saying thanks for coming. Jared looked around. He knew who some of the people were. There were lots of older couples. He supposed that they were people who had worked with the two in years past and retired. There were also people from all levels of the refinery's staff. The Summerfields and the Millers had already been there. He saw Ken Allison. He also saw some of the Petrotech people. While he stood on the outside of the building, everyone stood quietly or talked softly. But inside, Jared found that the people standing in line were talking—sometimes, he thought, too loudly to be respectful, and sometimes laughing. At first, Jared took offense at that. But then, he began to listen to what was going on. The people were telling the stories of what they remembered about Sarge and Deacon. In their own ways, they were celebrating their lives.

When Jared got to Maggie Christopher, she grasped his hand warmly and said, "Jared, I am so glad to see you. George thought so much of you."

Jared said, "Well, I thought a lot of him too. I can't tell you how much knowing him has meant to me."

Maggie introduced Jared to her daughter, who was standing by her side, and her son-in-law, and then she went back to talking very personally with Jared. She said, "George was telling me just before he went to work for the last time that he wanted to talk to you. He said he wanted to invite you to church. George always invited everyone to church."

Jared smiled and said, "Sarge had told me to expect the invitation."

Maggie said, "Well, then, on behalf of the Deacon, let me invite you to our church, St. Paul's."

Jared smiled and said, "Thank you. I just may be ready for that pretty soon."

"Well, then," Maggie said, "let me introduce you to one other person." Tim Mathis, the pastor, was standing nearby, and Maggie called him to come over. She introduced them.

Tim said, "Jared, I have heard of you. George mentioned you to me."

"I have heard of you too. I have heard that you are a mighty fisherman."

"Oh, someone has been talking about me. Do you like to fish?"

"Now and then. Maybe we can go together some time." Jared wondered why he had said that.

"All right, let's plan on it."

Maggie asked, "Jared, have you talked to Jane yet?"

"Not yet, but I will."

"Well, be sure and talk to her. She really wants to speak to you."

Jared said, "I will," and then he went to get in the other line.

When Jared finally arrived at Sarge's closed casket, Jane welcomed him especially warmly. She said, "Jared, there is something you need to know. Sarge had a special reason for taking a liking to you. We had three boys. The oldest of them wanted to be an engineer. He would have been just about your age."

Jared said, "Would have been?"

Jane said, "Yes, he died when he was a senior in high school. It was one of those freak things. An aneurism we didn't even know about ruptured while he was at football practice. Of course, Bill didn't say very much. He was a macho man. But he really grieved a lot. He enjoyed being around you because he thought you were probably what our son would have been like."

Jared was taken aback. "Well, I guess that is mutual. He reminded me of my dad."

"You are a lot like Sarge, you know. I heard that you were going back into the refinery to see what was wrong, just as Bill did."

"Well, yes. But when I heard the siren, I headed for the fence. I am not in his class at all."

"If you had thought you knew how to fix the problem, would you have tried to do it?"

"I hope I would have."

"Well, I like to hope that Bill and Bill Junior are together in a better place now. That gives me some comfort."

"I hope so too," Jared said, and then he wished he had said, "I'm sure they are."

Jane introduced Jared to her two other sons, Henry and Dave. They smiled as if they knew the secret. Dave said, "I think Dad wanted to adopt you as our brother."

Jared choked a little bit and said, "I would have liked that." Then he smiled at each of them and at Jane and said, "I am not as macho as Sarge. I cry."

Jane said, "So did Sarge."

After that, Jared left the funeral home and made his way back to his car, and sat there for a while—and cried.

After work on Friday, Jared met Deborah outside of the temporary office, and they drove to the community cemetery. It was a large, open space without many trees. It was not hard to find the funeral. A canopy had been put up and the casket and some chairs for family members were arranged under it. People were gathering—lots of people. There were already close to a hundred people gathered around the tent. Some wore suits. Some wore plant coveralls or other work clothes. People were still coming in. The response had been expected. The funeral director had arranged for a powerful public address system and for extra chairs. Jared and Deborah went by the tent to sign the guest book and then found a place to stand. People spoke to each other in hushed tones. Some people seemed to feel ill at ease about being there. Some of the men looked like they were on the verge of running away. The Summerfields and the Millers were standing near the tent. A reverent hush hung over the assembly.

By the time the family cars arrived at half past five, there were close to three hundred people gathered. Tim Mathis, the pastor, got out of the first car and escorted the Anderson family to the tent. Maggie Christopher and her children and Mac and Betty MacKinzie were also escorted to the tent and seated with the family. The funeral director looked around and then nodded to Tim.

Tim opened his prayer book and read the Twenty-Third Psalm and a prayer. Then he began his sermon. He told some familiar stories about Sarge, giving the people a chance to lighten up a little bit and relax. Then he said, "In spite of all of those things you know about Sarge, or maybe because of them, you all loved him. So is it so hard to believe that God loves Sarge too? That's what counts right now. None of us is good enough to go to meet the Lord counting on our own goodness. We all have to go counting on God's love for us. Jesus came to show us how much God loves us."

Then Tim added another thought. "Someone might ask, what about the judgment of God? The Bible does talk about judgment. In fact there's a passage about the judgment that ought to ring a bell with lots of us because it talks about refining. We know about refining oil, but this passage compares the judgment of God to someone refining silver and gold. Let me read it to you. It's in Malachi 3:2–4: 'But who can endure the day of his coming and who can stand when he appears? For he is like a refiner's fire and like a fuller's soap; he will sit as a refiner and purifier of silver, and he will purify the descendants of Levi and refine them like gold and silver, until they present offerings to the Lord in righteousness.' The old prophet is saying that when we meet God, that will be a time for judgment and for refining of our lives.

"Now, I may be a little bit of a maverick in the way I think about the judgment of God. I don't think of it just as something that happens at the end of time or at the end of our lives. I think it is something that happens again and again in the middle of our lives because God meets us in each moment of our lives and asks us to live up to the best that we are capable of. In those times I don't think God is looking for a reason to send us to hell. God is trying to find a way to bring out the best in us. I think that happens in a special way when life puts us into a situation where it will cost us a lot to live up to the loving commitments we have made. You all know something like that happened among us just this week. And Sarge and his friend George Christopher, the Deacon, rose to the occasion and gave the most perfect gift anyone can give to God and to us, a total commitment in love. Let's just pray that all of us can rise to the challenges that will meet us in life and experience the refining that comes from God."

After that, Tim said a prayer, mostly for Sarge's family, and closed the service.

As Jared listened to the sermon, he thought that nothing the pastor was saying related directly to the questions that had tormented him through the night after he heard about Angie. But he felt that he was in touch with a level of reality where the answers might be found. It helped.

Jared suggested to Deborah that, since they had already signed the register, they should not try to visit with the family. They would be exhausted after they had talked for a few minutes to all of their really old friends. By six o'clock they were in the car, out of the cemetery, and on their way to Galveston for some seafood. Both Jared and Deborah were quiet for the first part of the drive to Galveston.

Deborah broke the silence. "That preacher said a lot in a few words, didn't he?"

Jared said, "I've never heard it put just that way before." Then they were quiet again.

Eventually they began to talk about things that had no significance at all, as if they both knew it was time for a respite. Soon they were laughing again. Jared chose one of the famous restaurants by the seawall, where they could see the Gulf of Mexico. They laughed all through dinner. Then after dinner, Jared suggested that they go across the street and walk along the seawall to watch the breakers come in.

The sea was calm. Gentle waves were coming in one after another and breaking just before reaching the beach. The moonlight paved a glistening path from the moon to whoever was looking at it. A gentle breeze made the summer night comfortable. They got quiet again.

Deborah finally said, "Walking along the edge of an ocean kind of makes me feel small. It makes me think the things that are so big to me aren't really that big."

Jared asked, "Does it make you think the things that seem big to you are too big for you to do anything about them?"

"I guess so."

"I don't want to feel that way."

"Is that the dragon slayer talking again?"

"Nah! That's the engineer."

"Have you thought any more about calling Brown and Daniels and asking if they still want you?"

Jared said, "Yeah, I thought about it almost constantly, and I finally think I know what I have to do. It really is the job I want, but I don't feel like I can accept it right now. There is too much at stake. I feel like I have to stay."

"Are you feeling like you owe it to Sarge and Deacon to make your sacrifice to save the refinery?"

"It's something bigger than that. I think there is something even bigger at stake than one refinery. It's all of American business and industry; it's the American way of life. It's even bigger than that. It's the possibility of a better life for everyone everywhere."

"Wow! Are we ever getting global!"

"I know this sounds ridiculously idealistic. But there are other people out there making commitments to make things work. Joe Summerfield is going out on a limb. He is not risking his life, but he is risking his career—and I really think that is almost as important to him. And even the little guys, Brown and Pop and Tex, they are giving themselves to it. And you know what else? They are trusting it. And when it lets them down, they feel hurt."

"Trusting what?"

"They are trusting industry and business and government and the whole bunch of things that make up the world they see around them."

Deborah said, "I remember that we were taught in junior high school that the people who work and are productive will benefit from the results of their productivity and that if business and industry prosper, everyone will prosper."

Jared said, "Yeah, I remember being taught that too. But they have changed the rules. There are some powerful people in high places who are exploiting all of that trust and commitment. They are focusing on short-term profit. They are using their power to increase their power and to cut themselves a bigger and bigger piece of the pie, leaving less and less for the people who actually make things work. In the process, they are eroding away the very foundations of the whole productive system and moving more and more people toward poverty."

"You are finally seeing what I have been talking to you about since we first met. But I think you are seeing more of it than I have ever seen."

"I do seem to remember that we have been down this road before."

"Not quite. You are seeing it differently than I have seen it. I've seen it as something I have to survive. You are seeing it as something you have to fix."

"Yeah, I guess that is the engineer coming out in me."

"Or the dragon slayer. Now you have gone from trying to save one refinery to trying to save the whole world. What do you think you can do?"

"I don't know. Maybe nothing at all. Probably nothing at all. But I feel like I ought to be there in case there is something I can do."

"So you are not going to take the job at Brown and Daniels?"

"Not right now. It's not like I really have to throw my life at it, like Deacon and Sarge did. This is not my last chance. I have decided to write to Mr. Chung at Brown and Daniels and tell him that I really am interested in working for them, but that because of the present crisis, I feel a responsibility to stay at Apex for the time being. But I am going to ask them to remember my name for future reference. It won't hurt to pack a parachute."

"Good thinking. God only knows where all of this is going."

"Do you think he does?"

"What?"

Jared said, "Since you're a theologian now, do you really think God knows where all of this is going or do you think God is watching and wondering what we are going to do with it?"

"If God is like the one the preacher was talking about today, I think he has a preference."

"Yeah, so do I. And I feel like I have to do what I can. I'll know what I can do when the time comes to do it."

They were both quiet for a time, and then Deborah said, "There's something I want to say to you. I have a notion that Apex is going to have to start laying people off pretty soon. I suspect that they're going to need you but that they're not going to need me. Pretty soon now, I'm going to start looking around for something else to do. But I'm going to try to find something in the Houston area if I can." Then she stopped and turned to face Jared and said, "Because you are a special guy, and I want to stay in touch with you." Then she put her hand behind his head, drew his head down, and kissed him so that he would understand what she meant.

"You can move anywhere you want to. I'll stay in touch with you. You are a special lady." He kissed her again.

They held hands and walked on down the sea wall together. After a while Deborah said, "What time will you pick me up for the Deacon's funeral?"

"Do you want to go?"

"I think we should."

"It's at half past ten. I'll pick you up at ten o'clock."

A little later she said, "You're thinking about going to church on Sunday, aren't you?"

"How did you know that?"

"I guessed."

"You are scary."

"Well, if you do, you can pick me up for that too."

Jared looked at Deborah, shook his head, and said, "I don't have any idea where this is all going—but I'll bet it's gonna be one heck of a trip." They both began to laugh, and it was a long time before they could stop.

Chapter 11

Frederick Alexander stood by the floor-to-ceiling window in the board room of the offices of the Apex Oil and Refining Company, looking out at the place where the twin towers of the World Trade Center had once stood. He heard the members of the board of directors coming in for a called meeting to talk about the disaster at the Pasadena Refinery. Ordinarily, Alexander, as chief executive officer, would have been at the door, cordially welcoming the board members. But today he chose not to do that. There was sure to be lots of questions, and he wanted to keep it all contained within the meeting itself rather than letting things get started prematurely. Besides that, he really didn't feel like being cordial. He was brooding on the meaning of the things he was experiencing. He remembered the disaster of September 11. Terrorists had destroyed the magnificent buildings that once stood there, ending thousands of lives because of pure hatred. He had seen another disaster recently and wondered if it happened because of neglect or because of pure stupidity. Lots of people had reacted immediately to the hatred that brought down the World Trade Center, but very few people had given any thought to the origins of that hatred or to ways of doing something about it. Frederick Alexander wondered if anyone would be willing to ask questions about the real causes of the Pasadena disaster or to discuss doing something about those causes.

Frederick heard the people coming in and beginning their discussions. Then he heard William Stone's voice. He was readily giving his explanation of what had happened in Pasadena. Frederick knew that it was time for him to turn around and participate in what was going on. All twelve members of the board of directors were in their places. John Oliphant, the chairman of the board, called the meeting to order.

"Ladies and gentlemen, let us come to order. As you know, we have some very important things to discuss today. We have been furnishing you with information about the accident in the Pasadena Refinery as we have received it. It is incomplete, pending a thorough investigation of the causes, but it is the best that we have. Now, I believe you have all received a letter from the plant manager, Joseph Summerfield. We will be discussing that letter today."

William Stone spoke up and said, "I must apologize for that letter being sent directly to you instead of being directed through the corporate offices. That was Mr. Summerfield's idea. I can't imagine why he took it upon himself to send it directly to you. He knows the company policy."

Edward Ainsworth responded, "I have no objection to receiving this letter directly from Mr. Summerfield. I do not think that we need to have things predigested for us. We can read the input and analyze it for ourselves."

Oliphant said, "Well, in any case the letter is before you, and I am sure that you have all read it and analyzed it, but just as a formality, I am going to read it again so that the whole of it will be fresh in your minds as we discuss it. The body of the letter is as follows.

We find ourselves having to cope with a major industrial disaster. I know that you are calculating the cost of this disaster in terms of lost production, corporate profits, and stock values. So am I. All of my savings are invested in Apex stocks. But I must also look daily at the twisted wreckage that stands where the plant of which we were so proud once stood. I talk daily with people who are about to be unemployed. And I have visited with the families of those who died in the explosion and fire. I am feeling the depth of this tragedy in every bone of my body.

I believe very strongly that we should take this terrible experience as a time for learning important lessons and planning new and creative ways of doing our work.

I have believed for a long time that Apex, and much of the rest of American industry, has been penny wise and pound foolish with regard to maintenance and modernization of facilities. I suspect that, when the investigation of the causes of the accident is complete, the findings will bear that out. I hope that we will be ready to learn important lessons and to make important changes.

Furthermore, I hope that we will begin to do some creative thinking about how to rise to meet the demands of a new day in the refining and energy industry. Much of the Pasadena Refinery is going to need to be rebuilt. We could take this as an opportunity to replace old processes with new processes that will meet the needs of a changing world.

I have taken steps to bring in engineering consultants to work with our engineers to do two things. First, to analyze the damages to the plant and to design changes in the infrastructure that will get the undamaged parts of the plant back into production as soon as possible. Second, to suggest ways in which the parts of the plant that were destroyed could be replaced with new, state-of-the-art energy production processes that could make Apex an industry leader in meeting the needs of a changing world. I have asked them to have their preliminary report ready within one month. I will see that you have it to study as soon as it is ready.

I deeply regret that we are having to deal with this catastrophic situation. But I sincerely hope that we can bring something good out of it.

Respectfully,

Joseph Summerfield, Manager of the Pasadena Refinery, Apex Oil and Refining Company.

"He adds a personal postscript. 'Two of the people who died in the explosion were long-standing employees of the company who were evidently making a heroic effort to save the refinery. I hope that the company will find some appropriate way of honoring them.'"

For a long minute, there was silence in the room. Then William Stone commented, "I have never heard such a ridiculous jeremiad in my life."

Andy Long, an older fellow who delighted in trying to hide a Phi Beta Kappa intelligence behind a Texas accent, said, "What in the world is a jeremiad?"

Stone quickly responded, "It is a tirade of negativism that suggests that the whole world is going to hell in a hand basket and it's our fault."

"That's not how I understand it." Jim North, an old man with a mop of white hair who always sat next to Andy Long, was talking. "I am an old Sunday School teacher and that word makes me think of the Prophet Jeremiah in the Bible, who saw his beloved nation going to pot and spoke out to try to get them to change their ways before it was too late."

John Oliphant tried to recall the meeting to the subject at hand. "Friends, I know we are all good Christians but ..."

Bill Lieberwitz said, "I'm not a Christian. I am a Jew."

"So am I," said Eve Schwartz.

"So was Jeremiah," said Jim North. A little ripple of laughter went around the table, and the group seemed to relax a little.

Edward Ainsworth said, "Mr. Chairman, I would like to make a response to the letter. I do not consider myself a religious man, but what Mr. North said about the Prophet Jeremiah actually sounded like a good description of what I heard Mr. Summerfield trying to do with this letter. I have been on this board for two years now, and this is the first time I have heard anyone suggesting that we should take a critical look at what we are doing and do some creative thinking about how we should go to meet the future. I think we should take this letter seriously and support Mr. Summerfield in what he is doing. American industry needs some aggressive leadership, and I believe that we can give it."

"Oh, come now. Can't you all see what this man is trying to do? He's just trying to hold on to his job." The speaker was A. J. Vanderver, a major stockholder who had the support of enough other stockholders and representatives of holding companies to make anything he said prevail. His massive body and deep voice seemed to announce his dominance. "A major industrial accident has happened in the plant, for which Summerfield was responsible. Now he is trying to shift the blame and to present himself as the savior. If he could have made things better, he should have done it. It is clear to me that he ought to be fired outright. Of course, I know you are going to need to offer him a retirement package to make things look better, but we really ought to have already told him to clean out his desk."

William Stone added, "I have believed for some time that Mr. Summerfield is out of touch with the paradigms of modern business and industry."

Frederick Alexander spoke in Summerfield's defense. "I have to say that Mr. Summerfield has been an effective manager for a long time. And he has submitted several proposals for improving maintenance and safety practices and modernizing facilities, but we were not able to fit any of them into our budget."

Vanderver shot back, "His letter reminds me of the blame-America-first politics that we hear so much now. I am not about to let him shift the blame to this board of directors. The accident happened on his watch so it is his responsibility. And by the way, Mr. Alexander, it happened on your watch too."

Frederick Alexander's expression did not change. He had been expecting that attack. But he knew that he would be wise to keep quiet during the rest of the meeting.

Eve Schwartz spoke next. "It seems to me that it might be to our advantage to keep Mr. Summerfield in place at least until after he completes the first stage of the study he proposed, the part about bringing the undamaged parts of the plant back into production as soon as possible."

"I am sure that another manager could do that just as well," Stone said.

"Perhaps, but the transition could take some time, and that time could cost us money."

Vanderver always liked to defer to the ladies on the board. He made a statement that everyone knew would be final. "All right. Let him stay until he has finished the study. Tell him that we want it by our next regularly scheduled meeting, which is in three weeks. Then, when he has turned it in, can him and replace him with someone who can get things done."

Oliphant took Vanderver's statement as a motion and called for a vote on it. It passed with Ainsworth in opposition and Long and North abstaining. He asked if there was any more business. Vanderver reminded him that they were in a meeting called to attend to one item of business, and that was done. He was already standing as Oliphant adjourned the meeting. Everyone stood and started putting papers into their briefcases.

Ainsworth asked, "Wasn't there something in that letter about two employees that should be honored? What was that all about?"

Stone quickly said, "Oh, they were just a couple of old fools who didn't know when to evacuate."

At this, Frederick Alexander found his voice again and briefly told the story about how Sarge and the Deacon had lost their lives trying to save the plant. Everyone paused where they were in their packing up to go and listened politely. But when Alexander was finished, no one said anything more. As far as they were concerned, the meeting was over.

Edward Ainsworth followed Eve Schwartz out into the hall and spoke to her confidentially. "I appreciate what you tried to do in there just now. Do you think there is any chance that Mr. Vanderver will change his mind if the report is impressive?"

She shook her head. "I doubt it seriously. Once he has announced a decision like that, he is not likely to go back on it. He would think it would be a sign of loss of control. He has the clout to make anything he says stick."

Edward Ainsworth walked back into the board room and found Frank Oliphant still seated at the head of the table. He waited until the last hangers-on had left and then sat down beside him.

"Frank, I think you had better start thinking about finding someone else to fill my place on the board of directors. I have been thinking about doing something else for a while, and the meeting today helped me make up my mind. I will be directing my broker to sell off my Apex stock. I will have him do it gradually, in a way that will not cause a commotion in the stock market."

"Why in the world would you want to do that?" Oliphant asked. "You are a major stockholder, and your father served on this board for ten years. Why would you think of selling out and resigning when the price of our stock is as low as it is ever going to be?"

"There are lots of things involved. But just say that I remember Enron, and I don't want it said that I was an old fool who didn't know when to evacuate."

On his way out of the building, Frank Oliphant stopped at William Stone's office and asked, "What do you know about Edward Ainsworth?"

"He is a rich man's kid. He took advantage of his father's wealth to spend the first part of his life traveling around the world and going to college. He finally earned a PhD in political science and taught for several years at the University of Texas. He also served two terms in the state legislature down there. He was elected as a Democrat, but people who knew him there said he was sort of a maverick. Wouldn't stick by the party line. When his father died, he quit teaching and took over the family business. Why do you ask?"

"He just resigned from the board and said he plans to sell his Apex stock."

Stone shrugged his shoulders. "Good riddance."

Two hours after the board of directors meeting broke up in New York, it was lunch hour in Pasadena, Texas. Jared was working alone, completing the inventory of the damage done to Section F, Sarge's old unit. He decided to do something totally foolish with his lunch hour. He threaded his belt through the handle of his lunch kit and climbed to the top of the tower where Sarge had taken him on his first day in the refinery. It was a hard climb, but it was something he wanted to do. Once he was there, he walked around the platform and tried to take in all of the scenery around him. He couldn't do it. There was too much. In the distance, he could see the buildings of downtown Houston and of the Galleria area, where he and

Deborah had gone with her friends. He watched a tug leading a tanker down the ship channel toward the Gulf of Mexico and who knows where beyond that. Closer by, he again surveyed the panorama of petrochemical plants that he could see from there. Then he looked at the place where the fire had been. It seemed to him an awful sore spot in the body of something alive. The thought occurred to him that he hoped it was not a cancer. He wondered what Sarge would have to say about the things that were happening.

He opened his lunch kit, unwrapped his sandwich, and was about to eat when he heard someone else climbing up the ladder toward him. The distinctive scrape and ring of someone climbing a steel ladder was unmistakable. He wondered who in the world it could be. He didn't have to wait long to find out. Joe Summerfield's head came up through the opening in the platform.

"Mr. Summerfield! What in the world are you doing up here?"

"Looking for you. Al told me I might find you here. You sure have strange preferences about where to eat lunch."

"Yeah, I guess I do. Would you like a sandwich? I have plenty to share."

"No, I've already eaten." He looked around. "You can see a lot from up here."

"I guess it's kind of silly, but this is the place Sarge brought me on my first day in the plant to see if I was a sissy. Then when I passed his test, he introduced me to all of the channel industries from here."

"Sounds like Sarge, all right. It all looks good except for that big old ugly spot over there."

"That's just what I was thinking."

"What I really came up here for is to talk to you. I want to tell you what we are getting ready to do and to try to keep you interested in helping us do it. I just got the go-ahead from New York to put together an engineering team to make a study of the best way to get this refinery back into production and maybe to do some exciting new things too. Our first project will be to decide what it will take to get the parts of the plant that are still okay reorganized to get productive again."

"I suppose the first thing we will have to do is to clean all of the units up. I know that when you shut one of these babies down in the middle of a process, it gets all gunked up."

"Right. We have something going on that. Your old friend Mac is coming back. I am working through Petrotech to let him make up his own crew, using as many Apex people as he can and any Petrotech people he thinks he can trust and start that cleanup process right away."

"Great."

"In the meantime, you engineers, and a team of visiting experts, are going to figure out how we can connect this to that and move something from here to there to make an operating unit out of what is left. It will be a massive job of retrofitting."

"Sounds interesting."

"It should be. But the real fun comes when we go beyond that and start making recommendations about how to replace the units that were destroyed with some creative new units that will blaze new trails for the refining industry."

"That sounds fascinating."

"It will be. I am bringing in some outstanding consultants. One of them is Dietrich Schmidt. You have heard of him."

"Yes, I'll be glad to finally meet him."

"We will have to remember that we don't have any idea whether New York is going to run with the plan once we put it together, but I have just gotten the authorization to start the study. The reason I am telling you this is that I have an idea that you would have a lot to offer to that kind of a process. But a little bird told me that you may have gotten an offer from another company. I don't ever want to stand in the way of someone's career development, but I just wanted you to know what the next few weeks are going to bring, in the hope that you will consider hanging around, at least until we see where this project is going."

"I am flattered that you want me in on that. The truth is I have already decided to stay for a while longer. I hate to leave in the middle of something important."

"Good man."

"I don't know that I am all that good. I've got to tell you that I knew there might be trouble. Sarge and Deacon asked me to try to get some attention from the company. I did what I thought I was supposed to do, but it got lost in the chain of command. Ever since the explosion, I've been kicking myself for not putting my job on the line and marching into your office to tell you what I knew. I am not really feeling all that good."

"I understand. I have been feeling the same way about not marching into the office in New York and yelling at some people about the things that I knew needed fixing. Stay with us a while longer. Maybe we can make some things right. Come to the company office at seven o'clock tomorrow morning. We are going to get started right away."

"I appreciate having a chance to be a part of that."

"I have to tell you, though, that we are going to have to reduce our staff in some departments, and I am afraid that Deborah is going to be laid off."

"I think she is expecting it."

"Maybe we can bring her back on eventually. Well, I've got to go catch up with some other people I need to talk to. Glad you are going to be on the team." Joe Summerfield took hold of the ladder and started climbing down.

Jared thought about the things he had just heard. Gradually, excitement began to replace all of the heavy emotions he had been carrying around. He thought, *Man, I'm gonna get a chance to look for a cure for cancer!* He was just about to let out a shout, but he thought Summerfield was probably still right below him. He took an extra big bite of his sandwich instead and grinned silently.

At quitting time, Jared was walking across the parking lot and saw Deborah walking to her car with a large box in her arms. He caught up with her and said, "Hey, that doesn't look so good. Can I carry that for you?"

"Yeah, sailor. Things worked out like I was expecting them to. I have been laid off until further notice. Everyone was real nice about it. It was just something they had to do."

"What are you going to do now? Do you have a plan?"

"Yeah, first I am going to try to find out what happened to the report on that CPA exam that I took at school. I should have gotten my grade on that a long time ago. Then I am going to find out where the test is going to be offered next and get ready to take it again. Then I am going to start sending out some resumes."

"The lady has a plan. I knew you would. I have another suggestion for you to consider."

"Oh, what is that?"

"Since I am apparently going to have a job for a while longer, why don't you just marry me and let me take care of you?"

Deborah stopped and stared at Jared. There was a look of wide-eyed surprise on her face. Jared smiled at her over the box in his arms. But the look he saw on her face was not the one he was hoping to see. She seemed suddenly on the verge of panic.

"Oh Jared, I couldn't; I mean, it's not that I don't … I mean, I was just not ready for that. I guess I'm just not ready."

"I'm sorry I surprised you. I suppose this is no way to ask a girl to marry you. I just thought that was what the conversation on the sea wall was all about. And I really do want to marry you—for all of the right reasons."

"Oh Jared, that is the most beautiful thing anyone has ever said to me, but—but I am just not ready."

"We can think about it for a while longer. Don't be upset."

"Jared, I'm sorry. I'm sorry that I'm not ready. But Jared, please don't go away."

"I won't. It's okay."

Jared could not tell what Deborah was thinking. He only knew she was on the verge of panic—like she had been the night they sat in her car in the rainstorm. He put the box into the car, took hold of her hand and squeezed it, and said, "I'll call you."

"Please do."

Deborah got into her car, looked back at Jared one more time, and drove away. Jared didn't know what to make of what had happened. He drove home, waited a couple of hours, and called Deborah.

"Say, I forgot to ask you. I am going to have a really big day tomorrow, and I am going to need someone to tell about it. Can I take you to dinner? I have a notion that it may be late."

"Oh yes. Just call to tell me when you are coming to get me."

Jared could tell that Deborah was relieved that he had called. He thought, *Well, I messed up the first time, but apparently I did the right thing this time.*

At a quarter of seven the next morning, Jared walked into the company office with a laptop computer and his notes on his inspection of the damages. He felt a special kind of energy in the air. The secretary told him where the engineering team was meeting. Jared entered the room and was surprised to hear a chatter of loud conversation. It is a known fact that when engineers meet, their meetings are usually quieter than most professional meetings. That was not true of this meeting. There was excitement in the air. Jared looked around and saw all of the company engineers. Even Al

Scardino was there early. That just never happened. Jared spotted three strangers. There was a conspicuously beautiful young Indian woman, a tall athletic-looking young man with a burr haircut, and a short scholarly looking man with thick glasses and a mop of partially combed hair. Jared assumed that must be Dietrich Schmidt. He was wrong. The tall, athletic man came over to him and said, "You are the only one here that I haven't met, so you must be Jared Philips. I am Dietrich Schmidt. I've been wanting to meet you." They visited for just a few minutes. Five minutes before the announced meeting time, Joe Summerfield stepped to the lectern and said, "I believe everyone is here. We have lots of exciting things to do. Let's get started." A semi-circle of tables had been set up around the lectern, and a projection screen and chairs were arranged behind the tables so everyone could see. Everyone sat down. Jared sat down next to Al, and Dietrich came and sat with them.

Joe Summerfield took charge of the meeting. It soon became clear that he was an engineer and had not let his professional discipline lapse during his years in management. He knew the language. He started by explaining the project he had proposed to the head office. They would first make a study of the best ways to get the refinery productive again as soon as possible. Then they would propose ways of replacing the parts of the refinery that had been destroyed with creative new equipment that could make Apex an industry leader in the emerging new age.

At this point, Al leaned over and whispered in Jared's ear, "Save your Confederate money. The South shall rise again."

Summerfield went on to explain that all of that would have to be sketched in instead of developed in detail since they had only a little less than three weeks to do their work. But he warned that realistic cost estimates and estimates of construction time would have to be included. He said, "I hope you are as excited about this project as I am, because it should be obvious that you are not going to be able to get this job done working just forty hours a week." A murmur of agreement rippled around the room.

Joe then introduced everyone in the room. He started with the Indian lady. She was Dr. Mathilda Singh, a research scientist at Rice University. She had been doing research in the subject of what oil refineries will need to look like after people stop burning gasoline in their automobiles. The scholarly looking man Jared had mistaken for Dietrich Schmidt turned out to be J. T. Ogden, the assistant project manager on the biggest refinery construction project that had been planned in the United States in many years. He was on furlough while the company for whom the plans had been made studied the proposal and decided if they could afford it in an unstable economy. Everyone was impressed.

But Summerfield didn't stop there. He had each person stand while he read their list of qualifications. He told about their academic backgrounds, their majors in college, their research projects in graduate school, patents they had registered, and anything else he thought might be relevant to the project. It was obviously his intention to make sure that everyone knew what resources were present in the room and to see that everyone appreciated the talent of the others. Jared dreaded the time when he would have to stand and hear his beginner's background exposed. But when his turn came, he discovered that Summerfield knew more about him than he thought. He told the group about his specialization in the navy, the topic of his senior paper in college, and the scholastic honors he had won. He also mentioned his experiences watching the refinery burning from the air and his participation in the study of the damages. When Summerfield got through, Jared was actually convinced that he did have something to offer.

The last one to be introduced was Dietrich Schmidt. After reciting his impressive resume, Summerfield explained that Dietrich would be the project manager for this study. He would be in charge. Summerfield expressed his regrets that he would not be able to participate in the fun that the engineers were going to have while he was attending to his management responsibilities. He left, and Dietrich Schmidt took charge.

Dietrich knew just what to do. The morning was occupied with analysis of the extent of damages. The information that had been gathered had been assembled into a report by a team of Apex engineers. Printed copies were distributed. An illustrated presentation was made with time to discuss questions that needed further exploration. The team members were told how they could download all of the available information from the company computer system. Jared realized that someone had been "burning midnight oil" to get this information ready in a short time. By midafternoon the group was being divided into work groups and given assignments. Jared was impressed. This group meant business. They had a clear purpose and a plan for achieving it. The meeting broke up at six o'clock. Everyone was still excited. Jared did not realize until he was in the car that he was exhausted. He thought it would be good to go home and collapse. But he remembered that he had made a date with Deborah and that it would be important to keep it. He called Deborah on his cell phone and told her that he was on his way to her apartment.

Jared found Deborah waiting for him in front of her apartment. She had a smile on her face that he could see from a distance. He was glad to know that the embarrassment left over from the previous night was evidently gone. She hopped into the car and started talking immediately.

"I know that you have a lot that you want to tell me, but I have something I want to tell you too, and I can't wait. I decided that my project for today was going to be to find out what happened to the report on my CPA examination. I got on the phone and started trying to trace it. In about an hour, I found out that it was in the unclaimed mail box in the post office in my home town. I called my mom and asked her to go down and get it for me. The postmaster said he wasn't supposed to give it to anyone but me, but since he knew my mom, he gave it to her. In a little while, she called me back. She had it. I asked her to open it and read me the report. And guess what?"

"You passed it."

"I passed it—all sections—and my grade was in the top ten percent of the people who took the test."

"That doesn't surprise me a bit. I have been expecting that. I am sorry we are not dressed up. I would take you to someplace fancy to celebrate."

"I will take a raincheck on that—and I will remind you of it. And by the way, my mom is coming to see me next week, so you will have a chance to meet her."

"I will look forward to that. What happens next?"

"Well, I called Ginger Rayburn and got the name and number of that guy we met at her house who is starting a new subsidiary of Logan and Harley. Remember, his name was Rick Rogers. He said he would be looking for some people with accounting degrees. I called him. He remembered me and invited me to come to Houston tomorrow to fill out an application, and he made an appointment for me to come in and interview on Monday."

"You really don't waste any time, do you?"

Jared pulled into the parking lot at Applebee's, and they went in to eat. Deborah continued to chatter enthusiastically. "And oh, by the way, George Christopher's daughter saw that we were in church last Sunday and called to invite us to come again next Sunday and to come to their house for lunch. She said that her mom and Jane Anderson were going to come, and she hoped we would come to visit with them. What do you think?"

Jared said, "I think I would like that."

"All right, I will call her and tell her we will be there. Okay, now you tell me what happened today for you."

"Well, I thought I had a lot to tell you, but I don't think I can top that." Jared gave Deborah a brief report on the happenings on the engineering team. He told her how excited everyone was. They talked for a while more about both of their days. But as soon as the food was eaten, Jared said, "I am exhausted, and I'll bet you are too. Let's call it a day."

Chapter 12

On Sunday morning, Jared and Deborah made their second trip to St. Paul's Church. The week before, Deborah had been anxious about whether or not she would know what to do. Jared had assured her that anyone who could navigate a cocktail party in a Memorial Drive mansion could certainly figure out what to do in a blue-collar Protestant church. He was right. This time, she was more at ease.

They took advantage of their time driving to church to catch up on their respective adventures.

Jared said, "I'll bet you are really excited about going for your interview tomorrow."

"You bet I am. This sounds like the very sort of thing I have been wishing for since I started college."

"Are you scared?"

"Well, maybe a little, but I suppose that is natural. Say, an interesting thing happened to me Friday. Mr. Rayburn called me—you know, Ginger's father."

"Yes. What did he have to say?"

"Well, he said Ginger had told him that I had passed my CPA exam and that I was trying to line up an interview with the guy we met at his house. He wished me luck, but he also wanted to offer me another possibility. He said that if I should decide to set up my own accounting practice, he would like to hire me to do his external audits. He said he had some friends who sometimes needed some accounting services for their businesses, and he would be glad to put me in touch with them."

"How about that! It is good to have more than one possibility to choose from."

"It sure is. That was a real surprise. But really, if the thing in downtown Houston pans out, it is really what I want. What is happening in your end of the world?"

"Lots. We finished the analysis stage of our study, and we have been assigned to teams to do the preliminary designs for different parts of the plant modifications. I have been assigned to work with one of the mechanical engineers to design a new compounding department.

"All right, in plain English, what is that?"

"In plain English, that is the place where lubricants, oils, and greases are mixed with different additives to prepare them for various uses that the market needs. Al nominated me for that job because I had once had some ideas about how to improve what we had been doing in that department. Dietrich Schmidt also had some ideas about that, so he is going to work with us on Monday to get us started. It is not the most glamorous assignment, but it has the advantage of being something they probably will accept, since they are going to have to rebuild the compounding department. The old one burned, and it would be very costly to ship all lubricants to other refineries for compounding. There is no sense at all in building it back like it was. So I know that I am going to be able to contribute some creative new technology, even if the other plans get rejected."

"Sounds good."

"They have told us we can say goodbye to days off until this project is completed. We are to have our section assignments finished and ready to submit to the group by Friday. On Saturday, we start the stuff we are all looking forward to, designing the refinery of the future. We are to have a presentation folder ready to fax to New York by Wednesday so the board members can study it in preparation for the board meeting on Friday."

"Wow, they are really trying to get a lot of work done in a short time. Aren't the team members worried that their plans will be rejected?"

"No one is talking about that, but I suppose everyone knows it is possible that some things may be rejected."

Deborah changed the subject. "By the way, guess who called me yesterday."

"Who?"

"Adele Evans. We had a nice long visit. She told me about Andy's harrowing escape. I guess everyone has a story like that now. She said Andy has been laid off, too. He has signed up to be a substitute schoolteacher. Did you know he has a degree in physical education?"

"Yeah. He said he liked teaching, but he went to work in the refinery to make enough money to support his wife's teaching habit."

"She said to tell you that Andy is counting on you and the other engineers to get him his job back."

"I expect lots of people are depending on us."

"They are nice people. I hope we can get together with them sometime after the dust settles."

"Yeah, if it ever does."

"If it ever does."

Jared drove the car into the parking lot of the church. The building was a traditional-looking red brick building. In the foyer, an usher recognized Jared and Deborah from their previous visit. He welcomed them and handed them each a bulletin that explained the order of worship. He offered a little small talk and told them that they could sit anywhere they wanted to. Jared asked where George Christopher's family was. The usher said they had just come in and that they usually sat about halfway down on the right-hand side. They went into the sanctuary.

The sanctuary, too, was traditional. Pews were arranged in rows on both sides. An altar table stood in the middle in the front with a brass cross and candle holders flanking the cross. A pulpit stood on one side of the altar and a lectern on the other. Seats for the choir were behind the altar. One round stained glass window with a picture of Jesus praying in the garden of Gethsemane adorned the wall above the choir. The other windows were a kind of clouded glass that let in lots of light without being transparent. The room was full of light and, at this time, of motion and conversation. Nicely dressed people were coming into the sanctuary from the Sunday school rooms and from the parking lot. There were people of all ages, families with children and teenagers, older couples, quite a few older women who were alone. They greeted each other as they found their seats and visited. Phyllis Landry, George Christopher's daughter, saw Jared and Deborah and came to meet them.

"I'm so glad you could come today. Mom and Mrs. Anderson are looking forward to seeing you. Would you like to come and sit with us? We are all together right down here."

They joined the group. Maggie Christopher and Jane Anderson were already there. They met Phyllis's husband, Jack Landry, and their two boys, Georgy, who was ten, and Johnny, who was twelve. They exchanged pleasantries until the organ began to play. That was the signal to prepare for the worship service. The choir came in wearing red robes, and Tim Mathis followed, wearing a black robe. The service was very much like the ones to which Jared was accustomed. He knew most of the hymns. Deborah was able to follow along without any trouble. Tim preached a sermon on the importance of integrity. After the service, several people came up to greet the visitors and to invite them to come back. Phyllis suggested that Jared should just follow them to their house. She said that Tim Mathis and his wife, Martha, would be joining them later.

On the way to the house, Deborah said she was a little uneasy about being with the pastor. She could not remember ever having been in the same room with a clergyman except for the few times she had gone to church. Again, Jared assured her that she could just relax and treat him like she would any other person.

The Landrys' house was a large, older house that had been worked over. There were shrubs and flowers in the yard that looked as if they had been tended but not pampered. There was a basketball goal attached to the front of the garage. Jared noticed that Jack made it a point not to park too near the goal. He understood and did likewise. As the family was tumbling out of the Landry family van, Phyllis waved to Jared and Deborah and gave the traditional invitation. "Get out and come on in."

They entered through a small living room that was furnished formally but not pretentiously and then went into a large room that had been achieved by removing a dividing wall. The kitchen was in one end of the room. A fireplace and den furniture were in the other end, and a dining table was in the middle. This was obviously the family room. It was equipped with comfortable furniture and decorated with family pictures, Little League trophies, and one conspicuous fishing trophy, a large mounted bass. The whole house was full of the smell of a pot roast and vegetables that had been cooking while everyone was in church. Phyllis took charge.

"Why don't you boys sit down in the living room and stay out of the way while we get lunch on the table?"

Deborah asked, "Can I help?"

"Sure. You can tear up some lettuce for the salad."

Jack took his coat off and asked Jared if he wanted to do the same. Jack hung the coats up and they sat down in the living room.

Jack started the conversation. "I understand that you work at the Apex Refinery. I am an operator at the Lubrizol Chemical Plant. I suppose that what we do under ordinary circumstances is a lot like what you usually do."

"Yeah, I would guess so under ordinary circumstances. But circumstances are not very ordinary right now."

"What is going on over there? Since I married into an Apex family, I try to keep up with things."

"Well, most of the operating and maintenance staff has been laid off. Some of the office staff too. Deborah has been laid off. They have the engineering staff working with some consultants to develop a plan for getting the plant up and going again."

"Lots of good people are going to be looking for work."

"I have heard that Mr. Summerfield is going to try to bring Mac MacKinzie back to supervise the cleanup. We are going to need to have what amounts to a plantwide turnaround. Since they shut the units down in the middle of a process, they are probably in forty different kinds of messes inside even if they weren't damaged outside."

"Don't you know it!"

"I have heard that he is going to try to arrange for Mac to hire as many of the Apex people as he can so they can keep eating."

Jack asked, "Do you think the head office is going to let him do that?"

"Just between us, I suspect that he didn't ask New York, he just worked something out with Petrotech. Petrotech is in no position to argue. They have got to know that when the OSHA people finish their investigation, they are going to put a big piece of the blame in their lap."

"Yeah, I think everyone knows who is really to blame, but the companies are going to bend over backward to keep any of their people from getting hurt."

Jack lowered his voice and said, "Hell, I wish they had been a little more worried about trying to keep people from getting hurt before the explosion."

"I expect you know what Sarge and Deacon and Mac were thinking before things went haywire."

"Yeah. They told me. They told me that you were in on it with them but that none of you were able to get anything done."

"I lay awake at nights thinking about what I should have done but didn't."

"I expect a lot of people do. I even have thoughts like that myself, even though I am completely out of the loop."

"It sure would have saved a lot of lives and avoided a lot of suffering if someone had just listened."

"It sure would have."

"I hope that Mr. Summerfield can make his plan with Mac work. It can keep a lot of people working."

"Well, I can tell you from family gossip that Summerfield has asked Mac if he would be willing to do that and he has said he would."

"Good. I feel good about that. If nothing goes wrong with that plan, one important thing will be done well."

"Tell me about what they have the engineers doing that's interesting."

"Well, there are two phases of it. The first is to see what kind of redesigning will be necessary to get what is left of the refinery up and running again. That may take some creativity. Some of the units interfaced with units in Section C and D. We will have to see if we can redesign them so that they can interface with other units that are still okay. They may produce other products. We are just now beginning to get the picture of how that might work. We know we will have to design a new compounding department because, until we do, all of the lubricants will have to be shipped to other refineries to be compounded and packaged. That is going to be interesting. But the thing we are all excited about is the second phase. Mr. Summerfield wants us to come up with some plans for a dream refinery to be built in the place of Sections C and D. Everyone knows that refining is going to have to take some new directions in the very near future. He wants us to come up with a preliminary design for something that will blaze new trails."

"Has the head office bought into that plan?"

"Summerfield says that he has authorization to proceed with the study. Lots of us think that the first phase will be implemented with little trouble. But we suspect that the second phase is something that Summerfield will have to sell to New York."

"I can see how you are all excited about that. But the talk around the ship channel is that not many of the head offices are investing money in new construction of any kind, much less in blue sky projects."

"We are trying not to think about that. We are enjoying being excited about something for a change. Even my boss, Al Scardino, is getting excited. When I first met him, he was so disillusioned that he was just going through the motions of his job. Now he's showing up early for work."

At this point, the doorbell rang. Tim Mathis and his wife were there. Jack welcomed them like old friends. He took Tim's coat and introduced Jared to both Tim and Martha.

Jared said, "I have met Tim, but it is a pleasure to meet you, Martha."

Tim said, "It was good to see you in church again. I hope you will keep on coming."

"I probably will. The Deacon left me an invitation to church in his will. It will be hard to ignore that."

"He left us all a lot to live up to, including me. His expectations will be good for us."

Both Tim and Martha went back into the kitchen to greet the people there. Martha stayed in the kitchen and Tim returned. The three men sat down to continue the conversation.

Jack said, "We were just talking about what's going on over at Apex."

"Well, I hope you have come up with some encouraging news. We could all use some."

"I think maybe there is some. Mr. Summerfield has us planning for the future as if there is going to be one."

Tim turned to Jack and said, "While I have a chance, I want to ask if the company has made any arrangements to provide for Maggie and Jane. There was a time when we could just take that for granted. We can't be so sure any more. Some of us have been wondering."

"Yes, both Mr. Summerfield and Mr. Miller came to the house to talk to Mom Christopher last week. She asked Phyllis and me to come over so we could all understand what was being offered. They both made it clear that they knew no amount of money could compensate for anyone's death. But they said the company wanted to offer her a lump sum equal to the amount that George would have earned before compulsory retirement, and then they'd pay the regular retirement she would have gotten for the rest of her life, including hospitalization. They made the same offer to Mrs. Anderson."

Tim said, "I suppose that is as much as could be expected, but it really doesn't sound like much considering what George did."

"That is what we thought. But Mr. Summerfield gave us the impression that they were getting that much because someone at the top of the ladder had heard about what George and Bill did and argued for a generous settlement. We got the impression that some others were not in favor of being so generous."

Jared nodded and said, "I am not at liberty to say much, but I overheard a conversation that leads me to believe that is true."

"Mr. Summerfield said the heroism of George and Bill are probably going to help some of the other survivors get a similar settlement, too."

"I'm glad to hear that. I'll bet they would have felt good about that if they knew."

"Of course they said the company would want them to sign a paper promising not to sue the company."

Jared said, "I'll bet lots of people would think about doing that. I have heard of some."

"Mom Christopher asked us to come over at another time when a personal injury lawyer came by. He tried to get Mom Christopher to sue the company for five million dollars. He tried to get Mrs. Anderson to do the same thing. They talked with each other. Mom Christopher talked with us, and Mrs. Anderson talked with her children. They both decided that they didn't want to sue the company. They said that what the company offered was all they had expected, and they didn't want to try to capitalize on their husbands' deaths."

Tim said, "They are sweet ladies. I hope nothing ever happens to make them regret their decision."

"Yeah, we are all thinking that too. They both belong to an age in which workers were committed to their companies and counted on the companies to take care of them. But things are different now. Some companies seem to be thinking of nothing but how to cheat their employees out of their benefits. And what if whoever appreciated what George and Bill did retires or gets fired and is replaced by someone with a different attitude? And what if Apex is bought out by another company? That is happening all of the time now, and it seems that the first thing those big companies do when they buy out another company is to try to get out from under their responsibility to the retired people. Of course, Phyllis and I will see that Mom Christopher is taken care of so long as I have a job. But you really can't count on anything any more."

"Yeah," Jared said, "those are all things you have to think about."

Just then Phyllis came and called the men to lunch. The group gathered in the large room and Phyllis took charge of assigning everyone a place to sit. After everyone was seated, Jack asked Tim to return thanks.

Tim said, "Thank you Lord for food and for friendship and for all of the other things that represent your love to us day by day. Help us to receive them gratefully so that we can return love to you and to others. Amen."

After a brief pause, Johnny said, "You did that just like Grandpaw used to do it."

"Well, I'm glad I've learned to do it right."

Martha said, "I'll bet you boys really miss your Grandpaw."

Georgy answered, "We sure do. He was funny. We used to like to hear him tell funny stories. And when him and Mr. Anderson and Mr. MacKinzie got together, they would tell one story after another, and when they finished a story, they would all laugh and laugh, and we would laugh with them."

Johnny said, "Yeah, we would laugh with them even if we didn't know what was so funny."

Jared volunteered, "Lots of people will miss your Grandpaw and Mr. Anderson. I know you think they were great guys, but you are probably going to have to grow up a little before you will know just how great they were."

Platters of food were passed around the table. Pot roast, potatoes and carrots, salad, and rolls made up the meal. For the next few minutes the conversation was all about food. Then Jane Anderson said, "Tim, I want you to know how much my family and I appreciate all you have done for us in the past couple of weeks. We are all a bunch of backsliders, but you have treated us like we were among the faithful."

Tim said, "Well, it only seemed like the right thing to do since Sarge and I were old fishing buddies."

Jane said, "Yeah, George had to trick Bill into going fishing with you and him, but you would be surprised how often he talked about that trip."

Just then Deborah spoke up, as if she had been wanting to say something and had been watching for the right time.

"Reverend, I have not been a religious person, but I want you to know that your messages have been really meaningful to me."

"Please call me Tim; I am really glad to hear you say that. What in particular caught your attention?"

"Well, your message today was right on. You said that integrity is important because it is what holds things together. You would be surprised how much time Jared and I have spent talking about all of the things that seem to be falling apart in our world because of the lack of integrity."

Everyone around the table nodded, and Deborah went on.

"And the things you said at Sarge's funeral have stuck in my mind. It's not how religious you are but how much God loves you that really counts, and judgment day is any real life situation in which we are called to live up to the highest that we know."

Tim laughed and said, "You have just paid me the highest compliment anyone can pay a preacher. You remembered something I said."

"Well, to tell the truth, I have never spent much time in church, and I have never heard religion explained in that way before."

"That's interesting. I guess I may have put a little bit of a special spin on the idea of judgment day, but the part about God's love being the important thing is really pretty basic."

"Well, I just want you to know it meant something special to me."

Phyllis said, "Tim is good about saying things that mean something."

There was a long pause that signaled that it was time for another topic of conversation. Jack volunteered, "There is a big football game on television this afternoon. Anyone who wants to would be welcome to stay and watch it." The rest of the table talk revolved around football.

The dessert was chocolate cake and ice cream. The conversation shifted to favorite desserts. When the cake was eaten, the boys asked, "Mom, can we go outside now?"

"Yeah, you guys have suffered enough for one day. Go change your clothes before you go out." The boys departed unceremoniously, and in a few minutes, the sound of a basketball bouncing on the driveway could be heard.

After that the table was cleared. The dishes were put into the dishwasher and everyone moved to the sitting area at the end of the room. Maggie said, "Jane, I'm so glad you were with us today. You know I have thought of you as a sister for years. And Jared and Deborah, I am so glad you were here. George and Bill thought so much of you. Don't be strangers."

Jared said, "It will be an honor to be your friends. Besides being good at telling funny stories, George and Bill were real heroes. Someone ought to put up a monument to them."

"Oh, haven't you heard? They are actually going to do that. Mr. Summerfield said they are going to put up a marble monument near the place where they died. At first they were just going to have George and Bill's names on it, but we insisted that it should have the names of everyone who died in the accident. It is to be dedicated two weeks from last Friday, right at quitting time so everyone who wants to can be there."

"Thanks for telling us about that. We will be there."

Then the group began telling their favorite stories about Sarge and Deacon. After each one, everyone laughed. They knew they would have wanted it that way.

About two o'clock, Tim said, "Well, it's time for the football game to start, and much as I would like to stay and watch it, I had better go and visit the sick folks in the hospital."

Jared and Deborah took that as a good time to go too and so the party broke up, leaving Maggie and Jane to spend the afternoon together.

In the car on the way home, Jared told Deborah about the things the men had talked about before lunch. She said that pretty much the same conversation went on in the kitchen.

Then Jared said, "Say, I was surprised how much interest you seem to have developed in religion."

"I don't know that I am especially developing an interest in it. It's just that I have heard some things about it that I had never really heard before."

"Like the idea that God's love is unconditional?"

"Yeah, like that. I suppose I have heard that before, but I guess it just never soaked in. I wish I could believe that."

"Say, I've been thinking about something. You have always said that you have trouble believing in a loving God because your father let you down. What about your mother? She gave you dependable love, didn't she?"

"Yeah, I always knew I could count on her."

"Could you think of God being like your mother?"

"I never thought of a female God."

"Well, I think everyone knows that God is neither male nor female."

"Oh, I wouldn't have any trouble imagining my mom representing love to me. But I could never think of her being in control of everything like God is supposed to be. She was always up against it and struggling to make things work."

"Do you think God is really in control of everything? I've been wondering about that lately."

"Well, isn't he?"

"Do you think it was God who made the refinery blow up?"

"I certainly hope not."

"So do I. Lately, I've been thinking that maybe God really doesn't have everything under control. Maybe God is up against it too. Maybe God is struggling to make things work just like your mom."

"Now there is a new idea. I wish I had everything all put together like you do."

There was a long silence. Deborah looked at Jared and saw a pained expression on his face. She asked, "What's the matter, sailor?"

"Well, I'm not so sure that I have it all as put together as you think I do. I grew up in the Christian religion. I want to believe it. I try to live it. But sometimes, in the middle of the night, when I get to thinking about all that is going on, sometimes I wonder if there really is a God. And when I get to thinking about the things going on in my life, I wonder if he can really love me."

"We really have been having to deal with some heavy stuff lately, haven't we?"

"Yeah, we have. Stuff like that is bound to gnaw away at you and make you wonder."

"Stuff like what?"

"Oh, lots of stuff. Stuff like me letting other people down."

"I thought that was what that unconditional love is all about. Maybe you ought to get that preacher to go fishing with you."

"Maybe I will do that. Anyway, I just want you to know that your dragon slayer doesn't win all of his fights."

"Believe it or not, I'm glad to hear that."

Chapter 13

On Monday, Jared met with his partner from mechanical engineering and with Dietrich Schmidt to talk about their plans for the new compounding department. They talked about the kinds of lubricants that the newly reorganized refinery would be able to produce and about the demands that the market was likely to make. Then Dietrich told them about some plans he once had for modernizing the compounding department. Jared remembered seeing drawings Dietrich had made to propose his ideas. Those plans had been sent to the head office with the assumption that they would be considered by the technical department. Dietrich supposed that they might still be on file there, so they requested them. The reply came back that they could not be found. They had to start from scratch. First Dietrich told what he had planned. Then Jared told about some ideas that he had. Then they went to work making plans. Jared was surprised how readily things seemed to come together. They postponed quitting time by two hours, but by the end of the day, they knew where they were going. That felt good.

When Jared came home from work on Monday, he immediately called Deborah on the phone.

"Is this Deborah Olsen, CPA?"

"Hi Jared. I guess that is who I am. I'm glad you called."

"Somehow that is not exactly the response I had expected to get. I thought I was going to need to take you out for a celebration."

"I hope that will be in order but not right now. I'm still trying to figure out what happened today."

"All right, tell me about it. That will probably help."

"Well, I showed up early for my appointment, copies of application, resume, and CPA examination records in my hand, a big smile on my face, and enthusiasm pouring out of my ears."

"That's my ambitious lady."

"I was right in uniform. Everybody else was all smiles and enthusiasm. They are a new company. They are being spun off by Logan and Harley to offer business clients a new service. So far, so good."

"But …"

"Well, the first surprise was that they were not looking for someone to do accounting work. They were looking for someone with an accounting background to go out and call on businesses and sell their service."

"Sounds like outside sales to me. How do you feel about that?"

"Well, it was not what I was expecting, but I am not opposed to it. I began to warm up to it even more when Rick Rogers said I could make twice as much money doing that as I could doing accounting. He said that he remembered at the Rayburns' cocktail party that I seemed to have a talent for meeting people. He spent a lot of time showing me the office suite and telling me about the big plans that he and his investors had for their company."

"Sounds like just what you have been looking for."

"Yeah, it does, and I kept getting more and more excited until I realized that I had gotten halfway through the afternoon and Rick had not said anything to me about the service I would be selling—even though I kept asking. About four o'clock, he finally handed me a fat presentation folder and proceeded to give me the same pitch that he wants me to give to potential clients."

"And …"

"Well, do you remember that Congress passed a whole lot of new regulations for the finance industry right after the world economy cratered?"

"Yeah, I seem to remember hearing about that. I thought it was a good idea, but I couldn't begin to understand what they were all about."

"Well, it started right after the collapse of Enron and Arthur Andersen, everyone was clambering for some new laws that would regulate the accounting business and prevent the kind of misrepresentations that caused the Enron fiasco. Then when we had that avalanche of banking failures, everyone knew something had to be done. Congress haggled over that for a long time. They were caught between the voters and the business community. Finally, they came up with a new set of regulations. Everyone recognized that some new laws were needed, but almost everyone in business and accounting agreed that some of them were overkill. Business and accounting have been living with a lot of cumbersome restrictions and unnecessary expenses ever since. The new company is marketing an accounting procedure that will minimize the cost and trouble of conforming to the new regulations."

"Sounds good. If you can market a needed service, you can do some good."

"The problem is that I could never get him to explain the process in detail. All he wanted to talk about was what a great career opportunity it is to be in on the ground floor with an aggressive new business. Finally, I figured out that he was really not much of an accountant. He had moved from accounting to management as soon as he could and he hasn't kept up with developments in accounting. He didn't know how to explain the service in detail. He gave me a briefcase full of papers that he said would explain everything."

"Then you went home and started to study."

"Not quite yet. He took me to dinner at a fancy restaurant. Then, just to give me a taste of the success I could expect, he took me up to his apartment for a drink. It was really an elegant place with a spectacular view of the city lights. When he saw that I was impressed, he made the subtle suggestion that I could spend the night there with him if I wanted to."

"Oh? What did you say to that?"

"I pretended not to have gotten the message and told him that I had to get home and start studying the papers."

"And that is what you have been doing."

"Yeah. But it's pretty complicated. I'm getting ready to go to bed and start with a fresh mind in the morning."

"It is getting kind of late, isn't it?"

"Why don't you call me when you get home from work tomorrow? I may be ready for that celebration then. And, by the way, my mom is coming in on Wednesday. I want you to meet her."

"Wouldn't miss it. I'll call you tomorrow."

On Tuesday, Jared called Deborah and asked, "Are you ready for that celebration yet?"

"Not quite yet. But I do need to talk. Can you come and take me out for a hamburger? I'll buy."

"How come when you are going to buy, we eat hamburgers?"

"Remember, I'm unemployed."

"That doesn't sound too encouraging. I'll be over in a few minutes."

Settled at the back table in the Dairy Queen, Deborah began to share her thoughts.

"I've been studying the papers that Rick Rogers gave me all day. There are presentation folders and contracts and descriptions of accounting procedures. The first two were not hard to understand. They were full of promises of simplification of procedures and cost savings. But the descriptions of the accounting procedures we are selling are spelled out in very complicated technical terms. I thought they were unnecessarily technical. I was having a hard time understanding them. After I got it all sorted out, there were a couple of gaps in it. I called Rick and asked him to explain them. He couldn't. He gave me the name of someone at Logan and Harley who had developed the procedures. I kept him on the phone for about an hour. I think I have finally gotten the picture."

"And ..."

"I think that what they are going to do is legal—but just barely. They have found a gap in the regulations, and they are marketing a new way of misrepresenting a company's assets. I believe that when it comes to the attention of the regulatory agencies, they will close that gap."

"How do you feel about that?"

"Not good. I could go to work for this company and impress them with my eagerness and ambition, and maybe they would eventually move me up into a better position before the feds come down on them."

"Or they might find some way of blaming you for the misrepresentation and let you take the rap for them."

"I have thought of that too. I like the idea of moving up rapidly, but I really don't want to be a part of anything like that."

"So ..."

"So I am thinking about not doing it."

"Okay, what next?"

"Well, I can start reading the want ads again or I can give some thought to that suggestion that Mr. Rayburn made."

"Open your own accounting office."

"Yeah. That is not as glamorous as going to work in downtown Houston. I would probably spend a lot of time figuring income taxes for refinery workers. But it's honest."

"From what I know about you, I believe you could build your own business and maybe be the head of a first-rate accounting firm in a fairly short time."

"Thanks for your confidence. I had actually thought I would like to start my own firm someday, but I had thought that it would be good to work for a bigger firm for a while first. My only problem is that I would need to get a grub stake from somewhere to get started. Maybe I could get a small business loan."

"You are really thinking about this, aren't you?"

'Yes, I am. And you know what? I never thought about it seriously until Mr. Rayburn called and made the suggestion. I wonder what made him do that."

"I'll bet I can guess."

"Okay, what?"

"Ben Rayburn is smart. He makes it a point to know what is going on. I'll bet that he had heard about the new program and had some doubts about it. He wanted you to have some other possibility to fall back on so that you could say 'No' if you chose to."

"Why would he go to that trouble for me?"

"You are a friend of his daughter's. He was probably thinking he would like for someone to do that for Ginger if she was about to get into a tight spot."

"That would be sort of an unusual thing for a businessman to do, wouldn't it?"

"Maybe. But it would not be a novel thing for a dad to do. Dads sometimes start acting like dad to all their children's friends. My father once went to a lot of trouble to get one of my navy buddies a job at the plant where he worked. I'll bet that fathers of girls are even more solicitous of the well-being of their daughter's friends. I think if I ever had a daughter, I would be."

"That concept is really foreign to me."

"Deborah, not all fathers are like your father."

"I know you are right. What you're saying does make me feel good. I will think some more about his suggestion."

Jared made sure that he didn't have to work late on Wednesday. He was invited to dinner at Deborah's apartment. This would be his first chance to meet Deborah's mother. He had offered to take the ladies out to a nice restaurant, but they put that off until the following night. Deborah insisted that, since she was at home all day, she would cook dinner—just to prove she could.

Jared went home after work and changed into some nicer clothes before going to Deborah's apartment. He felt that this was a very special occasion. Deborah greeted him at the door wearing a casual outfit and an apron.

"There you are. Come on in and meet someone special. Jared, this is my mom, Rebecca Olsen."

Jared found himself looking at a very attractive, middle-aged woman who looked a lot like Deborah but a few pounds heavier. She took three steps toward Jared and held out her hand with a self-confidence that reminded Jared of her daughter. She wore a big smile and said, "Jared, I am glad to finally meet you. Deborah has told me so much about you that I was not sure you could be real."

"Deborah has told me a lot about you too. I am really glad to meet you ."

Deborah said, "Why don't you two sit down and visit while I finish supper. This apartment has a one-butt kitchen."

"Something sure smells good," Jared said.

"I am going to feed you some Texas country cooking."

"Do I smell chicken frying?"

"That's it. I see you recognize it."

"Oh yeah. That is a favorite everywhere. But it is never quite as good in a restaurant."

"Mom taught me to cook," Deborah said as she returned to the kitchen, "and I want to prove to her that I remember how."

"From what I understand, Deborah has learned a lot from you, Mrs. Olsen."

"My goodness, what?"

"Lots of things, like, for instance, survival."

"Oh yes, that."

"I also understand that you are a nurse."

"Yes, I am. It makes me feel useful. I used to work in a hospital, but now I work in a doctor's office. It is a little easier."

"But no less important. Tell me what you like most about nursing."

Rebecca shared anecdotes about nursing for a few minutes. Then Deborah announced that dinner was served. She had decorated the apartment's small breakfast table for a special occasion. Fried chicken, mashed potatoes and cream gravy, black-eyed peas, greens, and corn bread made up the Texas country dinner. Jared held the chairs for both ladies as they were seated, even though Deborah was up again in just a minute to get sugar for the iced tea. Jared obviously enjoyed the meal. He commented that it was just his third home-cooked meal since coming to Texas.

Mrs. Olsen said, "Deborah, shame on you. You should treat a friend better than that."

Jared bailed her out. "Well, I haven't cooked for her even once."

"Now you will owe me one."

"I promise to cook for you as soon as we get this big project done."

"I have been hearing about the exciting work you have been doing. As soon as you get through eating, I want to hear all about it."

Jared didn't wait. He mixed eating with talking until he had given a fairly comprehensive layman's explanation of the plant redesign project.

"I can tell how excited you are about it," Mrs. Olsen said.

"We are all excited about it. It gives us a chance to do something creative. We are designing something that will be built. We will be able to see it. And it will last for a while. I suspect that, in one way or another, Deborah is soon going to be doing something exciting too."

"Yes, she has been telling me about the two possibilities she has been thinking about."

"Mom and I have talked about that for several hours. I have just about decided that I am not going to go for the glamour job I told you about. There is something fishy about it, and I don't want to start out on the wrong foot."

"I'm glad to hear you say that. I thought that was what you were thinking. I'll bet there will soon be another job offer that will be just as glamorous, if that is what you want."

"You know, I'm actually feeling drawn to the possibility that Mr. Rayburn suggested."

"You mean opening your own office."

"Yes, as I told you, I had always thought I would like to have my own office, but I thought it would be best to work for someone else for a while before venturing out on my own. But with the promise of the beginning of a clientele, I'm wondering if this might be the time. I wonder if I can do it."

"I bet you can do anything you set out to do."

"So do I," Mrs. Olsen said.

"Boy! With that kind of vote of confidence, it would be hard to turn back. But I still want to think about it a little longer."

After supper, they sat around and chatted like old friends, mostly about things Deborah had done while she was growing up and about things Jared could remember from his family history.

At a reasonable hour, Jared said he had to go home and get rested for the next day's work. He promised to take the ladies to dinner the following evening. After he left, Deborah and her mother sat down to talk.

"Deborah, that one is a keeper. Don't let him get away."

"Oh, Mother!"

"How do you feel about him?"

"Good. You know, real good."

"He really seems to like you."

"He asked me to marry him."

"He did? What did you say?"

"Well, he kind of surprised me. I got flustered and told him that I wasn't ready to talk about that yet."

"You have some misgivings?"

"Not about him. About me. To tell you the truth, Mom, I just can't get over my resentment of Dad leaving us like he did. I am not sure I am ready to trust someone."

"Deborah, you have to put the past behind you and say 'Yes' to the future. I made a poor choice for a husband, but not all men are like that."

"I know. I have known some men I thought were different. The problem is with me."

"Deborah, I know you remember the Kirkland family."

"Oh yes. How could I ever forget them? Judy and Jane were two of my best friends in high school. Mr. and Mrs. Kirkland were sponsors of the tennis team. They were always taking us somewhere or having the team over to their house. I always loved being with them."

"They had a happy family."

"They certainly seemed to. Mom, I don't want to hurt your feelings, but the reason I spent so much time over at their house was that they seemed to have what we didn't."

"I know that. I was glad for you to spend time with them so you could see what a happy family could be like."

"It broke my heart when Mrs. Kirkland got cancer and died. It was just awful that she had to suffer so long."

"And Mr. Kirkland was right there taking care of her when he wasn't working. And the girls dropped out of Baylor and came home to be with her for her last year. None of them seemed to regret having done it. They will be graduating this spring."

"Oh good. I haven't seen them since the funeral. They had such a good mom."

"They have a good dad too."

"Yes, they do. I know you are telling me that there are some men like Mr. Kirkland."

"Yes, but that is only part of what I am trying to get around to telling you."

"Oh? What else?"

"Well, for the last couple of months, Bob Kirkland has been coming around and taking me out to dinner once or twice a week."

"Mom?"

"And I have been cooking dinner for him now and then."

"Mom! Short little bald-headed Mr. Kirkland?"

"Okay, so he's not a hunk like Jared. But he is a good man and he is nice to me and he makes me feel good."

"Mom! After all of these years, I can't believe you have a boyfriend!"

"I can hardly believe it myself. But I am not about to tell him to go away."

Tears welled up in Deborah's eyes; she hugged her mother and said, "Oh Mom, I'm so happy for you. I hope it all works out. I can't believe that I could have Judy and Jane for sisters and a family like other people."

"Whoa! Don't get carried away. This whole thing is in very early stages. But I am staying open to the possibility—and I think you should too."

At breakfast on Thursday, Deborah's mom reminded her that she still had almost $20,000 in the fund that she had put away for Deborah's education out of the child support that she had received. Deborah had been frugal in planning her education, going to a local junior college for her first two years and bypassing the sorority scene at the university. Deborah was saving that in case she ever wanted to earn a graduate degree. Rebecca reminded her that she could either use that money to start her business or borrow against it. Deborah had not thought of that. She had forgotten that the money was there. But now that she remembered, lots of things seemed to be falling into place for her to start her own business. She had the promise of the beginning of a clientele and start-up funds available. She decided to think more about it. It helped to have her mom there to talk with as she thought things through. Deborah realized that she had moved into an adult friendship with her mother. It felt good.

About midmorning, Deborah made two phone calls, one to Rick Rogers to tell him that she would not be accepting the position he offered her. The other was to Rayburn Supply to make an appointment for the following day to talk about the possibility of offering some accounting services. After that, Deborah and her mom went to Houston for lunch and shopping—mostly window shopping—at the Galleria. Dinner was late. Jared did not get away from work until after seven. He took the two ladies to dinner at the restaurant by the ship channel. He thought a lady from central Texas might enjoy watching seagoing ships pass by. Jared was excited about the way in which his project was coming together and talked about it for a few minutes. Then he listened to the ladies talk about their trip to the Galleria. He kept thinking how glad he was that he did not have to make that trip with them.

After taking Deborah and her mom home, Jared went back to work for a while. The team schedule called for the work groups to make presentations of their work for the critique of the whole team the next day. All members of the engineering team would be invited to make suggestions. Then the work groups would be expected to complete their work, including preliminary drawings, to be incorporated into the report that would be sent to the board of directors the following week. Plans had been made for graphic artists with Brown and Daniels to turn the preliminary plans into a presentation. Joe Summerfield planned to take Dietrich Schmidt to New York with him to make the presentation.

A huge amount of work had been done in a short time. But everyone was looking forward to what was scheduled to happen on Sunday. Dr. Singh was scheduled to take charge of the group and lead them in imagining what might be done to turn the Pasadena Refinery into an industry leader in new technology. Everyone knew that the plans would have to be so promising—and at the same time, so doable—that they would get the board of directors excited and win their support.

Jared remembered that he had once met a member of the board of directors, but for most of the engineers in the room, the board of directors was something like the assembly of Greek gods who were supposed to be living out of sight on the top of Mount Olympus and governing all of the affairs of men in keeping with their own capricious whims.

Chapter 14

On Sunday morning, everyone on the engineering team was in their place early. No one grumbled about missing a day off. This was the day they had been anticipating with great eagerness. This was the day when they would begin the process of trying to visualize the future of the refining industry and finding a place of leadership in it for Apex Oil and Refining.

Joe Summerfield reintroduced Dr. Mathilda Singh and reminded everyone of the scope of the remainder of their task. Jared had actually been wondering why Dr. Singh had been showing up every day for the last two weeks. She really hadn't been saying much. He soon found out. She had been listening. The whole morning was to be spent in an illustrated lecture summarizing the present and anticipated changes in the world's culture and demographics and the impact that those changes might have on the refining industry. Even though the lecture was obviously summarizing the research in a terribly broad field of knowledge, Dr. Singh frequently related aspects of what she was saying to different things that she had heard people saying during their two weeks of problem analysis and planning. Eventually, Dr. Singh began to tell the group about some of the experimental things that were being done at different places in the world to take first steps toward planning for the future. Everyone was fascinated. When they broke for lunch, they couldn't stop talking about the new visions they were seeing.

After lunch Dr. Singh resumed her lecture and began to set out in chronological order the steps the industry needed to take to move into the future. These steps were represented by a series of posters she hung on the wall across the front of the room. The engineers could actually see the future unfolding before them. About midafternoon, everyone took a break. When they returned, Dr. Singh gave each participant a copy of the outline of the stages of development represented by the posters. Then she broke them into discussion groups of three and asked them to discuss which of the steps they might most realistically begin to take first, second, and third. They were to consider the likelihood of emerging needs, the unique possibilities present in the Pasadena Refinery's situation, the state of the present research, and the probable cost. After two hours, they reassembled and reported on what their groups were thinking. It was apparent that some consensus was actually beginning to emerge. They worked together as a group to list three projects that could be included in the first steps of reconstruction of the Apex refinery and two that might be next in line. Jared was amazed at the skill with which Dr. Singh led the discussions and helped them to arrive at a consensus in their vision.

During this whole process, Joe Summerfield had been participating as one member of the group. Only when it appeared that they had reached a stopping place did he stand and say, "You people have really done a lot of work today. I thank you all for it. In case you haven't noticed, it is eight o'clock. I think it is time for us to break for the evening. I will see you all in the morning."

Early on Monday morning, Joe Summerfield placed a telephone call to John Oliphant, chairman of the board of directors of Apex Oil.

"Mr. Oliphant, this is Joseph Summerfield, plant manager of the Pasadena Refinery."

"Good morning, Mr. Summerfield. How are things going down there in Texas?"

"Really well. I have had an engineering team working with some consultants to prepare the report I promised you. Everyone on the team is excited about how things are coming together. We hope that the board will be as excited about it as we are."

"That is interesting."

"I want to check my plans for making the presentation with you. I understand that the board will meet at ten o'clock on Friday. I plan to have copies of our complete report sent by fax to each of the board members so that they will have it the first thing Thursday morning. Then I plan to bring my chief consultant, Dietrich Schmidt, with me when we come to make our presentation. How does that sound to you?"

"Let me check with the people in New York to see what they think about that."

"Do you know of any of the board members who will not be in their offices to receive the reports on Thursday? If you do, we will try to get a copy to them wherever they are. We want them to have an opportunity to review the report before the meeting."

"I will check on that. Why don't you go on and send the report now so they will have more time?"

"It is not ready yet. You know, you didn't give us much time to get this big job done. We plan to wrap it up on Wednesday and then have some people from Brown and Daniels Engineering working late to put the report in presentation form and to get it to the board members."

"Oh, I see."

"Do you see anything wrong with that plan for making the presentation?"

"Well, there are a couple of things I feel like I need to check on. I will be getting back with you after I talk to the people in New York."

"Thank you. I will be looking forward to seeing all of you."

On Monday morning, Deborah kept her appointment with Ben Rayburn at his office in LaPorte. His secretary informed Rayburn that Deborah was there. Ben came to the door of his office and invited her in.

"Good morning, Deborah. I'm glad you're here."

"Thank you for seeing me."

"I know this has been a busy time for you. How are things going?"

"You are right. I am trying to work my way through an important transition. I am exploring a possibility that you actually suggested to me. I am thinking about opening my own CPA office."

"I'm glad to hear that. Did you interview with the people at Logan and Harley?"

"Yes, I did. Their offer was attractive to me in many ways, but there were some things about it that made me a little uncomfortable. I think it may not be right for me."

"I understand. Logan and Harley is a good company, but to tell you the truth, I am also a little uncomfortable about the things I have heard about their new service."

"Well, even with that aside, I began to think about taking the big leap and opening my own office. I had often thought I would like to do that someday, but I had not thought about doing it right now, until you suggested it."

"Well, from all that Ginger has told me about you, I believe that you can make a go of it, and I would be really glad to have some more top-notch young professionals working in our area. As I told you, I have some work that I would like to talk to you about."

"You mentioned that, and I am eager to hear about it."

"I was hoping that was what you were coming for. I have asked my accounting department to prepare a schedule of audits and other services that we may need to get from someone outside of our own company. I would like you to give us a bid on those services."

"I will be really glad to do that. When can I meet with them?"

"Right after we get through visiting. I also mentioned that I have a couple of friends who have businesses in our area who might need your services. Here is a list of three. And there is a fourth name on the list that is a new business just starting up. Of course, they don't have an accounting department yet so they may be able to use even more of your services."

"I can't tell you how grateful I am for your help."

"I'm grateful that a really sharp young accountant is available for us to call on. I want to mention something else to you. Do you remember Dr. Ed Ainsworth from the university?"

"I remember him but not from the university. I met him at the reception at your house."

"Ah, good. Well, he is an old friend of mine and has decided to run as an independent candidate for the United States Senate. He knows it will be a long shot, but he has decided to try it, and I have decided to back him. On Thursday, I am going to have a reception to introduce him to all of the businesspeople I know in this area. It will be in my warehouse out here in LaPorte at five o'clock. I would like to invite you to come to it. It will give you a chance to get acquainted with some more of the businesspeople in our area. Bring your boyfriend too. I think he just may like what this fellow has to say."

"I don't know how to thank you for this. I am beginning to believe that I actually can make a success of this."

"I know you can. I will look forward to seeing you on Thursday."

As Deborah left the office, Ben Rayburn said to his secretary, "Please take Miss Olsen down to the accounting office. They are expecting her."

When Jared called Deborah after work, she told him about her conversation with Ben Rayburn. She said that she had decided to make a try at opening her own office. She was going to go for it. She told him about the reception. Jared said that by Thursday, he ought to have plenty of leisure time and he thought it would be interesting to go to a political rally. She said that her first task would be to find some office space, preferably in some suite of offices that provided a receptionist for their tenants. Then she would have some business cards made and start calling on prospective clients. Jared could hear the excitement in her voice. It made him feel good.

When Joe Summerfield came into his office on Tuesday morning, he found a fax waiting for him from John Oliphant. It said that some of the board members preferred to have a member of the company's technical department present the study and proposal from the Pasadena engineering team rather than having him and Dietrich Schmidt do it. It said that, so far as anyone knew, all of the board members would be able to receive the report by fax in their offices on Thursday morning. Oliphant suggested that Dietrich Schmidt call to the company technical department Thursday morning to review the report and then to expect a call from whomever was selected to make the presentation so that Dietrich could brief him on the details. The fax said that Oliphant was going to be out of his office until the board meeting on Friday.

Summerfield thought that was a curious response. He really didn't like it at all. He felt that he needed to make the presentation. He started to call Frederick Alexander to talk about the matter, but he had a gut feeling that he needed to go along. At the first break, he called Dietrich Schmidt into his office and showed him the fax. Dietrich said, "That sounds crazy to me."

"Me too. But I guess we had better be ready to do it their way. I would like for you to be sure to be here and available when the man calls on Thursday afternoon and then also during the time of the meeting on Friday morning in case anyone needs to get in touch with you."

"You've got it."

All day Tuesday and until noon on Wednesday, the engineers worked to develop plans for the five possibilities they had identified as the best first steps Apex could take into the future. On Wednesday afternoon, the group again assembled and shared with each other the plans they had made. Even though everyone knew that their plans were very preliminary, they knew that the things they were recommending were entirely realistic and doable. When they saw the comprehensive report coming together, they were unashamedly excited. They believed that they were seeing the future, even though, a few weeks earlier, most of them had wondered privately if there would be a future. And even better than that, they believed that they were going to have a chance to make the future happen. Joe Summerfield wrapped things up.

"All right, people, I think we've got something really good to offer the board. We will work from eight till half past four tomorrow and Friday. Let's all give ourselves and each other a hand."

Everyone began to clap enthusiastically.

Jared called Deborah and confirmed the tentative plans they had made to go out for a victory celebration that evening. Jared went home and changed into his suit. He had made arrangements for them to have dinner at a Clear Lake area hotel, where there was a band and they could dance for a while after dinner. It was beginning to get dark when Jared picked Deborah up, but she insisted that, before going to dinner, they drive by her new office space. It was a nice but unpretentious three-story building on Southmore Street in Pasadena. Jared pulled into the parking lot and stopped for a few minutes. The building was closed so they could not go in, but Deborah described her office to him and then presented him with a newly printed calling card: "Deborah Olsen, CPA, General Accounting Services." Jared smiled broadly at her excitement, congratulated her, and gave her a celebratory kiss.

On the way to the hotel, Jared told Deborah all that had happened with the engineering team since they had seen each other. His enthusiasm for the project they had all been working on was obvious. Deborah said, "I sure hope those company big shots are able to tell what a treasure you people have put in their lap."

"Well, I sure do too. Surely they won't let this pass."

Dinner, and then dancing, and then standing on a balcony and watching the moon rise over Clear Lake made the evening a celebration to remember. As Jared was about to say good night, Deborah reminded him of the political rally they were to attend the next afternoon. And Jared reminded Deborah that there would be a dedication for the monument in memory of the people who had died in the accident on Friday afternoon. Then they swept away the nitty gritty and held each other close for a few minutes before Jared kissed her good night.

Thursday was an easier day. Joe Summerfield came into the engineering room and distributed copies of the presentation that had been faxed to all of the board members. He said, "Ladies and gentlemen, I am sorry that these reports are not hard bound. They are something you are going to want to keep. It is one of the most outstanding pieces of engineering work I have ever seen. You have a right to be proud of having helped to prepare it."

Then the team went back to their plans for bringing the refinery back into production. Jared and his partner worked on plans for the new compounding department. That was not as exciting as planning the future of the industry, but Jared was interested in what he was doing. He was fairly sure that he was designing something that he would see being built. Dietrich Schmidt spent some time with them in the morning, but at ten o'clock, he went to his office to wait for a call from the technical department in New York. At three o'clock he had still not gotten a call, so he phoned the technical department and asked to talk to the person who was to present the plans from the Pasadena Refinery to the board of directors. A lady by the name of Roberta Winston eventually came to the phone. She explained that she was a senior engineer and said that she would be making the presentation. Dietrich asked if she had any questions. She said that she did not. She complimented him on the report and said that everything was self-explanatory. Dietrich urged her to give the proposal a good push. She said she would do her best.

Dietrich reminded her that he and Joe Summerfield would be standing by while the meeting was being held, in case there were any questions. She thanked him and hung up.

Dietrich went into Joe Summerfield's office and reported on the conversation. Joe asked, "What do you think? Is she going to do a good job with the presentation?"

Dietrich said, "I hope so. I got the impression that she had read the report, but I can't believe that she didn't have any questions about anything."

"That is strange. I just hope the board members will think the report really is self-explanatory."

On Thursday afternoon, Jared drove Deborah to the warehouse of Rayburn Supply Company. He and Deborah went in and found where the reception was happening. There was something special about seeing a lot of dressed-up people gathering and socializing in a warehouse that was mostly full of racks and shelves of pipe fittings and cardboard boxes. Nevertheless, the festive air was unmistakable. Ben and Sheila Rayburn were standing near the door. So was Ed Ainsworth. They were greeting each person as they arrived and introducing all of their guests to the candidate-to-be. That was the purpose of this gathering. Ginger was there too, but she was "working the room" and seeing that everyone got some food and drink and someone to talk to.

When Deborah and Jared came in, Ben introduced them to Ed Ainsworth, saying, "I believe that you met these two people at a reception at my house. They were both employed at the Apex Refinery then, but Deborah has recently ventured out into an accounting practice of her own. She is going to be doing some work for my company."

"Well, I know this is an exciting time in your life. I hope your business will be a great success."

"Thank you. It is a frightening thing to venture out, but I am looking forward to it."

"Jared, don't I remember that you were an engineer for Apex?"

"Yes, I still am. They have been keeping me busy working on the team to make plans for the rebuilding of the plant."

"Well, I used to be a member of the board of directors of that company. I resigned at the last meeting so that I could do what I am going to tell you about. But somehow, they didn't get my name off of the mailing list. I want you to know that you woke me up at six o'clock this morning. I had plugged my portable fax machine into the wall plug in my hotel room last night and left it on. About six o'clock this morning, that thing started chugging and woke me up. At first, I didn't know what it was. I don't usually sleep with a fax machine. Then I realized what it was, and I thought it would stop in a few minutes so I could go back to sleep. But it just kept on chugging. I finally got up to see what it was, and it was a copy of your team's report."

"Oh, I am sorry. On behalf of the whole team, I apologize for disturbing your sleep."

"Well, I admit I was a little miffed. But when I realized that I was not going to get back to sleep, I got up and started reading your report. It was really interesting. You people have done a really great piece of work in a short time."

"Thank you, sir. I appreciate that. I hope that, when the board discusses the report tomorrow, they will think it is something they ought to vote for."

"Well, I won't have anything to say about it, but I hope they will too."

About that time, another group of people came through the door. Jared and Deborah moved on to let them meet the guest of honor. Ginger spotted Jared and Deborah and came over to guide them to the refreshments. On the way, she stopped to introduce them to a couple of people, one of whom Deborah recognized as being on the list of prospective clients that Ben had given her. It was Andria Aimes who ran a company that serviced the communications systems for industries.

Ginger said, "Ms. Aimes, this is one of my friends from college. She is opening an accounting office in Pasadena, and she is going to be doing some work for my dad."

Mr. Aimes smiled warmly. "Oh, you must be the one Ben told me about. He said I might be able to get you to do some work for our company."

"I would certainly like to do that. Let me give you one of my calling cards. I think the ink is dry on it now. I would be glad to help anytime. I would like to make an appointment to see what services you might need." Deborah handed him a card. They visited a little longer and then moved on to the refreshment table. They really did not know many people there, but Ginger managed to steer them into two more conversations. About seventy-five people finally assembled. At one time, Jared looked up and saw Joe and Helen Summerfield coming into the room. But before he could go to greet them, Ben Rayburn called for attention and began to speak.

"Friends, I have invited you all together here to meet someone whom I think could be very important to you and to everyone you know. I want you to meet my friend, Edward Ainsworth. I met Ed when we were in college. We were in the same fraternity at the University of Texas. He was the smartest guy in our fraternity. He got several of us engineering students through our courses in English literature and history and government. When he finished the university, he went to South America and served two years in the Peace Corps in Peru. Then he came back to the university and earned a PhD in political science. He immediately went to do a postdoctoral fellowship in international studies at the Sorbonne in France. He came back to the University of Texas to teach, where he had the honor of teaching my daughter, Ginger. He served two terms in the Texas State Legislature. Along the way, he met and married Elizabeth, the second most beautiful woman in the world (the most beautiful girl married me). They have two children who are in high school: Eddie, who plays football, and Annie, who is editor of the school paper. Ed Ainsworth is a very special friend to me because, in spite of all of his accomplishments, he is the only guy I know whom I can usually beat in a game of golf. Now Ed Ainsworth has decided that he wants to return to politics. He is running as an independent for the position of United States Senator from Texas. I don't know anyone I would rather see in that position, so I am going to give him a chance to convince you. I am happy to introduce to you, Dr. Edward Ainsworth."

Ed Ainsworth told a couple of funny stories about things he and Ben had done in college and then launched into his message.

"I have been hearing lots of people talking lately as if we are living through the twilight of American history. They talk about the decline of American industry, the weakening of the American economy, the loss of American moral leadership in the world, and the disintegration of many of the structures of American community life. I understand what those people are talking about. I have seen the things they have been looking at. But I don't believe it has to be that way. I still believe in the American people. I believe that we have the ability to act creatively, to do what is right, and to give leadership to the world. I believe that there are American people who are committed to making this nation work. I recently heard of two of your local men who risked and lost their lives trying to save the Apex Refinery in the recent catastrophe. That story really impressed me. Frankly, it helped me to make the decision to do what I am doing now. I believe there are lots of Americans who are willing to make heroic commitments to American industry and to the American way of life.

"But if you are going to commit yourself to something, you need to have something that you can trust. Recently, we have all witnessed the failure of many of the things that the American people really need to trust. We have witnessed the failure of business and industry structures, and the failure of government structures, and the failure of community life structures. In most cases those failures happened because someone took a shortsighted or greedy approach to something and exploited something that they should have been caring for. You can all name the examples. Many have been in the papers. I have seen some that haven't made the papers. But they are a burden on my heart. I believe the American people will come through if we give them something they can trust. That is what I want to do. I know that running for the Senate as an independent is a long shot, but whether I win or lose, I can make enough noise to call attention to the things that I think need fixing in American life."

Ed Ainsworth spent a few more minutes rounding out his presentation and then invited people to ask questions about specific issues. He answered as if he had thoroughly thought through each of the issues. Then he stopped talking and began to mill around and visit with people. Jared and Deborah found Joe and Helen Summerfield and went to visit with them.

Jared said, "Excuse me, sir, haven't I seen you somewhere before?"

"Yes, almost constantly for the last three weeks."

"It has been an adventure. I hope some other people feel as good about the work we have done as we do."

"Well, the report has been sent off on its way. I hope it gets to the people for whom it is intended."

Jared said, "I can set your mind at ease. It got to at least one of the people to whom it was sent." He told Summerfield about how that report had arrived in Ed Ainsworth's hotel room in time to wake him up. "Did you know that Dr. Ainsworth is not on the board of directors any more?"

"No, I did not know that. Now that I have heard him speak, I am sorry he is not."

In a few minutes, Ed Ainsworth came around to speak to the little cluster of people who were talking with the Summerfields.

"I am Ed Ainsworth. Who are you folks?"

Summerfield introduced himself and his wife; he added, "I think you have met Jared Philips and Deborah Olsen." He introduced the other people who were standing in the group, but Jared was surprised to see that Ainsworth had fastened his attention on Summerfield.

"Are you the plant manager of the Apex Refinery?"

"Yes, I am."

"I have never met you, but I have a high regard for you. I was a member of the board of directors of Apex until last month. I resigned then for several reasons, mostly to avoid any conflict of interest in my political campaign. I got the letter you wrote to the board, and I want you to know that I appreciated it very much. It was from your letter, and from something Frederick Alexander said, that I heard about the two heroic people I mentioned in my talk."

"I am very glad to finally meet you too. I have heard your name many times."

The two men were shaking hands again, even though they had already done that. They were looking intensely into each other's eyes. Jared had the feeling that each word that was being said had more meaning than appeared on the surface and also that important things were being left unsaid.

Joe said, "I understand that you have seen a copy of the report that we sent to the board of directors."

"Indeed I have. It is brilliant. I've never seen anything that was at the same time so practical and so visionary. Who produced that report?"

"We had three excellent consultants. They served as resource people and facilitators. But most of the creativity actually came from the people on our own engineering team who know the refinery. It is visionary. But you are right in saying that it is practical too. It is not some impossible dream. Everything in that report is something that can be done right now. It is something that can work."

"You are justly proud of it, and of the people who produced it."

"I hope that the members of the board of directors think so too."

"So do I. Say, I would like to hear more about the two heroic pipe fitters you mentioned in your letter."

"Jared could probably tell you more about them than I can, even though I have known them longer. We are going to dedicate a monument in memory of them and the others who died in the accident about this time tomorrow. You are welcome to come if you want."

"I would like to, on one condition. That is that nobody will introduce me as a political candidate. I think it is inappropriate to politicize an occasion like that."

"All right."

"If you will excuse me, I need to speak to some more of these people. I will see you tomorrow."

As he drove Deborah home, Jared asked, "What did you think of Dr. Ainsworth?"

"I really liked what he said," she answered. "I liked what Mr. Rayburn said about him, too. I think he just might be a part of the solution for the problems of our world."

"He solved a problem for me. I was beginning to think that I would have to go back to school and study law and run for Congress to solve the problems of American business and industry. Now that I know he is going to do it, I can keep on being an engineer."

"I have been thinking that I would have to go to a seminary and learn to be a preacher to solve the problems of our world."

"Really? You?"

"No, not really. I suppose I'll always be an agnostic accountant. But I am beginning to think that it will take some kind of a religious solution to solve the world's problems. Most of them have to do with the basic values and commitments that people let govern their lives."

"You just never stop surprising me with the stuff you come up with. Say, did you notice anything strange about that conversation between Joe Summerfield and Dr. Ainsworth?"

"No. What?"

"I think something was going on there under the surface. Something I can't put my finger on."

"Now who is coming up with weird stuff?"

"Yeah, you are probably right. Just forget it."

Friday morning came in a surprisingly normal sort of way. The members of the engineering team came on time and got to work on their projects. The other Apex Oil employees started the day doing the things they would ordinarily do on a Friday morning. Jared and his partner were working on some details of the new compounding plant. Deborah was setting up a computer program in her new accounting office. Helen Summerfield kept herself busy around the house so that she would not be far from the telephone. Yet everyone knew that an important decision was being made somewhere beyond their sight. It was a decision that would determine the meaning and value of the things they had been doing and maybe, to some extent, of the catastrophe that was still hovering in the backs of their minds. All of them were hoping that something good was about to happen. All of them were trying to ignore the possibility that something disappointing could happen.

Joe Summerfield was in his office waiting for the phone to ring. Michael Miller was there with him—waiting. At nine o'clock they knew that the board of directors of Apex Oil and Refining Company was convening in New York. They made small talk while they waited.

A little after ten, the secretary came to the door with two faxed letters in her hands, one for Joe and one for Michael. They took them, closed the door, and sat down, looking at each other. Joe said, "I have a bad feeling about this." They both read their letters silently, and then looked at each other with expressions of shocked disbelief on their faces. Joe read his first.

Dear Mr. Summerfield:

The board of directors is very appreciative of the good work that the engineering team has done on the study in preparation for the rehabilitation of the Pasadena Refinery of Apex Oil and Refining Company. The board has approved the report. We expect that the plans made for bringing the undamaged parts of the refinery back into production will be followed. The very interesting suggestions for replacing the parts of the refinery that were destroyed will be referred to our technical department and may be used at some time in the future, either for rebuilding parts of the Pasadena Refinery or for constructing new facilities in other locations. The board asks that you express their appreciation to the engineering team for the good work that they have done.

Since the Pasadena Refinery is about to enter a new phase of work, with rehabilitation and construction projects that are likely to be going on for a long time, the board has reached a consensus that it would be best for the refinery to move into this phase of its life under new leadership. It is also the consensus of the board that it is good to move the top management of the refineries around from time to time so that the situations in each refinery can be looked at with fresh eyes. For that reason, Anthony Jacobs will be arriving on Monday to replace you as plant manager of the Pasadena Refinery. Please have your office vacated so that he can occupy it at that time.

As for your relationship to Apex Oil and Refining Company, you qualify for retirement. We are prepared to make that option attractive to you. But, if you prefer, we will find a position for you somewhere in the organization. Please let us know your preference in this matter.

Respectfully,
Frederick Alexander
Chief Executive Officer
Apex Oil and Refining Company

The two men sat in silence and looked at each other for a long time. Then Joe said, "We should have seen this coming. The way they have been acting in the last few days, and the fact that it took them less than an hour to make their decision, tells us that decision was either made at a previous meeting or brought to the meeting ready made by some powerful person or group. But why in the hell didn't they tell us that? Why didn't they just send their new man down here to do the part of the planning that they wanted and forget the rest?"

"My guess is that they knew you could get it done quicker and better so they just let you run with the ball until you got it a little further down the field before passing it to their new star."

"Probably."

"From what I remember about our visit at Ellington Field, I would guess that this letter sounds more like William Stone than like Frederick Alexander."

"It's neither of those. They are just spokesmen. They have to do what the board tells them to. It is some powerful person or group on the board. But you can bet that Stone is their spokesman. He is cultivating their patronage and may be the next CEO."

"Well, there is a thought that ought to make retirement look more attractive."

"Yeah, it does."

"In case you are wondering, my letter is all full of appreciation and assurances that I am in line for promotion when the next opening for a plant manager comes up. It repeats their policy of moving top management around to get fresh insights. And it asks me to do all I can to help Anthony Jacobs get started."

"Well, I am glad. That is good for you even though I don't see it being good for the plant."

"Do you know anything about Anthony Jacobs?"

"Not a thing. His name started appearing on company correspondences about two years ago. I bet I know what kind of training he has."

"MBA."

"Yeah. And I'm betting that what they are saying about the fresh approach of fresh management really has something to do with implementing the board's policies without arguing about them."

"I'm seeing something else that doesn't look good to me. My letter was full of affirmations. Yours didn't even say thank you for anything. That makes me think they are going to hang at least part of the blame for the explosion on you. You may be the scapegoat."

"That doesn't feel good. There is enough blame to go around, and I have been feeling my part of it, but they had better be careful how they come down on me. I may come back on them. I can tell the world about those OSHA recommendations they kept putting off. If they had followed those recommendations, it would have changed history."

"You should do that."

"Well, now I need to cuss a little bit and then I need to call Helen. Then I need to get my head together and go out there and tell those engineers what has become of all of their good work."

"Call me before you go out there. I want to go with you."

Thirty minutes later, Joe and Michael walked out into the room where the engineers were working. Everyone immediately stopped and looked at them. They could tell from the expressions on the two men's faces that the report was not favorable. Joe Summerfield spoke.

"Ladies and gentlemen, I have the response from the board of directors of Apex Oil and Refining Company to the presentation you have worked so hard on the last three weeks. The report is not all that we had hoped it would be, but it is, by and large, a positive response that promises action on at least part of what we have proposed. Let me read a part of the letter that I just received from the company CEO: 'The board of directors is very appreciative of the good work the engineering team has done on the study in preparation for the rehabilitation of the Pasadena Refinery of Apex Oil and Refining Company. The board has approved your report. We expect that the plans made for bringing the undamaged parts of the refinery back into production will be followed. The very interesting suggestions for replacing the parts of the refinery that were destroyed will be referred to our technical department and may be used in the future, either for rebuilding the Pasadena Refinery or for constructing new facilities in other locations. The board asks that you express their appreciation to the engineering team for the good work they have done.'"

There was a long pause. Then Al Scardino stood up and said, "Mr. Summerfield, we have all heard that wording before. We all know what it means and so do you. The company is not going to do any more than they have to."

"Al, I know what you are thinking. A lot of good suggestions have gotten lost in the company technical department. But this time they have to do at least part of what you have planned or else shut the refinery down. And you never can tell, someday after there have been some changes of leadership and history makes it clear that the refining industry is going to have to change or perish, they may find our plans for the future and put them to work somewhere."

Al was still standing so he spoke again. "We thank you for what you tried to do. At least for a while we felt like we were doing something really significant."

"I feel guilty for setting you up for this disappointment. Remember, part of what you have planned will be done. You have done something very significant."

Someone else volunteered, "Well, we want you to know we will be backing you as you try to get this refinery up and running again."

"Well, there is something else I've got to tell you. It is not me that you will be backing. I have done about all I can do for you and for the company, so I am going to retire. Come Monday morning, there will be a new plant manager here on the job. His name is Anthony Jacobs. I hope you will all give him the same kind of cooperation that you have given me all of these years."

Someone else volunteered, "We all know what that means too. There are some chicken so-and-sos on the board of directors that are going to try to blame the explosion on you."

"No, that is not really what that is all about. I have been thinking about retirement for a long time, and I can see that this is a logical time for the plant to have a change of leadership. I want to thank you all for your support. I think it is getting close to lunchtime, so you can all knock off a little early. And as one of my last acts of authority, I am going to give you the rest of the day off as comp time for the overtime you've been working. I hope you will come back for the dedication of the memorial monument at five o'clock."

Joe and Michael left the room. Everyone else gathered up their things and left, either silently or grumbling to each other. Jared couldn't bring himself to get up and leave. He sat at his work table, thumbing through the copy of the presentation folder that was in front of him. Dietrich Schmidt saw him doing that. He came and stood in front of him and said, "Jared, I know how you are feeling right now. I have felt that way many times. But remember, Apex is not the whole industry. And today is not the end of human history. There are major refining companies that are planning new facilities to be built in this country. And there are some who are looking forward to the future and planning creative ways to go to meet it. As soon as you get through with what you feel like you have to do here, I hope you will apply to Brown and Daniels again. I don't think it will be too long before they have a place for you."

Jared looked up at Dietrich and said, "Thank you for that. I will do what you have said."

Dietrich walked away, and soon after that, Jared left. And the room where the engineering team had met was empty and quiet.

About half past four in the afternoon, people began to find their way through the company gate and down through the shells of burned-out refinery units to where a granite monument had been placed. The company street leading to the monument had been cleared, but the effects of the fire were still visible. The asphalt that had covered the road had been melted to fluid and then reconfigured as it cooled. It was not easy to walk on. Those who approached the monument had to watch where they stepped. The immediate area had been cleared of wreckage, but charred and twisted remains of refinery units still surrounded the scene and towered over the group that was gathering. It looked like a scene from a science fiction movie.

But the day was clear, and a little bit of breeze found its way past the wreckage to make the things a little more comfortable. The monument was about six feet high, made of rough red granite; the side with the inscription was smooth. The inscription read, "This monument is placed here in loving memory of the sixteen people who died in a tragic industrial accident. Their names are listed below ." And carved on the monument on either side of the list of names was an image of a pipe wrench. The wrenches were the only special recognition given to Sarge and Deacon. A lectern with a public address system was set up by the monument. Arrangements of white flowers were placed on either side of the monument. In the drab surroundings, they seemed to glow.

When Jared and Deborah arrived, there were already several people there. Jared did not know most of them. He had only really known three of the people whose names were on the monument. Jared found himself being churned up with all sorts of mixed emotions. The three weeks of euphoria working on what he thought was to be significant had given him some relief from the memories of the disaster, the flames, the news about his friends who had died, the nights full of grief and guilt and remorse. Now all of those feelings were tumbling back in on him.

Jared saw the little Hispanic lady with her two children coming in with a Hispanic couple, who interpreted for her. They went to the monument and she found her husband's name, Guadalupe Salazar. She traced the letters with her finger and then hid her face in her hands and cried. Somehow, she represented to Jared all of the millions of impoverished and dislocated and oppressed peoples of the world. The event was beginning to take on some broad, mythic significance. Jared saw Sally Williams, Angie's friend, with two families; he assumed they were her family and Angie's family. Jared was ready to deal with that now. He thought, *Poor, pretty Angie. She wasn't very smart, but she knew how to dance—and it's important to know how to dance.* He saw Deacon's family coming in together, and Sarge's wife and their sons, with their wives. They stood together. The people with whom Jared and Deborah had so recently shared a Sunday dinner now seemed like images on a distant tapestry. For some reason, Jared felt separated from all that was around him. It was as if he were seeing everything from a distance. And everything was silent, so silent. Things are never silent in an oil refinery—unless, Jared thought, unless it is dead. He felt the same way as he watched Pop and Tex and Brown come in and stand together beside the two families of their old friends. The people with whom Jared had joked and drank beer seemed like part of the scenery. Jared grieved that Hog was not there. He understood but regretted it.

Each person or group that arrived went to the monument, found the name of someone they knew, and then withdrew and formed a circle around the monument. Al and Maria Scardino did the same. Jared was feeling deeply connected with each person who came, but he did not feel any desire to go to speak to them. He did not want to intrude upon their grief—or to have anyone intrude on his. He stood as still as he could, his jaw set, trying to choke back any tears that might come. A few minutes before five, he saw Ed Ainsworth walk up and take an inconspicuous place in the crowd. At exactly five, Joe and Helen Summerfield came in, followed by Michael and Ann Miller. They went directly to the lectern, and Joe began to speak.

"Thank you all for coming here today. I guess that, by now, most of you have heard that this is the last thing I am going to do as plant manager of this refinery. But I think it is something very important that we need to do. I know this seems like a pitiful little thing for us to do to remember the people whose names are on that stone. Nothing we could do would be enough. But doing something that is too little is better than doing nothing. Each of these people whose names are on the stone was someone special to many of us. They will be terribly missed."

At this point, Summerfield choked. He turned to Michael and asked him to read the names from a list. He read them slowly, leaving time for those who heard to call their faces to mind and to remember something about them. Several times, someone broke into sobs after a name was read. When he had finished, he said, "If anyone wants to say anything about any of these people, please come here to the lectern and use the microphone." Someone Jared did not recognize went first.

"I just want to say that my father's name is on that stone. He had worked for Apex for almost thirty years and he had big plans for his retirement. He and my mother were going to travel and enjoy life. That is not going to happen now. But we want everyone to know that we loved him and we appreciate all of you who were his friends."

Sally came to the lectern next. "I want to say how much I loved my friend Angie. We are all going to miss her."

Jared felt a twinge of guilt, but he pushed it away.

Another young man Jared didn't know stepped to the lectern and said, "My brother died in this fire. He left a wife and two little children. I am going to say something that a lot of people are thinking, especially some of those who are not here today. This thing shouldn't have happened. These people ought to still be alive. I am mad as hell. So are a lot of other people. I hope someone will do something to see that this sort of thing doesn't ever happen again."

Jared felt himself attacked by conflicting feelings. He was mad as hell too. But he was also feeling that he should have been able to do something to prevent all of these deaths. He wondered who would say something about Sarge and Deacon. To his surprise, Pop Slovacek stepped to the lectern.

"I am going to say a few words about two men who were my best friends. We all knew them as Sarge and the Deacon. They were best friends to lots of you. They were regular guys and fun to be around, but they were a lot more than that. I was a soldier in Vietnam. I saw lots of people do heroic things, and I saw lots of my friends die heroic deaths."

Jared thought of his brother, Arthur. He thought, *The heroic suffering is still going on.*

Pop went on. They died because they believed in something. They died for us. They were war heroes. Their deaths were precious gifts to us all. And they set us an example to live up to. My two friends, Sarge and Deacon, died that same kind of death. I suppose there is still some kind of a war going on. I feel it going on, even though I couldn't say who it is that is fighting, or what they are fighting for. But we are all called to be ready to step up and do our duty when the time comes. Sarge and Deacon evidently felt it was their time to step up. They did. And they died. As far as I am concerned, they are war heroes. They have made a precious gift to us and we ought never to forget it. And they have set us an example of the kind of commitment we should all be willing to make when the time comes for it. I will always remember them with those other heroes. And I will always try to be ready to follow their example."

After that, no one had anything else to say. Joe Summerfield stepped back to the lectern and said, "Thank you for the things you have said, all of you. I think each of you spoke for all of us. Right now I am feeling remiss because I did not ask a clergyman to come and end this ceremony with a prayer."

Brown walked over to the lectern and said, "Mr. Summerfield, I believe I could say a prayer if you would let me."

"Thank you, Mr. Brown. I think we would all appreciate it."

Brown began, "Dear Lord, we are just a bunch of your children gathered here with heavy hearts."

Jared wanted to pray, but he did not bow his head. He looked around at the faces of the people he could see as Brown said the words of his prayer. It seemed the right thing to do.

"Lord, we are sad, and we are angry, and we are feeling all sorts of bad things because so many of the people we love and so many of the things that are important to us seem to keep on dying."

Jared looked at the families of his two friends and then at the other family groups that were bowing with arms around each other and crying. He tried hard not to cry. He knew he must have been looking like a stone face. He was feeling very alone. Then he felt Deborah's arm around his waist. He put his arm around her shoulder.

"Lord, sometimes when there seems to be so much dying we feel like we are dying too. We don't feel like going on. We don't feel like trying any more."

Jared looked at Al Scardino. He saw several others from the engineering team and he thought, *That is how they all must be feeling.*

"But Lord, we know you are in the resurrection business."

That came as a surprise to Jared, and he found himself looking at Joe Summerfield.

"So Lord, help us to put those beautiful people who died here in your hands. And help us to put all of the things we are worried about in your hands. And help us to put ourselves in your hands. And help us to go on doing the best we can at whatever we have to do. Amen."

Nobody said anything more. Everyone seemed to need to pause for just a few more minutes in silence, and then everyone began to walk away.

Jared and Deborah walked back toward the parking lot holding hands. About halfway there, Jared finally spoke. "You know, I don't think this is really the end of the road for American industry or for the way of life that goes with it. Lots of things seem to be trying to stifle it. But there are too many people committed to it. Lots of the people there were living out of commitments just like those that made Sarge and the Deacon do what they did. Those commitments will keep things alive."

Deborah said, "I think you are right. I have never been very good at making commitments, but I am learning. I suppose it is something I am learning from the company I am keeping."

"I think you just made a pretty big commitment in the past few days."

"Well, I am thinking about an even bigger one."

"Oh? What's that?"

"If a certain engineer I know ever asks me again to marry him, I am going to say yes."